Out From Silence

A Thornton Mystery

by
C. L. TOLBERT

LEVEL
BEST BOOKS

First published by Level Best Books 2019

Copyright © 2019 by C. L. Tolbert

Richie Arpino (Author Photo Credit)

Bailey Toksoz (Cover Photo Credit)

First edition

ISBN: 978-1-947915-42-8

For my children, CHARLES L. DESPORTE, JR.
and LAURA DESPORTE AKIN, M.D.,
who have always been my inspiration...

1

August 15, 1990

The man drove along the deserted gravel road to the Patrick farm and stopped, just short of the entrance to the pasture. His hands shook as he turned off the lights and coaxed his vehicle through the open gate, inching onto the grassy field. He cut the engine and checked his watch. Almost midnight. In the next few minutes, if things worked out as planned, the girl and her father would both be dead.

He scanned the field. The full moon hung low over the horizon, its beams skimming cedars and illuminating puddles in the red Georgia clay. This was the first break in a near week of steady rain. The clear night was a good omen, but it didn't calm his nerves or ease the pounding in his chest.

He grabbed the rifle from behind the seat, and for a moment watched the wind blow through the trees along the fence line. Then he slipped out of the cab, dug his boots into the soggy earth, and darted toward the fence along the north side of the field. He dragged himself under the wire and stood, stealing his first glimpse of the modest clapboard house through the trees.

The lights were out. Exactly what he'd hoped for.

Clutching the rifle to his chest, he dashed across the gravel road between the back pasture and the entrance to the farmhouse. Crouching, he crept along the sodden path, hugging the ground so closely he could smell the oil embedded in the dank soil.

He had rehashed their plan a thousand times, but what if something went wrong and his partner, who'd plotted every step of everything that was to happen tonight, didn't show? A hundred other things could go wrong. Inhaling deeply, he shook the hair out of his eyes, rubbed the sweat from his palms on his pants and pulled himself up. He spotted the silhouette of a shadowy form as it stepped out from a stand of trees, raised his hand in their agreed-upon signal, and waited for the response. The strobe of his partner's flashlight let him know they were moving forward. He clutched the butt of his rifle, checked the magazine, and began his rush toward the farmhouse, barely keeping his footing as he scrambled up the driveway's slick incline.

The carport was uncluttered, giving him easy access to the telephone lines. Falling to his knees, he pulled a Buck knife from his back pocket, snapped it open, traced the phone wires along the side of the wall, and cut them. Then he turned to the front of the small frame home.

Ten steps took him to the window ledge of the first bedroom. He peered inside, squinting through the panes. Barely visible against the soft white glow of the sheets, the girl seemed even younger than her eighteen years. So peaceful, almost childlike.

His partner, gripping an assault rifle, skirted a protective cluster of trees at the side of the house. Then, clambering over puddles and sludge which had collected from the week's rain, emerged to stand beside him, next to the girl's window.

Edging sideways toward the father's room, he stared down at the hand that grasped his rifle. It felt as if someone else was holding the weapon. He clicked off the safety. With a nod from his partner, they raised their weapons simultaneously, and took aim, each at their separate targets.

His partner's AR-15 aimed at the girl, fired.

A dull click told him that his rifle had jammed and misfired. For a few seconds he panicked, his body frozen. Forcing himself to move, he turned and dashed back down the driveway. He crossed the field to his truck, and zigzagged to the back gate in a hasty getaway.

His partner also fled, protected by the canopy of the trees, leaving behind the girl's lifeless body, and the casings scattered under her window.

2

August 16, 1990

The wail of the siren pierced the night air. Emma Thornton sat up with a start, sending the casebook she'd been reading crashing to the floor. She'd fallen asleep studying—again. The alarm clock next to the couch glowed 12:30. She stood up and stumbled to the living room window to peer into the deep indigo sky, catching a brief reflection of her disheveled blonde hair and bleary eyes in the glass. Other than a lone pickup truck traveling toward town, she saw only the blue flashes of a sheriff's car as it emerged from the inky landscape headed toward her apartment. And the moon. A moon so full it seemed to have burst and spilled its glistening contents over the hillside.

Emma stared at the night sky for a moment. Can't you make wishes on a full moon? She glanced at the stack of bills on the kitchen table. If so, she'd wish for lots of cash, and fast.

The siren made another trill as it passed her apartment.

This was the first siren she'd heard in the two years she'd been at the law school. Sirens and alarms always put her on edge, so she tiptoed down the hall to check on the twins. When they'd moved to Jonesburg, she'd promised the boys they'd have separate bedrooms, just like the ones they were leaving behind at their old home. Only eight years old, they still giggled and talked through the night when they were in the same room. Keeping them separated was essential for her sanity and their sleep, and since she couldn't afford more than a two-bedroom apartment, she was on the couch for the entire three-year law school stint. She peeked in Bobby's room. The moonlight outlined his golden hair and the baby-like roundness of his cheeks, making Emma's heart ache. Time was passing so quickly. He slept soundly, his favorite baseball glove curled under his chin. Billy snored lightly in the next room. The siren hadn't bothered either of them.

She padded into the kitchen and brewed a cup of herbal tea, hoping its calming effects would coax her into a few more hours of sleep. Juggling the twins, third year law school and a part-time job with a local attorney didn't leave much time for study or rest.

She stirred her tea and scanned the stack of bills on the table. She didn't know how she'd pay some of them, but at least the boys' dentist was easy to work with. She stacked the envelopes in a neat pile, stepped over to her desk and slipped them into a cubby hole. She'd deal with her accounts another day. Her mornings started early and she needed sleep.

She heard Bobby cough, and carried her tea down the hall, checking on the twins one more time. She tended to worry about them, but the boys were the best part of her life. Her ex-husband hadn't seen them in years. He didn't know what he was missing, and probably never would. Yet in the long run, she thought his absence was probably for the best. Some people only cause pain.

Exhausted, Emma settled back on the sofa, smoothed the sheets and opened her casebook. As she read, she listened for more sirens in the night air but the world was blissfully quiet. In less than five minutes, she was asleep again.

3

By the time Deputy Ren Taylor got the call, David Letterman had introduced his second guest of the evening, and Ren's three-step flossing ritual had begun in earnest. When he picked up the phone, he didn't expect to hear Sheriff Colson's voice crackling on the other end.

"What? The Patrick place? Good God. Just the girl? I'll be there. Right away, Sheriff." Ren placed the receiver on the hook and walked through his tidy house to make certain all doors were locked, and the blinds were drawn shut. He was dressed and on the road in less than ten minutes.

The drive to the Patrick farm would have been quick if it hadn't been on twisty back roads at night. Instead, it took nearly twenty minutes. Ren couldn't recall another murder in the tri-county area in his lifetime, and certainly not during the seven years he'd been the chief deputy sheriff. Armed robberies were the most heinous crimes he could remember, and there hadn't been many of those. He'd trained for a night like this for years, but his heart was racing. He gripped the steering wheel so tightly his hands hurt. He took a deep breath and exhaled, trying to shake off the feeling. But he knew he'd never want to grow accustomed to homicide investigations, or live in a community where murders weren't a rare and awful thing.

Ren's car traveled up the Patricks' steep driveway. His tires crunched on the gravel as he pulled behind Sheriff Colson's truck. He wasn't sure what to expect, except that Lyle Patrick's daughter, Jennifer, was dead. He slid out of his car and avoided a shallow puddle as he approached the sheriff's vehicle, guided by the light over the front door of the small house.

A portion of the front yard had already been sectioned off with yellow crime scene tape. The sheriff was standing outside of his truck, leaning against the roof of the vehicle, speaking to someone who was seated inside. As Ren approached the vehicle, he could see that Lyle Patrick was in the front seat, his shoulders and head leaning against the passenger door. Colson was speaking in hushed tones. Lyle, a hulk of a man, his face crumpled by convulsive sobs, held a tissue in his massive hand as he tried to catch the tears that ran down his face. Colson was doing what he could to comfort him. The sheriff had known Lyle for years, although Ren didn't think they were close. Still, in these parts, time and acquaintance added up.

Colson stepped back from the truck and, motioning for Ren to come closer, murmured instructions under his breath. "First room on the left. Eyeball the area, but don't go in the room since no one's taken photos yet. Just take notes. You know the drill. It's step by step. The same process as any other crime. I'll be with you in a minute. Forensics and the ME will be here shortly." The sheriff turned his focus to Lyle.

Ren returned to his car, donned gloves and protective coverings for his shoes and approached the house, careful to stay on the driveway, or the concrete entryway to avoid leaving footprints in the soft ground. The door, which had once been a cheery robin's egg blue, was now peeling and faded, a sad reminder of its former warm and welcoming façade. It had been left ajar.

The Patrick home was simply furnished, but threadbare. The living room seemed untouched by the night's events, with its plaid couch and wooden paneling still clean and intact. The small kitchen and office areas were modest but pristine. Ren trudged toward the girl's room down the hall.

Notebook in hand, Ren couldn't bring himself to describe what he saw. Shattered by gunfire, Jennifer Patrick lay sprawled like a broken doll in the middle of her blood-soaked bed. Unable to move, Ren stared at what had once been Jennifer's silky blonde hair. It was now matted with blood, goose down, and flecks of cotton, and feathered across her face like crudely-spun crimson Spanish lace. A stuffed toy, her school's mascot, lay aslant next to her head. One hand was raised next to her forehead, fingers curled, as if she had been sound asleep. Ren closed his eyes, overcome by the sight and the slightly metallic smell of blood.

He took in a deep breath and noted the other details. The bedroom was painted bright pink. With its ruffled curtains and pom-pom decorations, it was a room any girl would have been proud of if it hadn't been cruelly demolished. The window had been blown out and edges of the frilly curtains were blood-spattered. The cornice of lace at the top of the casement and ribbons of pink tatters danced with macabre glee in the breeze. The remaining glass shards added a menacing bite to the scene. The white wicker headboard, once a charming feminine touch to the room, had exploded into a thousand fractured pieces.

At first, Ren was unable to process what had occurred. What kind of deranged person would attack a beautiful young girl? Jennifer's death would not only crush Lyle, it would devastate friends, neighbors, and others across the county. Ren knew that until the killer was apprehended, the shock of Jennifer's murder would prevent the people of Greendale County from feeling safe, even in their own homes. Everyone's life changed with one vicious act.

Jennifer was Lyle's only child. Her mother had died ten or twelve years earlier, following a lengthy battle with cancer. Ren remembered Jennifer sitting on her mother's lap during church services. Sometimes the two wore matching dresses. He closed his eyes, recalling a Sunday school picnic by the river not long after Mrs. Patrick had died. Jennifer was probably about six. He had watched Lyle comb tangles out of little Jennifer's wet hair. The comb was dwarfed by his huge hands, but his touch was as delicate and light as a hummingbird's.

Ren strode back down the hall, and out of the front door. Reluctant to approach the tenderhearted giant again, he hesitated before walking back to the sheriff's vehicle. It was tough to look at so much hurt. Taking a deep breath, he plodded back to the truck, stood next to the sheriff, and noticing the condition of Lyle's sodden tissue, handed him his handkerchief.

Lyle blew his nose and struggled to speak. "I know who done this. It had to a' been Adam. Adam Gannon." Lyle's huge fists balled up like massive ham hocks.

"Why would you think Adam Gannon would want to harm Jennifer?" Sheriff Colson sat down in the driver's seat of the truck.

"He used to be Jennifer's boyfriend. She told me she broke up with him a couple of days ago. I never liked her seeing that boy. After she broke everything off, he was real upset. I know he done this...she was probably the first person who'd ever refused him anything."

"Robert and Darcy Gannon's kid?" Ren said.

"That's right." Lyle nodded.

The Gannons were one of the wealthiest families in the state. They owned a former cotton plantation in Greendale County which they'd converted to a horse farm with stables and thoroughbreds worth a fortune. Robert Gannon, the father, was one of the best college quarterbacks the state had ever produced. He and his wife Darcy were often in the local newspaper for social or charitable events. The family's wealth set Adam apart from other kids in the area, especially since his parents tended to spend excessively on their only son. Ren remembered that something about the kid was unusual, though he couldn't put his finger on what it was.

"I been knowin' the Gannons," Lyle continued. "I used to sell hay to 'em from the back pasture. I remember Adam from when he was a little kid. He's deaf, you know."

Ren nodded, remembering that the boy was always quiet.

"Jennifer wouldn't a' had it any other way but to have Adam as her boyfriend." Lyle heaved his throbbing head into his hands.

"This is a terrible tragedy. I'm so sorry, Lyle. You may not remember, but we all attended the same church at one time. When did Jennifer start seeing Adam?" Ren said.

"I'm not sure. Beginning of her senior year, I guess. I didn't want her around that Gannon kid at all, and she resented me for it. But she was a good girl. She studied hard and was planning on going to college. I just don't understand it. She didn't deserve this." Lyle's chest heaved. He broke into sobs so hard he could barely catch his breath. "I'm sorry. I just can't believe this happened."

Ren leaned toward Lyle. "Did you ever see anything that would make you think Adam was capable of something like this?"

Lyle shook his head. "Not really." He wiped his nose with Ren's handkerchief. "I know he didn't like it when they broke up. There's always been bad blood between our families. Jennifer didn't really care about none of that. Can't speak for Adam. But Jennifer was kind to Adam. Helped him. Now look at what he done." Lyle snuffled and wiped his eyes.

Colson nodded. Most people in town knew that Robert Gannon's father had taken advantage of Lyle's mother during the war by talking her into selling the best part of the Patrick farm to the Gannons while Lyle's dad was away, fighting. Now, as a result, the Gannons were prospering and the Patricks were barely making it, their stock and crops wasting away to nothing. Lyle managed to raise some corn and hay for feed and had a few head of cattle, but little else.

"Let's take a look at the outside of the house," Colson said.

Lyle wiped his face with his sleeve, and then opened the door of the truck and led them, flashlight playing across the grass, up the driveway. He stopped at the edge of the carport, resting against the side of the house for support.

"The shots came from outside the window," he said. "They woke me up. By the time I got out of bed and figured out what was going on, no one was there but Jennifer. That's all I could see. She was all by herself in her room." He hung his head, dug his fist in his eyes and wept.

Ren took Lyle by the elbow and helped him sit on the front stoop.

"So where's forensics?"

Colson shrugged. "Should be here any minute."

"Who called in the shooting?" Ren asked the sheriff, pointing to the severed telephone line.

"Lyle drove his truck to a neighbor's to make the call." Colson nodded toward a beaten-up Toyota truck parked haphazardly across the front of the yard.

"Whoever did this knew where the phone line was, even in the dark." Ren peered around the corner to the laundry room behind the carport.

A few minutes later, the medical examiner and forensics team pulled up to the farm, blue lights flashing. Ren tiptoed to Jennifer's window, careful to step only on stones and little grassy knobs, ignoring the sheriff's glare. He directed his light on the ground under the ledge, catching the glint of spent casings. There was also at least one perfect shoe print in the softened mud.

"This is what we need, Lyle," he said, gesturing for the newly arrived investigators to finish marking the site with yellow crime-scene tape. "We've got a decent shoe print here since it's been raining for the past week. If we're lucky, we'll find the rifle, then the owner, and match up the two pieces of evidence. If we get all that, we've got him."

Colson strode over to Lyle and put a hand on his shoulder. "I know this is difficult, but you can't touch anything in Jennifer's room or disturb the area outside the bedroom windows or the carport. You should stay somewhere else tonight." The three men were illuminated by the strobing lights of the county cars. "These men'll get all of the evidence they can tonight. But we'll all come out again tomorrow at daylight. The casts from the shoe prints should be dry in the morning, and we can make sure we didn't miss anything."

Lyle nodded. Colson stood up and squinted into the nearby pasture as if he was trying to imagine the killer's escape route.

"The ME will take Jennifer. He has to examine her." Ren said, indicating the ambulance next to Colson's truck. He walked toward his car, then stopped and turned around. "Somewhere we can drop you tonight, Lyle?"

Lyle climbed into Ren's car, unable to name a destination other than a local motel. Within the last hour, he had become a man with no family, no comfort, and nowhere to go.

4

Awakened by her 5:30 a.m. alarm, Emma pried her eyes open and winced as she rolled off the sofa and grabbed her robe. She was getting too old to sleep on a couch. Checking her backpack, she realized she'd left half of her notes for Civil Procedure at the office and would have to run by work before class. She mentally updated her to-do list as she brewed her morning caffeine.

Gulping down her first cup of coffee, she felt a familiar jolt as her brain kicked into gear. She jumped into the shower before she got her kids up and hopped out ten minutes later. Then, clearing a spot on the surface of the foggy bathroom mirror, peered at her face before she got ready for the day. Without makeup she still looked as if she was in her twenties. She'd inherited her mother's olive complexion, which didn't seem to wrinkle, and her father's deep brown eyes, which were now wide open, thanks to the Sumatran dark roast and her shower. She slathered moisturizer on her skin and scooped her blonde hair into a quick pony tail. A dash of mascara and a touch of red lipstick completed the look. She slid into a pair of slim black pants, a black and white striped shirt, and some loafers. Now for the kids.

"I don't want to wear that, Mom," Bobby mumbled as he watched Emma take jeans and a tee shirt out of the closet. "I want to wear my Death Star shirt."

"Sweetheart, you can't wear that every day. For one thing, it needs to be washed," Emma said, bending down to give him a kiss. Her brother had given the twins matching Star Wars shirts for their birthday, and, given the chance, Bobby would wear his every day.

Billy was halfway dressed before Bobby stirred. He was the first to react to the ringing phone, scurrying down the hall to answer the call with a brisk "hello, Grandmother." He handed the phone over to his mother with a smile as he headed for the bathroom. Billy had already honed the art of avoidance, especially for his grandmother's calls.

"Is everything okay, Mom?" Emma said, her voice rising half an octave.

"I was calling about Labor Day. Thought we'd meet you in Augusta on Thursday, then drive the boys over to Savannah. That gives you a little break since we're driving about a half an hour longer. But that's okay." Her mom sniffed. Emma hated her Mom's sniffs. "Then we'll drive back and meet you in Augusta again after the holiday." The statement was more a command than a proposal. "They don't need to be with you when you're distracted by studying," she added.

"That's two weeks from now. It's also a four-hour drive in the middle of a tough work and study schedule." Emma didn't try to hide her sigh. "I'll talk to the boys and see what they'd like to do. I have to get them ready for school now."

Emma hung up the phone and shook her head to expunge her mother's disapproving tone from the morning. She'd needed her parents' help with the boys since her divorce and now that she was in law school, she leaned on them even more, especially during exams. Her parents loved the boys. There was no doubt of that. And her dad was a good influence on them, which was important, especially now that she was a single mom. Her mother had disapproved of her divorce and hated that she'd enrolled in law school, even though she knew all about the problems Emma had had with the boys' father, and even though she knew Emma needed a better paying job. Her mom, who belonged to another generation of southern women, treated Emma's divorce as her own personal failure. Law school for women had been unthinkable in her day.

"Get a move on, boys!" Emma began cracking eggs for breakfast. She smiled at their freshly scrubbed faces when they scuffled in ten minutes later, shirts half-way tucked in, elbows and knees flying, and plopped down at the tiny round table.

"Would you two like to go down to the coast for Labor Day?" Emma slid plates filled with scrambled eggs and toast to each of the boys.

"Are you going?" Bobby asked between gulps of orange juice.

"No, hon," Emma said. "You know I need to study all the time now, and I should work even harder when I have time off."

Emma avoided Bobby's disappointed scowl. She hated time away from her kids. Even when she had to study, she had difficulty concentrating when they weren't there. Her kids were her anchor; she floundered without them. She didn't want them to leave, particularly on a holiday. But Emma's mom usually got her way. And this time her mom was right, she needed to study. Her shoulders slumped in resignation.

"I don't like going there without you." Bobby fiddled with his napkin, turning it into little white balls until Emma scooped it and the remnants of his breakfast into the trash.

"But you'll get to swim and do a lot of other fun things you wouldn't get to do here. Don't you agree, Billy?"

Billy nodded between bites of toast.

"Okay, it's decided, then," Emma said.

Emma marshaled the boys toward their toothbrushes while simultaneously combing their cowlicks. Mornings were crazy, and the time they had together was short. A part of her heart broke every day she watched the boys saunter down the sidewalk to catch their bus. They were growing up so quickly. Moments with her kids were sacred, and were probably as close as she ever got to prayer. But she wasn't kidding herself. She knew she was making mistakes. She chose law school, challenging even for a childless person, and a ridiculously demanding profession. Half the time she felt as if she didn't know what she was doing. Most of the time she felt as if she wasn't paying enough attention to anything in her life, not to her kids, or her studies, or her job. She felt as if she was doing everything wrong. Maybe her mom was right after all.

Emma watched the boys board the bus, grabbed her purse and books, and dashed to her beaten up Audi. She was determined to avoid the morning traffic, grab her notes, and still make it to class on time. She took the shortcut through campus and managed to make it to the town square within the ten minutes she'd allotted.

All in all, Emma liked Jonesburg. She liked college towns in general, and this place was as charming as a Eudora Welty novel. Great oaks canopied the streets of the city and dotted the campus. Spanish moss draped the trees, sending an elegant lacy shade to the late summer days. Cottages in lovely pastel colors decorated the hills. Daffodils sprouted by the thousands in springtime. Jonesburg loved its eccentrics too. Drunken writers, poets, and musicians gathered in its watering holes, and there was live music every night somewhere on the square. The town was idyllic. Perfect, almost.

Rounding the corner of Jonesburg's Civil-War-era square, past the bright red-and-yellow painted used book store, Emma noticed a large gathering of cars at the sheriff's office. She pulled into a parking space and waited for her car to stop sputtering before hopping out.

Emma worked for Silas Steele III, a respected defense attorney. Silas was following his father's and grandfather's well established legal legacy in a refurbished fire station across the street from the sheriff's department. Emma loved the old building with its high ceilings and creaking stairs. She secretly planned to slip down the pole that was still in the center of the station some late evening when she was there all by herself.

She unlocked the front door and bounded up the stairs to the second floor to grab her notes. She had a clear view of the sheriff's office from the window by her desk and peeked through her blinds as deputies filed out the front door and packed into Greendale County's four patrol cars. Perplexed, she watched the vehicles careen down the road like off-kilter land barges. This was the first time she had seen local law enforcement responding to an emergency during the two years she'd lived in Jonesburg. Whatever occurred last night had happened out in the county, outside of town. Otherwise, the Jonesburg city police would have been involved.

Emma had some misgivings about the sheriff and his men. To be fair, she had a similar sense about the entire town. If a community had never really been exposed to crime, it couldn't have a sophisticated response to it. Half of Jonesburg's citizens still left their doors unlocked and kept their keys in their cars while they were grocery shopping. She loved the innocence of the place, but she often felt as if Jonesburg was stuck in another era. That had to be even more true for the people who lived on farms and in rural neighborhoods outside of town.

Emma grew up in a community where serious crime was widespread and frequent. Not that that was a good thing. But it changed the atmosphere of a place. It created an awareness—an edge that was missing in Jonesburg. Emma suspected that same edge was missing in the sheriff and his officers.

But one of the deputies had managed to attract Emma's attention for an entirely different reason. He stood out in the crowd of bustling, frenzied officers. He was composed, good-looking, although a little more spit-polished than she usually liked. His crisply ironed shirt must have been unwrapped that very morning from the laundry's paper packaging. His shoes caught the sunlight. Somehow, she knew he'd smell good. He was tall, well over six feet. His straw-colored hair reflected the light of the sun as he moved. He had a strong jaw and shoulders to match. As she watched him leave the office with the sheriff, she noticed she liked the calm steadiness of his walk. And Emma, who didn't have time for friends outside of work or the baseball team's mom's group, never noticed the way men walked.

5

en and Sheriff Colson pulled up to the Patrick farm and parked the sheriff's truck on the gravel road next to the fence. Ren watched as small gnats, reflected in the sunlight, swarmed around the hood. A handful of deputies, comprising the Greendale County forensic team, parked behind the truck, and scrambled out of their cars, eager to continue their investigation. One of them hustled over to the sheriff's truck.

"We're heading over to the house to pick up the shoe impressions and make sure we didn't miss anything," an oversized deputy mumbled through a massive plug of chewing tobacco. Colson signaled his approval with a hasty nod. Ren noticed darkened saliva drying in the corner of the deputy's mouth.

"You'd think that stuff would curb his appetite," Colson said.

Ren watched the heavyset man lumber down the road. He shuddered as he recalled Coke bottles full of nasty brown tobacco spittle that littered the floor of the sheriff's office.

"Yeah, well, I never noticed it affecting yours," Ren said.

Colson had given up the practice only about a year ago, partly to please Ren. Colson jabbed Ren playfully on the shoulder as he stepped out of the truck.

Ren's father, who had been an investigator with the sheriff's department, had died of lung cancer some fifteen years earlier. Colson stepped in then to help out Ren and his family when he could, and they'd grown close over the years. Ren was younger than several of the other deputies. He knew his promotion to chief deputy meant not only that Colson trusted him, but that he was also grooming him to take over as sheriff one day. Colson was gradually allowing him to take the reins in several cases.

Ren slid out of the truck and watched from a distance as deputies began to gather around Jennifer Patrick's window to remove dried shoeprint casts from their metal frames. Some of the group had already focused their cameras on the ground under Jennifer's bedroom window to take photos in the daylight. At Colson's request, he stayed behind in the field.

"Years ago, when I was still a boy," Colson began, "my granddad taught me how to track wild animals in the woods. Mostly raccoon, rabbits, and fox." He paused a moment. "He told me once that fear can be more dangerous than size or strength. A scared animal, no matter how small, can be extremely dangerous."

Ren nodded, not quite sure where the sheriff was going.

"What do you think was the most valuable lesson I learned from my granddad?" the sheriff asked him.

Ren shrugged his shoulders, but curiosity kept his attention focused.

"To trust my own instincts," the sheriff said. "What do your instincts tell you about this murder, Ren?"

Ren contemplated the question. It was a strange case, all right. It was hard to imagine how anyone could cause the sort of destruction and mayhem he'd seen last night. Who could have done this? The easiest answer was the one suggested to them: Jennifer Patrick's former boyfriend, Adam Gannon. But Ren wasn't so sure about that, and he wasn't about to jump to conclusions because a grieving father thought he knew who the killer was.

"The person who did this might've been disturbed, or maybe even deranged, but it's obvious he'd carefully planned his attack," Ren said. "This wasn't an impulsive act."

"What makes you think that?" the sheriff said.

"Well, the telephone line was cut. That shows a plan. And he seemed to know where the girl slept. I doubt if he spent much time looking through windows to find her."

Colson nodded and squinted toward the pasture.

"You may be right," Colson said. "But there was such an uncontrolled spray from the gun. He was obviously not a trained shooter. This doesn't seem to be the work of a typical teenager either."

"I don't think a typical teenager would have anything to do with this sort of thing." Ren shaded his eyes to get a better view of Colson.

Colson shrugged. "Unless there's a deeper problem, and that's what we may be looking at here. When kids get into this sort of trouble, it usually starts out as a robbery, or a harmless prank that goes bad. This has an entirely different footprint."

Ren nodded. "You also said something about fear," Ren said. "Who could be afraid of an eighteen-year-old girl? Do you get the sense the shooter was afraid of something or someone else?"

"I only meant that fear is a motivator. It can compel people to do things they wouldn't ordinarily do. It's important to keep the motivation for this murder in mind. Lyle's blamed Adam, and he's a likely suspect. Would anyone else have a motive or a reason to kill Jennifer? That's something we need to keep asking ourselves."

Ren watched as Colson surveyed the damage to the land caused by two weeks of near solid rain. The early sun beat down on his head as he peered across the field, his hand shielding his eyes from the blinding light. The pasture still smelled of freshly cut hay and alfalfa. The odor of manure drifted over from Lyle's dwindling herd, grazing in an adjoining meadow. It was hot, dank, and steamy from the morning dew.

Ren followed Colson's gaze across the field, checking the markings embedded into the furrowed ground. Two sets of tracks led from the side gate halfway to the fence at the end of the north pasture. The morning sun had begun to dry the larger ruts into clay-like ridges. The first set appeared to have been made when the driver entered the pasture. The ground was lightly indented along these tracks, with no rutting, and the recently cut hay was bent but still intact. Those tracks had likely been made by a large pickup, judging by the size of the tires. The second set completely destroyed the field where the tires ripped up the turf in a hasty getaway.

Ren watched as Colson walked along the tire tracks until they ended. The sheriff stooped over and moved slowly for another twenty feet. He stopped in that same crouched position for a while with his eyes closed, looking like a khaki-clad Buddha, his hair wafting in the breeze. Then he stood up and waved Ren over.

"Get the guys to make a print of these boot impressions and, once they're dry, compare these to the ones found at the front of the house."

He pointed to some other indentations in the mud. "What do you make of that?"

"Looks like marks made from the toes of a shoe. And those smaller ones could have been made by fingers or knuckles," Ren said.

"Yeah," the sheriff said. "He must have been crouched over as he made his way to the house," he said. "And judging the size and depth of the markings, the killer was the size of a full-grown man."

Ren pointed out similar boot prints leading back toward the tire impressions. "By the length of the gait, looks like he was running on his way back."

"Well, wouldn't you?" Colson asked. "Let's get molds made of the rest of these tire marks and shoe prints. And get photographs too. Get a couple of the guys over here to help," he added as he headed off toward the house.

6

Arousing shake jolted Adam Gannon from a fitful slumber. For a moment, he was caught between two worlds, uncertain whether he was dreaming or awake. Blinking his eyes open, he sat up, startled, his heart pounding as if it were about to explode. He didn't like surprises. His father, Robert, reached over his bed and tugged the cord of the Venetian blinds. Bright white light angled its way across the room. Adam threw himself back on the bed, shut his eyes, and pulled the covers over his head. Even though his eyes were closed, he could sense the unforgiving glare of the morning sun.

He should never have given his dad a key to his apartment. But he'd needed a place near the junior college and his dad, who was paying for everything, had insisted on it. He clenched his jaws. He'd get the key back, one way or another.

Adam pulled the covers back, squinted his eyes open again, and, for a few seconds, watched the shadows from the oak tree play across his wall. He caught a glimpse of his dad's flushed face and knotted forehead, which could only mean one thing—he was upset. Adam's second clue was his father's clenched fist pretending to knock on a door. Was someone coming by? Now? Or later? He couldn't be certain.

Deaf from infancy, Adam was a lip reader, and although he only under-stood a fraction of what others said, he'd learned to observe body language and facial expressions. From that, he developed a better understanding of speech, and people's idiosyncrasies. An expert mimic, he was also an artist, and a quick study in most sports. His skills convinced others that he understood what was being said when he often didn't. By the time Adam figured out the context of a conversation, most people had already moved on. He missed subtleties. The misunderstandings that resulted caused a disconnect that made Adam feel isolated and alone. Even his parents had little patience with him. He felt as if he was living underwater and everyone else was up top.

His dad was still talking, then pretended to rap on a door, his lips wagging in his familiar way. Adam couldn't understand most of it. He knew someone might be coming by—or maybe they'd dropped by his father's place earlier? He didn't get the name of the person his dad mentioned, although he thought he picked up the word "sheriff." Since his father pointed to his eyes and then back to Adam, it seemed pretty clear someone wanted to see him. But his dad wasn't easy to follow, especially when he was worked up about something.

Adam turned his back on his father to begin hunting for his notebook and pen, hoping to encourage him to explain. Adam strode over to the kitchen and opened the junk drawer, reached back, and ripped out his notebook. He handed it and a pen to his father.

Adam used the written word as a last resort. Math came easy to him, but he struggled with reading and writing. The only deaf student at his school, he was reluctant to reach out for help. He hadn't been taught to speak, and, even though he'd learned through trial and error to say a few words, he was usually too embarrassed to try. He quickly grasped concrete concepts, easily understanding most nouns and verbs, anything tangible, but abstract ideas, or the relationship of one idea to another could be difficult, if not impossible.

His dad scribbled:

A deputy came by the house this morning looking for you. I gave him your address. He'll be here soon.

Adam struggled through his dad's message and handed it back to him, raising his eyebrows, questioning the meaning of the visit.

His father continued speaking, his lips punctuating each word with jerking staccato-like emphasis. Tiny beads of perspiration formed along his hairline.

Adam studied his dad's words as they were formed. *What was he saying? Why did I pull you out? Do you know what is out? Oh...Do you know what this is about?*

Adam shook his head, turned around, and shuffled down the hallway, breathing slowly in an attempt to ease his nerves. He grabbed a towel, stepped in the shower and turned on the water as hot as he could stand it.

A towering man in a tan-colored uniform stepped into Adam's tiny apartment, filling up the space in the front room. A couple of men in matching uniforms remained outside in the breezeway. A badge pinned to the man's shirt pocket identified him as Chief Deputy Sheriff, Greendale County. The name TAYLOR was etched on a brass bar over his pocket, and a gun was worn on a belt at his waist. When his dad let him in the door, Adam noticed that they didn't shake hands, and neither man smiled.

Deputy Taylor turned toward Adam. "Adam, I'm told you're deaf. Can you understand me, or do I need to write down my questions?" The deputy pointed to his ear and pretended to write with an imaginary pen.

As Adam stepped toward the deputy with his notebook and pen, his father moved next to him, interrupting the deputy. "I can help."

Adam threw his notebook on a nearby chair. The pen skittered along the floor.

"Is there a place we can sit?" the deputy asked as he stepped toward Adam.

Adam showed the deputy to a small table in the kitchen.

"I'm Deputy Ren Taylor." He pointed to his badge, then pulled a card from his wallet and handed it to Adam. Typed across the top of the card were the words "Miranda Rights." The deputy began to read and Adam followed along, occasionally glancing up to watch the deputy's lips for clues.

When he finished, Ren looked up from the card. "How do you want to proceed, Adam?"

"We'll answer your questions, Deputy," Robert said.

"That was a question for Adam. Adam, are you willing to answer my questions?"

Adam looked at his dad, then the deputy and nodded. "Last night, there was a murder off of Highway 17 in Greendale County." Deputy Taylor sat down in the chair offered by Adam, his legs protruding from under the table into the tiny kitchen. "Jennifer Patrick was killed."

"Did you understand that, Adam?" His dad hovered next to Adam, studying his face.

Adam nodded. His cheeks flushed a deep crimson. He blinked back tears.

"Where were you around midnight last night?" The deputy leaned back in the kitchen chair and folded his arms across his chest.

Adam turned away from Ren and stared out of the window above the sink.

His dad reached out and touched Adam's shoulder. He turned around to look at his father.

"Did you understand what he said?" Robert asked, pointing to his head as he spoke. Adam nodded, dropping his gaze to the floor. "I mean no disrespect, Deputy, but you must be out of your mind to think Adam could do something like this."

"Mr. Gannon, I'm not accusing Adam of anything. But Lyle Patrick, Jennifer's father, not only believes Adam is capable of murder, but since Jennifer recently broke up with him, he's convinced Adam actually did it. So, right now, Adam's a primary suspect. We've got a Consent to Search form I'd like Adam to look over. Then, if he signs it , I'd like to search his apartment and truck."

The deputy faced Adam. "Adam, I need you to read this, and if you agree to the search, sign it." Deputy Taylor handed the form to Adam.

"I'm sure we've got nothin' to hide." Adam's dad turned toward him, catching his eye. "Let me know if you need help."

Adam nodded and scanned the form the deputy handed him. He signed his name at the bottom and handed the document back to the deputy.

"Adam, do you understand what's going on here?" The deputy pointed to the form Adam had just signed.

Adam studied the deputy's lips and shrugged. He knew the deputy was going to look at his apartment and truck, but he wasn't sure why.

Deputy Taylor leaned toward Adam. "Adam, how old are you?"

Robert answered, "He's nineteen."

"Look, Mr. Gannon, you need to understand that Adam's old enough to answer these questions himself."

"Yes, but he's deaf. I won't let you bully him because he can't understand what's going on."

"I'm trying to make certain he does understand what's going on, but instead, you seem to be answering for him. He's not a minor; he's deaf. There's a difference. How can I make sure he knows what's going on here?"

"Well, he can read lips. So, talk to him like you have been. If that doesn't work, you can always use his notebook and write things down for him."

The deputy handed the consent form back to Adam.

Adam watched the deputy as he spoke, but his lips moved in an exaggerated manner, which made it difficult to follow.

"It's better if you don't speak so slowly," Robert Gannon said.

The deputy started again.

Adam watched as the deputy formed his question.

What was that? Her father...something... He shook his head to let the deputy know he didn't understand. *Her father thinks I...he thinks I killed Jennifer? No!*

Adam frowned and looked down at his hands, which were beginning to shake again. He raised his head as the deputy moved his chair closer.

"You've just given us permission to examine your apartment and truck. Do you understand that?" Deputy Taylor nodded his head toward the form.

"I'll make certain he understands," Robert Gannon said, walking over to the table where Adam and the deputy sat.

Ignoring his dad, Adam peered at the deputy across the table. *What did he just say? Sam in my apartment? What?* He scanned the consent form again and handed it back to the deputy with a shrug.

Deputy Taylor motioned for the deputies to begin their examination of the small apartment. He noticed muddy boots next to the bedroom door and picked them up as well as some jeans in the corner next to the closet.

"I need to take these in to be tested." The deputy placed the boots in a plastic bag and sat them next to the door.

Deputy Taylor completed his search of the apartment and directed the other deputies to examine the truck in the parking lot. Several minutes later, one of the deputies walked back into Adam's apartment carrying a large semi-automatic rifle.

"We found this behind the seat of your truck, Adam. Do you know anything about this weapon?"

Adam stared at the deputy, not knowing how to respond.

"Is this gun registered in your name?"

Not understanding the question, Adam diverted his gaze, then glanced back at the officer.

"Is this your rifle?"

He nodded.

"We're taking the firearm to the sheriff's office with the other evidence we found today. We also need to seize your truck so we can get the tires tested. We'll need to make imprints of each of the tires so we can compare them with the tire treads found at the scene. To do that, the tires have to actually be on the truck at the time we make the imprints. Do you own the truck, Adam?"

"Yes, he owns the truck. It was his eighteenth birthday present. Do what you have to do, Deputy. But he'll need his truck back," Robert said.

"We'll take the impressions and check to see if we need the truck for any other reason. We'll probably need to take some dirt samples, that sort of thing. Here's a receipt for the vehicle. It may be able to be returned, but right now I can't promise that. One thing, though, Adam shouldn't leave the county." The deputy headed out of the door.

Adam crawled back in bed after the chief deputy and his men left, and closed his eyes, finally giving in to tears. He'd never forget the first time he met

Jennifer. It was at the lake the summer before their senior year. Jerry, one of his teammates, had invited everyone to meet at his parents' camp for water skiing. Someone was bringing watermelons. Jerry had made a special effort to invite Adam, writing out directions to the place, so Adam decided to drive out. When Adam pulled up to the dock where everyone was gathered, Jennifer was all he saw, even though she was surrounded by a crowd of at least fifteen or twenty people.

She towered over all of the other girls, and some of the boys. Her blonde hair was what he noticed first. It shone silvery-white in the sunlight, casting a light so bright it almost hurt his eyes. He knew she was the only girl he'd want to be with from that day forward. But he didn't know how to approach her. How could he introduce himself, or even carry on a simple conversation?

Too many people came to the lake that day for them to all board the thirteen foot Chris-Craft at once, so they took turns skiing, four on the boat at a time. Others were milling about eating watermelon, throwing the football, or sunbathing. Adam sat down on the dock with his sketchbook and began drawing a scene from the shoreline. He realized someone had sat down next to him and when he turned, he was surprised to see it was the girl with the silvery blonde hair.

She said something to him. He indicated he couldn't hear.

She picked up a pencil and wrote in his sketch pad:

My name is Jennifer.

He wrote, *Adam,* then pointed to his chest.

They both smiled.

She wrote, *grade?*

He wrote the number twelve. She smiled and pointed to herself. They both laughed.

She wrote, *school?*

He wrote, *Greendale Christian Academy,* then pointed to her.

She raised her eyebrows and wrote, *Greendale High School and we beat you last year.*

They both laughed.

Adam wasn't as embarrassed as he thought he'd be. She was easy to be with. She promised to come watch him play basketball at some of his games.

Adam felt his face flush red when he picked up the pencil, accidentally brushing her hand before he wrote his question.

Pizza?

She nodded.

Friday?

She smiled.

6:00. Moe's. Where house?

She shook her head and touched his hand.

I'll meet you there.

Adam asked if he could draw her, and Jennifer posed on the dock for him as he sketched. When he finished, he showed her the drawing. She smiled when she saw it, and wrote:

You are so talented! I love the sketch. Can I keep it?

He tore the sheet of paper out of his notebook and gave it to her. He'd never felt so happy.

At the end of that day, he held her hand as he walked her to her friend's car.

They were together their entire senior year, through all of his basketball games, and all of her dances and parties. He visited her at her house, and, even though her father didn't know it, he often sneaked into her bedroom window at night and left the same way, sometimes after midnight.

Until a couple of days ago.

He didn't understand why she'd broken it off. She had never really explained.

7

August 17, 1990

When Emma Thornton first learned about Adam's case, she wasn't concerned with his guilt or innocence. His defense was much more interesting. What did Adam understand at the time of his arrest? Did he even know why he was in jail?

"I think I can help you talk to Adam or get someone who can," Emma told Silas on the phone. "I would bet he didn't understand what was going on at the time everything was taken from his apartment and truck, or at the time he was arrested. That's a good argument for the suppression of that evidence, at least. Plus, I'm pretty sure that under state law, they should have had an interpreter present. I don't think his dad qualifies. You should have some solid defenses there. If you've decided to take the case, I'll help you." Emma penciled in the case on her active litigation list.

At first, Silas wasn't sure he wanted to represent Adam. He had several trials coming up which nearly filled his calendar for the remainder of the year. Plus, he'd never been around the deaf, and didn't know what to expect. He didn't know if he and Adam would ever be able to have a meaningful conversation, which worried him. He'd had challenging clients before. He'd been lied to more times than he could count, but this was different. He wasn't sure how to approach a client who couldn't hear, and had little patience for complications. He rubbed his head, finally deciding to take the case if they'd agree to his price. He wasn't one to run away from difficulties.

"Come down to the courthouse this afternoon. Adam's already been indicted since the DA pushed his case through to the grand jury with everything else they had. I filed a motion for a hearing on the bond, and it's been set for today at 2:30."

"That was fast. But I can't make it. I've got class at 2:30, and it's one I can't miss."

"Then come on down to the office after the hearing and meet Adam and his parents. I feel certain I'll be able to get Adam out on bail. Try to get there by 3:45."

Emma rushed through the office door at 4:00, letting it slam behind her.

"They're in the conference room." The receptionist scowled.

Emma breezed through the lobby and headed toward the back of the office. Although Silas had upgraded the wiring when he moved from his father's old offices and refurbished the fire station, the space still seemed dimly lit. She peered into the room, trying to read the faces in front of her.

"Nice to see you could make it," Silas said, not looking up from the Gannons' information form.

Emma ignored Silas's sarcasm. She knew he was a perfectionist, always testy when she was late, reminding her that no judge would cut her slack in the courtroom. Which, of course, was true. But her classes had to take priority while she was still a student. She knew he'd get over it.

"As we planned, we got Adam's bail set." Silas stacked the Gannons' recently completed papers in front of him in a neat pile.

Emma scanned the room, more interested, for the moment, in the people seated at the conference table. The only woman, sitting next to Adam, had to be his mother, Darcy Gannon. Visibly shaken, her delicate features were swollen and red from crying, but Emma could tell she was a stunning woman. She had dressed for the arraignment in a navy blue silk suit, tailored to glide over her trim body perfectly. It was complimented by a double strand of pearls worn closely at the neck. Her blonde hair tumbled over her shoulders, catching the scant light of the wall sconces in the room. Emma detected a tremor in Darcy's delicate, tapered hands when she dabbed her eyes. Her skin, which was so pale it seemed nearly translucent, had the glistening, creamy texture of whipped meringue. Emma swallowed her envy. How could anyone be so perfect? When Emma entered the room, Darcy's eyes darted in her direction, but she immediately returned her gaze to her trembling hands, as if willing the shaking to subside.

Her husband, by contrast, paced around the room, his fists shoved in his jean pockets. He didn't look up as Emma approached the conference table.

The difference between the two was startling. Robert Gannon, although attired in an expensive tweed jacket, wore cowboy boots and a gold chain around his neck. His black hair was long for a man of his age, reaching well below his starched collar. Well-tanned, with the bulky muscles of a former athlete, he reminded Emma of the men she saw hanging around the bars at Hilton Head, back in the days when she could take vacations. Emma's dislike for him was immediate.

Adam Gannon sat with his hands folded in his lap, mimicking his mother's posture. Stoic, silent, and still, Adam's eyes barely flickered in Emma's direction. He'd only been released that afternoon. His composure puzzled her. She'd expected to see signs of anxiety, but he remained calm, his face completely devoid of emotion. She grabbed the bond documents. Bail had been set at half a million, which meant that his parents had paid fifteen per cent, or seventy-five thousand dollars to the bail bondsman. And they'd also guaranteed the remainder of the bail. That was a lot of money, even for the Gannons. Emma wasn't sure Adam understood the trouble he was in.

Early in her teaching career, Emma worked next to deaf educators, where she learned more about teaching language skills than when she was taking university courses on the same subject. She was fascinated with how the deaf were able to learn to speak, read, and write, even though they couldn't hear. Emma had learned a few basic signs and how to finger spell, but she wasn't proficient. Most of the deaf students she knew wore hearing aids, which enabled them to pick up segments of a few words if they had any residual hearing. She was surprised Adam didn't wear one. Even stranger, his parents rarely looked at him when they spoke and no attempts were made at sign language.

"Adam's always been a good boy," Darcy said, lifting her chin. "He played basketball and soccer in junior and senior high school and was also on the wrestling team." She attempted a shaky smile.

Adam was a handsome, well-muscled nineteen-year-old, sleek like his mother but with his father's darker coloring. Wearing a striped oxford button-down shirt and jeans, he was neatly dressed, his hair perfectly styled. That haircut alone must have cost a small fortune to maintain, Emma thought, suppressing her resentment.

Silas moved closer to Adam, and glanced at the Gannons.

"We'd like you to stay in the room while we question Adam, but to avoid a waiver of the attorney client privilege, we will need you to act as our agent, and interpreters, or communication assistants for Adam. If you agree to do this, you will not be able to discuss anything you hear today with anyone else. Can you do this?"

The Gannons both nodded.

Emma touched Adam's arm. "Adam, is it okay for your parents to stay in the room while we ask you questions about the case? They're staying to help us."

Adam shrugged and nodded.

Silas leaned toward Adam, for once seeming unsure of himself. It was obvious he'd never spoken to a deaf person.

"Can you tell me where you were the night Jennifer Patrick was killed?" He shouted at Adam, loud enough for the people in the next building to hear.

Adam turned away from Silas, folded his arms, and set his jaw like a boxer entering the ring. Robert struck the same posture with near syncopated timing.

"Do you know why you're here?" Silas shouted even louder, flailing his hands and long arms in the air.

Even though he was quite slim, at six-foot-four, Silas was an imposing figure. His red hair jutted out at odd angles on the top of his head from several cowlicks over which he had no control. His Army days left him with such an air of authority that every question sounded like a command.

Emma had seen deaf students place their heads down on their desks, or pivot around in their seats if they didn't want to pay attention to their teacher. If they couldn't see, they couldn't do what their teachers were telling them to. It was obvious from Adam's behavior he didn't want to "listen" to Silas.

"Does Adam sign? Does he understand American Sign Language?" Emma asked the Gannons.

"Well, no." Darcy stared at her hands again. Her voice was so soft and lilting that Emma strained to hear her.

"We sent him to a school for the deaf when he was little, but pulled him out when they started to teach him sign language."

Emma, stunned, adjusted her face to hide her disapproval, hoping Darcy hadn't noticed. "Why'd you do that?" she asked, hoping she didn't sound rude.

Darcy ignored Emma's question. "When Adam was born, he seemed perfect. We don't know if he was born deaf or not. He was a quiet baby, and never cried much."

"When did you realize he couldn't hear?" Emma asked.

"Right before his first birthday." Darcy shifted her gaze to the conference room window.

"He got the flu sometime before his first birthday, and his fever spiked a few times, but the doctor just said to give him plenty of fluids and some Tylenol. Now they're thinking he may have had meningitis, and that caused nerve damage," Robert said as he stepped closer to Adam. "They call it a nerve hearing loss."

"What made you realize he couldn't hear?" Emma said.

"One day he was in his playpen and our housekeeper knocked over a large potted plant from the table right next to Adam. Darcy was on the back porch and said it was so loud she could hear it all the way back there. She jumped up and ran to where they were. Right?" Robert glanced at his wife for approval.

Darcy nodded and turned toward Adam, who hadn't taken his eyes off of his father. Although Adam's expression hadn't changed, Emma sensed he understood what his father was saying. There was a look in his eye. A certain intelligence, or knowing.

"When she walked in, the housekeeper told her that Adam didn't notice the pot falling over, even though the crash was so loud. They clapped their hands next to Adam after that, but he didn't seem to notice."

"So what did you do once you suspected he was deaf?" she asked.

Robert turned his head away from Emma, ignoring her question.

"We took him to all the best doctors and audiologists in Atlanta, and they confirmed that he was deaf." Darcy folded her hands and placed them in her lap. "'Profound hearing loss,' they said. I didn't believe it at first. I thought maybe he had an ear infection or something. I guess we didn't handle it very well. Robert punched the doctor who told us right in the face. He couldn't accept it." Darcy dabbed her eyes. Her face grew redder, and pink blotches flushed along her neck. Robert Gannon's features were locked in a frozen stare.

"We'll need to get an audiologist on board, Emma. There should be one at the university you can contact to test Adam to verify his level of hearing or lack of hearing. That will be important for several of our defenses."

Emma made notations in her legal pad to follow up on Silas's instructions.

"We didn't want Adam to suffer by being different from the other kids." Darcy shifted in her chair and re-crossed her legs, smoothing her skirt toward her knees with a move that caught Silas's attention.

"When he was nearly three, we sent him to a school in Atlanta and the teachers there taught him to lip read and speak some. He was there until he was five, or through his kindergarten year. Then we put him in Greendale Christian Academy, a private school closer to our house," she said.

"Do any other deaf kids attend Greendale?" Emma asked.

"Not that I know of."

"Was there a special teacher there for Adam, or an interpreter?"

"No. He was treated like all the rest of the kids. That's what we wanted for Adam."

"Do you know how much he understands from lip reading?" Emma asked.

Darcy shook her head. "He seems to follow what his teachers tell him to do in wrestling classes. I've seen him do that. He has to learn to communicate with hearing people, not with deaf people. He's going to a good school and is being taught by good people. We believe we are doing the best we can for him."

Even though Adam's parents insisted that he be treated like everyone else, he was a lip reader who didn't use sign language. He wasn't like everyone else, and the law required that an interpreter be present during searches, seizures, arrests or any legal proceeding. There seemed to be serious problems with the seizure of evidence from Adam's apartment and truck. Since Adam was a lip reader the law also required that the interpreter do an "oral interpretation," or mouth speech to Adam at the time of the search, mimicking what the deputy was saying so his lips could be read easily. As far as she knew, that wasn't done. Still, Emma needed to see what Adam could understand from normal spoken or written speech.

"I'm guessing that there's a lot of physical demonstration in a wrestling class that would be easier for him to mimic. Is he able to read and understand written questions?" Emma asked.

"I'm not sure. You can try." Darcy reached over and moved a lock of hair out of Adam's eyes. Adam jerked his head back as soon as his mother touched him and moved his arm away from her simultaneously.

Emma sat back in her seat. Her eyebrows, arched ever so slightly upwards, revealed her surprise. Her boys found affectionate gestures embarrassing, and they were only eight. It didn't surprise her that Adam recoiled from Darcy's touch. She was more surprised Darcy seemed uncertain about Adam's ability to read.

"Does he read? Do you know his reading level?"

"He reads, but I wouldn't have any idea about the level." Darcy smiled at Adam, then Emma.

Emma grabbed a legal pad and wrote: *Do you know what happened to Jennifer Patrick?* She pushed it toward Adam.

Adam picked up the pad, read Emma's question, and wrote: *she dead*

Emma then wrote: *How did she die?*

Adam paused. His hands shook as he reached for the pencil, then scribbled: *man shot*

Emma grabbed the pencil. *Who is the man? What do you know about him?*

Adam shook his head.

Emma scrawled: *Did you see the shooting? How did it happen?*

Adam hesitated, then wrote: *Man shot gun*

Emma shoved the pad over to Silas, who read the exchange. Their eyes locked for an instant. They'd both read the police report. Adam's brief account revealed that he might know something about the night of the murder. If so, he could be holding back important information.

Do you understand that the sheriff thinks you killed Jennifer?

After reading Emma's question, Adam slammed his hand on the table. "Nah!" he shouted, his face contorted with emotion. His voice was uncontrolled, guttural. He shoved his chair back, stood up, and began pacing the room. Forcing himself to sit down, he picked up the pad and wrote: *not Adam bad man shot. he shot gun. not Adam*

Emma then wrote: *Who was the man? Who killed Jennifer?*

Adam picked up the pad: *not Adam.*

His face was flushed crimson and little veins appeared along his temple. His jaw rippled as he clenched his teeth and glared at Emma.

Where were you at midnight last night?

Adam read the question, shoved the paper aside, bowed his head into his hands, and refused to make eye-contact with Emma or Silas.

Realizing she wasn't going to get more information from Adam that day, Emma shut down the session, determined to discover the key to communication with Adam, and to gain his trust.

Emma cleaned and chopped broccoli as she mulled over her interview with

Adam. Had he actually revealed details of the murder scene today? He'd also insisted on his innocence, which wasn't necessarily inconsistent with the truth, but she knew she needed much more information. One thing was certain, Adam couldn't know the murder scene details unless he was there. And, if he were there that night, chances are, he was guilty.

She began chopping chicken. That must be why he wouldn't tell them where he was at the time of the shooting. She put the chicken in a pan with some olive oil, garlic, a dash of salt, basil, and green onions. The recipe began simmering on top of the tiny apartment stove and savory odors soon filled the kitchen.

Emma couldn't ignore that Adam was isolated by his communication skills, both by his struggles to speak and his difficulty understanding what others said. That sort of seclusion had to have affected him. But something pulled him through high school. An innate intelligence, perhaps? And why was he stoic one minute, then reactive and volatile the next? Was the "man" Adam described, the one he said shot Jennifer, imaginary or real? At this point, Emma had no clue.

In a separate pan Emma whisked together chicken broth, heavy cream, and a little tarragon, then added some chicken drippings from the pan. She took the broccoli out of the microwave, and hesitated for a moment before she called the boys. The investigation would be difficult. Adam was fragile and she was new to all of this. One mistake and Adam could refuse to communicate with any of them. She needed to be able to get to the truth, but should she launch a full blown excavation into the underpinnings of his mind? Did she even want to know that much? A part of her wanted to uncover what secrets, if any, Adam might be harboring, but she realized that could be dangerous. Especially if she discovered information she would rather not know.

8

August 18, 1990

E mma's Monday morning class concluded at 11:00 giving her just
enough time to make it to the sheriff's office before lunch. The
Greendale Sheriff's Department occupied a boxy, red brick building
filled at that time of the day, with deputies completing affidavits for warrants
before the courthouse closed for lunch, and citizens with traffic violations.
Clutching her notebook and Silas's expensive camera to her chest, she
approached the officer at the front desk, identified herself, and handed him
her driver's license.

A deputy led her down a dark hallway to the back of the complex, into
a small room. The space was intensely bright. Based on all of the cop
movies she'd seen, she expected the evidence room to be dark and dank,
with lockers lining the walls. Instead, sun reflected through open windows
onto the floors of the small chamber and up onto the ceilings, bouncing
about from pane to pane in a checkerboard pattern. The trees stirred outside
as lazy morning breezes blew rag weed pollen through the air and into the
windows, which were gaping open. She sneezed and squinted through the
sunlight as she looked around the space.

Tables lined the walls. Bloodstained bed linens, stuffed envelopes, shoe casts, and crime scene photographs were piled up on top. Molds of tire imprints, tires, clothes, and a rifle were stacked on one side of the room. Two deputies stood across the room at attention, like mismatched bookends, carefully monitoring Emma's movements. One of them, the thin one, seemed friendlier than the other.

"Come on in," the smiling officer said. "Take as long as you need to look at this stuff. We gotta stay here with you to make sure nothing leaves the room." He grinned through tobacco-stained teeth, holding up a pair of oversized rubber gloves for her to put on.

Emma nodded at the deputy. She grabbed the gloves, slipped them on, and approached the wads of bloody bedclothes without hesitation. She knew why the windows were open after a few minutes of examining the stained bedspread and sheets, and quickly snapped a few photos of the more grossly damaged linens.

"You got a mighty strong stomach for such a small girl," the deputy said, raising an eyebrow as he stepped over to one of the benches. "Name's Frankie," he said, extending a hand.

The officer, a lanky, tobacco-chewing man of about thirty, wore a .357 magnum slung down low alongside his spider-like leg. Massive key chains and handcuffs jangled loudly when he sauntered about the room. His shoes, which looked like spit-polished U-boats poking out from under his pants, made little tapping noises when he stepped. He seemed to like the sound. He was a one-man band.

Emma shook the deputy's hand and turned her gaze back to the sheets and other evidence in the room, suddenly feeling the need to sit down. Her hands shook ever so slightly, and she could feel the blood leave her face. She kept her back turned so the deputies wouldn't notice and began listing each item in her notebook.

"Do you know who took these photos?" Emma asked.

"We got a few guys. They usually put their initials on the back." Frankie pointed to the back of one of the photos.

Emma nodded and noted the initials "R.T." on one of the eight-by-tens.

"Who's that?" She pointed at the initials.

"That'd probably be Ren Taylor, the chief deputy."

"I'd like to speak to him."

"I'm sure that can be arranged." The deputy smiled. "Just leave me your phone number and I'll make sure he gives you a call."

Emma shook her head. "I'll call later and make an appointment to see him."

She walked over to the bench where the rifle was leaning, picked it up and examined the evidence tag. The detail from the tag indicated the weapon was found at 1123 Milton Circle, Apt. B., driveway, A. Gannon, Chevy C/K truck, behind driver's seat. She was certain the deputies didn't have a warrant when they conducted the search of the truck. She glanced at the description of the rifle: AR-15. She snapped another photo.

"Isn't there a missing piece? A clip?" She peered under the butt of the firearm as if she were looking for something.

"The magazine?" The chatty deputy treated her to a slow smile and nodded toward the bench. "It'd be there if they found it."

She noticed graphite residue on the barrel.

"Looks like they dusted for fingerprints."

"Yep. And you might want to ask if they tested the casings found at the scene against those fired from the gun. They usually do that too."

"Okay, Ever shot an AR-15?"

"Yes, ma'am," he replied. "Used one like this at the academy in training. Pretty smooth. No recoil to speak of."

"Where can you get a rifle like this?"

"You can just about get them anywhere." He glanced over his shoulder at his colleague and lowered his voice. "I think a guy out at a place in Bentwood's been selling them to kids."

Emma flipped through the photographs again. A spray of bullets had broken through the window and destroyed Jennifer's wicker headboard, splintering it into fragments. The killer was obviously a poor shot, but with a weapon like the AR-15 it didn't seem to matter. Although only a few of the rounds actually hit Jennifer, the exit wounds left ragged, gaping cavities in her body.

Emma stacked the photos in a neat pile and started to place them back on the bench, but hesitated. She brought the top photograph closer to examine, and noticed, for the first time, one shot in the middle of Jennifer's forehead. That alone could have killed her. If it was intentional, she'd have to reevaluate the shooter's skill level.

"The shooter may not have had much control over that rifle of his. The entire room was demolished." She laid the photographs back on the bench.

The deputy shrugged. "Could'a been what they call a 'hammer follow.' It's a defect in some of the models. The hammer follows the bolt and firing pin into the battery, which causes the firing mechanism to function faster than it's supposed to. Happened to me once at the academy. You go to shoot the thing, and it changes from a controllable semi-automatic to an uncontrollable automatic. It's crazy. Or it could'a been deliberate. You never know."

"Sounds like a person could easily lose control if there was a defect. Or, like you said. Maybe it was deliberate." Emma scribbled furiously in her notebook.

"Yes, ma'am. Usually, you find that hammer follow problem in a rifle with a little more wear and tear."

Emma photographed the plaster casts that the deputies had made of the shoe and tire imprints found in the pasture and under Jennifer's window. The shoe impressions all seemed to match the boots seized from Adam's apartment, with the exception of one which had a peculiarity of the left foot. A greater depression was created in the ground on the left side of that mold, as if each step listed slightly off center. The person who wore the boot may have favored his right leg.

She went back to examine the photographs of Jennifer's room a second time. She knew she had to do everything she could to keep them out of evidence. The scenes were horrific. Any jury viewing them would want to find against the only defendant sitting in the courtroom. It was only human nature.

But the photos also told Emma something about Jennifer, once she looked past the blood and violence. Her bedroom walls were pink, her linens were a flowery design, and her walls were covered with high school honors and photographs of friends. Emma doubted Jennifer's room had changed much since childhood. She was a very pretty, unusually tall girl. In a more sophisticated city, she could have been a model. She appeared to be popular, but no photographs of Adam or any other boy were displayed, which Emma found interesting.

Emma opened the plastic bag holding a small collection of letters from Adam. A few photographs fell out of the bundle. Most of them were of Jennifer and Adam. Emma also found another larger bundle held together with several rubber bands. The letters came from Adam's apartment and were from Jennifer. She opened one and began to read.

April 30, 1990

Dear Adam,

I don't understand why you won't write. We can't talk on the phone. So, it would be nice if you'd write me back. It was good seeing you last week, but I'm beginning to wonder what we are doing. This fall, I am going to begin my freshman year in college, but you have no plans. I don't even know if you are doing anything in the fall. Will you start working at your dad's farm? Will you go to school? Have you ever thought about Gallaudet in Washington D.C.? That could be a great place for you. I think we need to see each other and talk about some of this.

Love, Jennifer

May 5, 1990

Dear Adam,

I was amazed by your drawings. I hope I really look that beautiful. It is nice that you think I do. You are on my mind all of the time. I miss you and I can't wait to see you again.

Love, Jennifer

August 13, 1990

Dear Adam,

I am so sorry to write this letter, but I think it is best that we stop seeing each other. I will always love you, and even though I can't explain right now, I want you to know that you were a wonderful boyfriend and I loved the time we had together. I will try to explain things to you some day. Always remember how talented and special you are. I believe in you.

Love, Jennifer

Emma picked up the first bundle of folded papers bound with the pink ribbon. Tucked in among the photographs and scant notes were several drawings executed in exacting detail. Most were pencil sketches, although there were also a few small watercolors. Each was signed at the bottom "Adam." Emma held her breath for a second. The drawings were refined, revealing the dedication and skill of a mature artist. Jennifer was right. Adam's renderings were stunning. Her eyes shown luminously and her hair seemed so soft Emma was tempted to reach out and touch it. He drew the long lines of her neck and curve of her shoulders in graceful compositions. The care and tenderness Adam took with his drawings alone was proof of the depth of his feelings for her.

There were two letters from Adam to Jennifer in the papers.

May 10, 1990

Dear Jennifer, I happy you like drawing. You my wish come true. See you Saturday. Adam

The second letter was even shorter, and even though it wasn't a clear threat, it didn't help Adam's criminal case. It was dated August 14, 1990——the day before Jennifer's death.

Jennifer. You be sorry if you break with me. Adam.

Emma read the remaining letters from Jennifer, put them back on the bench in the evidence room, and, with a nod to the deputies, walked out of the sheriff's department across the square to Silas's office.

Silas was at his desk reading. Emma peeked in the office, and rapped on the doorframe. If he was too busy, he'd ignore her. He glanced up from his casebook.

"Got a second?"

"Yeah." Silas held his finger to mark his place on the text.

"I looked over the evidence at the sheriff's today." Emma flopped down in one of Silas's comfy office chairs. The walls of Silas's office were made from brick which some said pre-dated the Civil War. The leather furniture and wooden book shelves gave the place a warm glow that was cozy and inviting. Emma liked the smell of the old leather-bound books and found herself finding excuses to do research there when Silas wasn't in the office.

"I'm not sure what to make of some of it, but none of the evidence found at Adam's apartment helps his case, except maybe his sketches of Jennifer. They were exceptional. But the rifle could be enough to convict him if the casings they also found match up. Then there are the tires from his truck. On top of that, Adam wrote a hostile letter to Jennifer. Said she'd be sorry she broke up with him. So, it's not looking good for Adam, even though it seems as if he cared for Jennifer. But I'm bothered by something else too."

"What's that?"

"I can't get a clear sense from him of whether or not he's guilty."

Silas shrugged. "It's not your job to decide that. It's only your job to defend him. Anyway, if he is, he wouldn't be the first guy to kill a girl he was in love with. Prisons are full of them."

"Adam doesn't seem to have the disposition for it in some ways. He's so sensitive. On the other hand, he can be reactive. Still, his feelings toward Jennifer are tender. I have a hard time imagining he did anything to harm her."

"You seem impressed by Adam's drawings, but aren't they a little obsessive? How many were there?" Silas cleaned his glasses on his sleeve and held them up to the window for inspection before placing them back on his nose.

"I didn't count them. More than ten, I guess. Obsessive? I didn't think so. Do you mean Adam was so obsessed with Jennifer that he killed her when she broke up with him?" Emma shuffled her notes.

"I'm not saying anything one way or the other right now. I'm just trying to get you to think like a prosecutor so we can begin to prepare our defense. The DA will use the letter you mentioned—the one where Adam threatened Jennifer—against Adam. Don't be surprised if he also uses the drawings against him. By the way, have you begun to think of a theory for Adam's defense?" Silas stood and stepped to the credenza to pour a glass of water.

"Not yet, really. I've got a few ideas, but we've got a lot more work to do on the investigation. For one thing, I tried to contact the audiologist as you suggested, and he doesn't have any openings for the next few weeks. Our procedural motions are coming together though."

"Good, we need to file them next week. And I'm going to ask the DA if Adam could get his truck back. They've got the tires. That's all they need. If Adam can see we're doing all we can for him, maybe he'll be a little more cooperative." He shrugged. "It's worth a shot." Silas returned to his desk, sloshing his water glass along the way.

"Okay. I'll get the motions ready. I hope something makes him more helpful. I'm not sure what would work at this point. He never confirmed where he was the night Jennifer was killed, unless he was at the scene. We need some explanation if he was." Emma slumped down in her chair.

"Right. Why did he say 'a man' shot Jennifer, unless he was there?" Silas placed his wet glass on the edge of a coaster and picked up the case book he'd been reviewing.

"I'll ask Adam about that again." Emma wrote the question in her notebook, placing stars around it so she could find it easily when she reviewed her notes.

"That's got to be explored. For one thing, we need to know if we're going to put him on the stand. Right now, it doesn't look like we can." Silas pushed his glasses to the top of his head and peered at Emma. "Are you having second thoughts about the case?"

"No. It's just that Adam's an enigma. Stoic and sweet one minute and sullen and reactive the next. I wish I understood him."

"You do much better with him than I do." Silas marked the case he'd been reading with a yellow Post-it.

"Not really. We're not exactly carrying on a conversation yet. I wonder whether Jennifer Patrick made Adam feel more accepted, like he belonged. If she did, their break up could have been devastating to him. He may have had a hard time coping afterward."

"So, do you think Adam killed Jennifer?"

"I have no idea, " Emma said.

"Let's wrap up the motions. I'd like to read them soon. Maybe finalize by next week?"

"Okay. But I also want to visit Adam's mom."

"What do you hope to accomplish by that?" Silas shut his casebook and leaned back, anticipating her response.

"Family is important, Silas. And who knows him better than his mother?"

9

August 20, 1990

Emma pulled up to Mayfair, the Gannon's estate, feeling as if she had drifted into another era. She was raised along the coast of Georgia, and before now had never visited the scarce mansions and former plantations which still dotted the middle section of the state. Properties of this vintage were rare since most of them had burned during the Civil War. Mayfair wasn't a farm, or the sort of place where a few acres of corn were raised. It was a magnificent property, stretching out past the horizon, over hills and rolling fields, encompassing thousands of acres. Emma passed barns housing a dozen tractors with glassed-in cabs. A couple of matching Lincoln Town Cars were angled in front of the stables along with a number of over-sized pick-up trucks. Huge boll buggies decorated with the white cottony remnants of the farm's main product lined the fields.

The entrance to Mayfair was lined with ancient oaks grandly welcoming visitors to its wide-open verandas. This estate was a part of the Old South, the age where mint juleps were sipped on front porches, and horse-drawn carriages lined the cobblestone entrances to the main houses. The portico was lined with massive Greek columns. Its shuttered windows were taller than the doors to Emma's apartment by several feet.

She parked her sputtering vehicle at the end of the curved driveway and stepped out of the car, thankful that her shoes, at least, were decent. A uniformed housekeeper welcomed her at the elegantly carved front door. As she moved past a curved staircase, Emma was ushered into a smaller side parlor where she was asked to wait. Gazing upward, she estimated the ceilings were an elegant fourteen feet in height. The walls were papered in a silvery blue, reminding Emma of the ceilings in one of the old Savannah cathedrals. Silken settees lined each side of the massive fireplace. Its carved marble mantel boasted a crystal candelabrum that sparkled as if it was on fire. The gilded Rococo mirror over the mantel reflected a great paddle fan in the hallway that maintained a flow of cool air throughout the front corridor. At any second Emma expected to see Darcy Gannon floating down the staircase in vast billowing skirts.

"How nice to see you again," Darcy said in her whispery voice as she extended her hand and walked toward Emma. Emma started, surprised by Darcy's entrance from the side door. "Why don't we step into the library? It's my favorite room in the house. I always feel so cozy there. The side parlor's too formal."

They moved into one of the loveliest rooms Emma had ever seen. Its walls were painted a warm spring green and lined in beautifully burnished wooden book cases.

"Those book shelves were built from several cherry trees that were removed from the property more than seventy years ago," Darcy said, motioning for Emma to sit down in one of the chintz-covered over-stuffed sofas in the room. "The men on the farm built them. We've always had a few carpenters on staff to handle what goes wrong in this old house."

Emma gazed out of the window and watched while the gardener dead-headed roses from rows of lush bushes in varied colors. The library windows were draped from ceiling to floor in the same English rose fabric as the sofas and were sashed back to show the grounds outside. The beauty of the room was a reflection of the garden. The roses were duplicated in the print of the drapery and the sofas. The spring green walls were echoed in the lawns and fruit trees. Bits of yellows, crimson, fuchsia, and pale pink were spotted here and there in window boxes outside and in other prints in the room.

"You have quite an eye for detail, Mrs. Gannon," Emma said.

Darcy smiled as she sat down. She was as impeccably dressed as before, this time in well-fitted linen pants and shirt tailored to fit her lean body to perfection. She wore the same pearls at her neck and her lustrous hair was worn loosely about her shoulders. But she looked thinner. Even though her creamy-soft skin was unblemished, the hollows under her eyes were lavender-tinged and deeper. She welcomed Emma graciously, but Emma questioned the sincerity of her hospitality. Darcy reminded Emma of the women from First Baptist Church back home. Her smile seemed strained and insincere, like a beauty pageant contestant who'd been on the stage fifteen minutes too long. Her face twitched with the sheer effort it took to be pleasant. Detached, despite her sunny façade, Darcy didn't maintain eye contact, and her handshake was a cold and clammy grasp.

"The painting is of Robert's grandmother. She was a beauty, wasn't she?" Darcy followed Emma's gawking gaze to the portrait over the fireplace.

"Even though you said she was *Robert's* grandmother, she seems to resemble you," Emma said.

"That's what Robert thought the first time he saw me. He never met her, but her painting has hung over this fireplace his entire life. I think she became the ultimate image of beauty for him. And Robert has always reminded me a bit of my father. They share some of the same vices," she said with a soft laugh.

"Are you from this area as well?" Emma asked.

"No, I'm from Tennessee. My family was not well off, but we had a few horses. I used to ride, and I met Robert at a horse show. My daddy worked as a trainer when he wasn't gambling and drinking too much. Later he became the trainer for the Gannon family. That's the one thing Robert and I have in common—our love of horses—not drinking and gambling."

Darcy shifted the books on the coffee table so that the edges of the stack and the table were in perfect alignment. Satisfied with her arrangement, she sat back, crossed her arms across her waist, the corners of her mouth tilted upward.

Emma cleared her throat. "Mrs. Gannon, I wanted to speak to you today because Mr. Steele and I need to develop a better understanding of how Adam communicates, and what he understands when other people speak. That way, we can put together a stronger defense."

Darcy held up her index finger as if asking Emma to wait, and motioned for her housekeeper. As if she'd been waiting for her cue, the woman marched to the tea cart in the corner of the room, picked up a tray filled with a variety of tiny desserts, and strode back to the sofa where they were sitting. She placed the tray on top of the coffee table next to a sterling silver coffee urn. Darcy nodded at her housekeeper who made a swift departure to the next room. Darcy handed Emma a small delicately-patterned Limoges plate and gestured for Emma to choose from an assortment of brownies, lemon squares, pecan tarts, miniature cheese cakes, strawberry parfaits, and tiny carrot cakes. Emma, dazzled by the selection, was speechless.

As if she'd read her mind, Darcy said, "You know you can choose more than one." Emma chose three desserts from the tray as Darcy offered her a coffee.

"I can't recall the last time I ate something as wonderful as this. You certainly know how to appeal to a person's sweet tooth." Emma dabbed her fingers with a lacy napkin.

"Well, that's easy. I have one too. I always have something sweet in the house. Baking is one of my favorite pastimes. I bake a cake for every new member of the church and deliver it to their home as soon as they move in. It helps take my mind off of other things too, sometimes. I found that especially helpful this week." Darcy brushed a lock of hair from her eye.

"Did you make these?" Emma swallowed and coughed quickly to avoid choking on carrot cake crumbs. "Everything I've tasted is incredible."

"I made most of them. Lola Mae, the housekeeper, helped with the cheesecake. She's become expert at them."

"Well, I'm impressed, and I'm sure the newcomers to the church are too. But getting back to the reason for my visit, like I said, I'd like to ask a few questions about Adam. I noticed he doesn't wear hearing aids. Could you tell me why? Wouldn't they help?"

"I don't think they really would help that much since he has profound hearing loss. He'll never be able to hear speech. When Adam was little, they tried to fit him with hearing aids, and explained that he might be a little more verbal if he wore them. But we still thought it would be better if he tried to communicate without them." She bit into a miniature lemon bar.

"Why is that?" Emma said, stifling a cough behind her hand.

"He didn't like them. I think they felt strange. But then, we never saw hearing aids as something that were good for him. They made him look different and you know how cruel kids can be. When I was young I was tortured by my classmates for wearing the same clothes every day. I didn't want Adam to stand out as different in any way. I still don't."

"But wouldn't it have been better for him to be able to hear as well as possible? He might have been more fluent if he'd had hearing aids."

"I'm not so sure about that," Darcy said, raising a napkin to her lips. "We don't know that Adam could have done better with hearing aids or sign language. Frankly, Adam does very well. Don't you think?"

"I haven't had much of a chance to observe him. But I've noticed neither you nor your husband write anything down when you're speaking. Do you think he understands what you're saying?" Emma said, hoping she didn't offend Darcy. She knew there was a heated division between families and schools who believed in teaching sign language to the deaf and the "oralists," or those who thought it was better if the deaf learned to communicate with the mainstream community through lip reading. She also knew that deaf students who learned sign language had a much greater vocabulary.

"We decided a long time ago not to spoon feed Adam. That way, he's forced to figure out what's going on. It's not been easy. We think he understands most of what we say. But he brings a notebook with him most places, and we use it sometimes."

"Have you ever had Adam tested to see exactly what he understands?"

"Not since he was five, in that school in Atlanta."

"Did Adam's teachers at the Academy ever test his ability to understand language, spoken or written?" Emma asked.

"He had to take English tests and spelling tests just like everyone else. I remember that most of the writing was taught in history class. That's where they did their term papers." Darcy stood up and began pacing back and forth in front of the fireplace.

"How did he do?"

"He usually passed his subjects. He didn't study much, but he's smart. He did great in math." Darcy stopped pacing, faced Emma, and beamed, obviously pleased when she recalled her son's accomplishments.

"Did you or your husband help him much?"

"Not really. We thought he should do it himself or it wasn't right, you know?"

"Do you know how he did on those term papers?"

"I don't really recall what sorts of grades he made on those, no." Darcy shook her head.

Emma took advantage of the lull in conversation. "How did he do in English?"

"He always passed."

Emma didn't know if she should ask the next question but plowed ahead. "How much is tuition at Greendale Christian Academy?"

"Why do you ask?" Darcy asked, walking back to the sofa and picking up another dessert from the tray. Consuming it in two swift bites, she brushed a few crumbs from the coffee table into the palm of her hand and sprinkled them back on to the platter. "I think it's ten thousand dollars a semester, but we've donated so much to Greendale that we're on the board of directors. But you didn't answer my question. Why do you want to know?"

"Adam's school and his work there are part of my investigation. I need to know as much as possible about how he communicates and what he's able to understand. I plan to retrieve Adam's school records and speak to the school administration and Adam's teachers, too."

"Okay. But you don't need my authority for that since Adam's nineteen. He's considered an adult now, right?"

"You're right. But could you suggest the name of a teacher who worked with Adam on his language skills?"

"I can't think of one right off the top of my head. I left all that sort of thing up to the school. I didn't interfere." Darcy wiped her fingers on a linen napkin.

Emma glanced down at her list of questions. She was nearly to the end. "How well did you know Jennifer Patrick?"

"I didn't know Jennifer at all. I never even met her. Robert doesn't feel comfortable around her father. There's some sort of land issue between the two families. I'm not certain of the story. So, we never had Jennifer over. Robert even tried to get Adam to stop seeing her. Robert doesn't like to talk about the Patricks, but he has a nephew, Ben Bailey, who seems to keep up with all of that. He's the family historian. I don't have much to do with Ben, so I couldn't give you any more information on that. But I can arrange for you to meet him."

"If you don't mind my asking, if this tragedy hadn't occurred, did Adam have any plans to go to college? One of Jennifer's letters to him mentioned Gallaudet. I hear that is an excellent university for the deaf. Did you have plans to send him there?"

"No, we never had plans to send Adam to Gallaudet. We never wanted Adam to attend a school for the deaf. That's why we took him out of the school in Atlanta when he was five. It's difficult to explain." A tiny frown marred Darcy's near perfect forehead for a second, then she smiled. "Like I said, we believe we're doing the right thing here. And we've thought about it a lot. Most of the world can hear. Adam has to adapt to that, not vice versa."

"I do understand." Emma adjusted her position in her chair. "Did you have any plans for Adam to go to any college?"

"We didn't think it was important since he could stay here and work at the farm. But he planned to attend a local junior college this fall. That's why he has an apartment. His school is a few miles away."

"Has he changed his plans since his arrest?" Emma asked.

"He'll put school off for a while and help around the farm until the trial is over. Adam enjoys working in the stables. He should; his dad just bought him a new mare. He spent nearly a hundred thousand dollars on her. She came from an incredible line. As far as we're concerned, he doesn't need to do anything more than work here."

"You said Adam's smart, and I'm sure you're correct, but what, specifically, makes you say that? His language skills seem low."

Darcy Gannon's smiled sweetly.

"Just watch him, Ms. Thornton," she replied. "He's a very talented young man. You'll see."

Emma pulled away from the Gannon's driveway realizing that other than Adam's deafness, and what seemed to be his substandard education, the two biggest problems she faced in defending him would be his parents. She tended to look to women for clues as to what made a family tick. Here, the mom, Darcy, was a child of an alcoholic father, who'd had her own struggles in childhood. Emma knew the type. Darcy apparently meant well, but she was a perfectionist, a control-freak, dead set on imposing her ideals on her son. It was obvious she cared about Adam, and that she didn't want her childhood repeated, yet she had unwittingly married a man who had many of the same vices as her father. And, from what Emma observed, Adam's father wasn't involved in Adam's life. Not on any level. Adam might be deaf, but Darcy seemed blind to what was right in front of her, good intentions or not.

Adam's parents leaned toward an oralist philosophy, which was accepted by many. Yet they also prevented him from wearing hearing aids, even though the devices could have enhanced his ability to understand language. His skill at lip reading alone wasn't enough for him to keep up with most conversations. Emma doubted he ever initiated friendships or had many, if any. He had no deaf peers and had a limited relationship with his parents. Even though he was surrounded by his family, the workers on his family's farm, teachers and classmates, Adam was alone. Adam was more isolated than anyone she knew.

10

August 21, 1990

By the time Emma arrived at the office, she was a few minutes late even though she'd left class early. As she pulled up, she noticed Adam's truck in the parking lot, pleased that the DA had agreed to release it late yesterday afternoon. She hoped Adam would have a new and improved attitude today. He was waiting for her in the reception area, hands folded and feet crossed. If she didn't know better, she'd think he didn't have a care in the world.

Emma had asked Silas if she could speak to Adam alone. She'd convinced Silas she'd be more successful with the interview if it took place one-on-one, and he'd agreed. At their first meeting, Adam and Silas had bowed up at each other like a couple of rutting rams. Adam's reticence and Silas's frustration seemed to be a bad combination, but it was early in the case. There was plenty of time to work on that.

Emma sat down across the mahogany refectory table from Adam.

"Can you tell me about your relationship with Jennifer?"

Adam lowered his head. He reminded Emma of a young buck in the forest, quietly observing hunters and other creatures, never quite sure who was friend or foe. He seemed as skittish as a deer too. Even though he could lip read, she sensed language needed to be broken down into simpler components. She directed Adam's attention to her face and watched his eyes. If he understood what she said his eyes would spark as if someone had turned on a light behind them.

"I'm going to talk to you without writing anything down," she said. "No paper, no pencil, okay?" she asked, holding up a page of paper, and a pencil, and shaking her head in a crude pantomime. "Read my lips."

Adam indicated his understanding.

Taking a photograph of Jennifer from her file folder and placing it on the table, she asked, "Was Jennifer your girlfriend?"

Adam nodded.

"Did you break up with her?"

Adam stared at her, not responding.

"Did you," Emma mouthed, pointing to Adam, "break up," she broke a pencil from the table, "with Jennifer?" she pointed to the photo again.

Adam frowned as he watched her.

Emma got up from the table.

"Did you," she said, pointing again to Adam, "break up with Jennifer," as she reached for a piece of paper from the silver tray in the middle of the table. Showing Adam the paper, she made an exaggerated effort at tearing the page in two.

"Nah," Adam said, shaking his head "no." His voice sounded as if it were trapped, or as if he had swallowed half of the sound before it could come out of his throat. But she could understand him. Unlike Adam, the deaf students she'd known were very animated, and would either simultaneously sign, or pantomime while speaking with people like her who were not fluent in sign language. Instead, Adam grabbed a pencil and the torn page and wrote:

She break with me

"Tell me why." Emma walked over to the side of the room to turn on the lights. The sun was beginning to go down. Emma squinted to see the subtleties of Adam's facial expressions. Silas's interior decorator girlfriend had designed the elegant conference room, but the charcoal walls and ceilings plunged the space into a cave-like darkness in the late afternoon. The floor-to-ceiling matching silk drapery didn't help.

"Why?" she said again, stepping back to the table and drawing a big question mark on a piece of paper.

"*I do not no.*" Adam wrote on the page.

"Can you say that?" Emma asked pointing to her mouth. "Can you say 'I do not know?'"

Adam shook his head.

"Tell me," Emma said, gesturing toward her head, "what you understand. If you understand me, write down what I say. If you don't, say no, okay?"

Adam looked at her again, this time without a glimmer of understanding.

Emma took out two more sheets of paper. On one page she wrote "NO," on the other she wrote "YES" and handed them over to Adam.

"Now, Adam," she said, "tell me if you understand what I'm saying."

Emma moved to the other side of the room and squared her chair in front of Adam.

"Do you know why the sheriff took your clothes?" she asked.

Adam hesitated.

"Did you understand that Adam?"

Adam picked a piece of paper and a pencil and skillfully sketched a pair of jeans in life-like detail.

"That's right Adam, jeans. They took your jeans, right?"

Adam nodded.

"Why?" Emma pointed to the large question mark she had drawn earlier.

Adam shrugged his shoulders.

"You don't know?" she asked.

Adam shook his head.

"Do you know who killed Jennifer?" Emma asked.

Adam looked down at the floor, his fingers absentmindedly tracing the hand-carved flowers along the side of the table.

"Adam," Emma said, stomping her feet. He looked up. Teachers of deaf students at the school where she previously taught often stomped the floor to get the attention of their students. It was an effective method since the students could feel the vibrations through the floor even though they couldn't hear the pounding of a shoe or a shout.

"Why did you say a man shot Jennifer?"

Adam glanced out of the window next to the fireplace.

Emma wrote the words down on a piece of paper. She laid it on the table and banged the floor again with her foot, getting his attention.

Pointing to the paper on the table, Emma asked, "Why did you say a man shot Jennifer, Adam?" Adam shrugged and picked at a place on his thumb.

Emma scribbled something else on the paper and pointed to the words: *Where were you the night Jennifer was killed?*

Adam read the question and looked away from the page.

Hoping to avoid another of Adam's shutdowns, Emma switched to a completely different line of questioning.

"Where did you get the gun?" She pantomimed the shooting of a rifle.

Adam looked at her and wrote *"fish stor man"*

"Man?" Emma said. "You didn't buy it at the store?"

Adam didn't respond.

"Adam, did you buy the gun at the store?"

Adam looked at the floor and folded his arms, then picked up the pencil again and began drawing a lake surrounded by trees. Then he drew a man with a gun, and another younger man, bearing a resemblance to himself with his hands outstretched toward the gun. He looked up at her.

"That's a good drawing, Adam."

Adam shrugged.

Emma wrote: *I have a minor in art from the university. If I say it's good, it's good.*

Adam's face began to flush and a slow grin began to form along the corners of his mouth.

Emma pointed to the drawing. "You met the man by the lake?" Emma asked.

Adam nodded his head.

"Why, Adam? Why did you buy the gun outside of the store? Didn't you know that was wrong?" Emma asked.

Adam looked down at his hands, refusing to respond. Emma began pacing up and down the length of the conference table. The overhead lights flickered slightly and for the first time she noticed that the sky was deepening into the deep azure of twilight. She hadn't realized it was so late. After-school daycare closed at six and she had to pick up the twins.

"Adam," Emma said, moving her hands to get Adam's attention. "How did you know Jennifer was shot?"

Adam looked up long enough to shake his head, and then looked back down.

"Adam, who killed Jennifer?"

Adam refused to look up, but Emma saw a tear drop onto his jeans.

Emma wrote:

Did you love Jennifer?

Adam read Emma's question, picked up a pencil and wrote:

I ask her marry me. she say no.

"How did that make you feel, Adam?"

Bad, he wrote. He crossed his arms and hung his head. Emma sensed their conversation was over.

Adam climbed into the cab of his truck and slammed the door shut, resting his head on the steering wheel for a moment before he buckled his seat belt. He didn't want to cry but couldn't stop the flow of tears. He needed to talk to someone, but he couldn't. Not now and maybe never. He knew things weren't good, but he didn't know what to do. He wiped his face on his sleeve and turned on the engine.

Emma rehashed her afternoon with Adam as she drove down University Avenue to pick up the boys. It was clear he could read lips, but he missed a lot. He didn't understand complex sentence structure. He had no clue what was going on when they'd taken evidence from his apartment, and he wouldn't be able to understand the context of a trial or any of his hearings.

He'd never be much help, if any, with the preparation of his defense. So, in addition to having evidence suppressed, there was even a chance they could get the entire case thrown out based on his lack of competency to stand trial.

Communication with Adam would be extremely difficult for anyone, but must have been particularly frustrating for Jennifer. Emma suspected Adam's proposal of marriage was sudden and unexpected. She couldn't imagine that Jennifer, who was also very young, gave it serious thought.

Adam was easily frustrated, quick to anger, and cried impulsively, which could be a normal reaction to his circumstances and isolation. Yet, his drawings were beautiful and deeply mature renderings, demonstrating the depth of his intellect and passion. Even though he was emotionally reactive, and often explosive, as an artist, he had a brilliant recall for detail and impressive control in the execution of his work.

When she taught learning disabled students, Emma discovered that the brain will find a route for the expression of intelligence even when it's thwarted by learning problems or challenges. Most of her students couldn't read, but they had an average intelligence or higher, and often could paint, or play musical instruments. Some of them won awards for extracurricular activities. Some were star athletes. Emma had come to believe that having a disability might even hone or distill a talent. She thought of it as a focused stream of brilliance—a white light finding another path in the brain, a path toward expression, a voice.

Adam's drawings were perfect articulations. Emma wondered if he had more. If so, she wanted to see them.

11

August 22, 1990

Greendale Christian Academy, Adam's alma mater, enjoyed an excellent reputation, and was celebrated for its winning basketball and soccer teams. So when Emma pulled through the school's gravel entrance she was surprised to find a converted but worn, post-modern church behind the school's placard, in need of repair. The drab, beige-brick exterior of the building was mildewed, and the shingles on the roof were torn. The grounds were littered with McDonald's bags and were in need of a trimming. She parked her car and followed hand-painted signs to the entrance of the administration building.

The administrative wing was feebly lit with conical-shaped fixtures suspended from the ceiling like so many dangling megaphones. Emma introduced herself to the receptionist and was directed to take a seat in one of several olive green plastic chairs set out in a row by the door.

Within minutes the receptionist tapped her on the shoulder, led her into another poorly-lit, cavernous room, which at one time must have been the church's fellowship hall, and introduced her to Mable Grayson. Mable, who had been waiting for Emma at a long craftsman-style oak table, hands in her lap, nodded when Emma entered.

Emma extended her hand, which was ignored. Mrs. Grayson, who sat at the head of the table like the figurehead of a ship, was shellacked in countless layers of hair spray. Her elaborate coiffure, swooped into a Dairy Queen-like up-do, was frozen to a crackling shine. Her dress, patterned with a sprinkling of pastel summer flowers, was cinched in the middle, a little string trailing down the center. Emma eased her unshaken hand back down by her side. "Thanks for agreeing to talk with me about Adam Gannon. What subjects did you teach Adam?" Emma sat down next to Mabel.

She met Emma's gaze with a steely glint in her eye. "I was his history teacher in the tenth grade. And I didn't have much choice about meeting with you."

Words erupted from Mabel Grayson with a force formed deep within her diaphragm. A sturdy woman with ample lung capacity, any drill sergeant would have been envious of the attention she could command with her voice alone.

Emma smiled, hoping to soothe Mrs. Grayson's irritation. "I'd like to ask you a few questions about Adam and how he coped with his deafness."

"Adam waddn't deaf."

Emma paused for a moment. "What makes you say that?"

"He always did everything just like everyone else. When the bell rang in between classes, or at the end of the day, he would get up with everyone else and go about his business. So, I figured he could hear."

"Didn't anyone ever tell you he couldn't?"

"All I was ever told was that his parents wanted him treated like the other kids. No special treatment."

"Didn't you think that meant he had a learning problem of some kind?"

"I wasn't told about it if he did."

"How did he do on tests?"

"He never was a good student. Didn't score well on tests. Also, in history class, students work on their term papers, learn how to research and write. You either do the work on that kind of thing or you don't. He didn't. Didn't even turn in a paper."

"How did he do when you tested them orally in class?"

"I don't remember if I ever gave them oral exams."

"Did you ever give pop quizzes orally in class?"

"I may have, but I don't really remember."

"Do you recall how you communicated with Adam? Did you ever write down what you wanted to say to him?"

"I don't remember speaking to him one on one. I may have, but I don't recall."

"Do you recall Adam's reading level, or his ability to write?"

"We don't read out loud in tenth grade. But the students do a lot of independent reading. He never talked in class, but he did blow up a time or two. I remember he couldn't write a complete sentence and he couldn't spell. Like I said, he just wasn't a very good student."

"What do you mean he blew up?"

"If he didn't like what was going on in class, or didn't get his way or something he'd get upset. One time he wadded up his paper and threw it in the trash can. I sent him to the principal."

"Was this the only time anything like that happened in class?"

"No. He had a bad temper."

"What sorts of things would make him upset?"

"He'd get upset if he didn't get his way, best as I can remember."

"Was that the only time you sent him to the principal's office?"

"I might have sent him another time. I don't really remember."

"Did anyone work with him to help him with his term paper, or with any of his assignments?"

"Not in my class."

"What makes you so certain he could hear?"

"Like I said, he did everything like the other students. He knew when class was over. No one told him. And he got up and went to lunch in the cafeteria like the other students." She nodded. "He could hear."

"If there isn't anything you'd like to add, Mrs. Grayson, I'll see the next teacher."

Mabel Grayson pushed her chair back, and exited the room, her dress swaying as her feet pounded out of the door.

Jerry Smithfield greeted Emma with an outstretched hand before he sat down next to her. Although he coached high school basketball, his tweed sport coat, wire rimmed glasses, which he wore perched on the end of his nose, and his longish salt and pepper hair gave him the distinguished air of a college professor.

"I can see by the shocked expression on your face that you've met Mrs. Grayson."

"That's right." Emma adjusted her position in the ladder-back wooden chair.

"Welcome to Greendale Christian Academy."

"I thought private schools usually had a superior roster of teachers. Present company excluded, I'm beginning to wonder about that."

"Depends on the school. At Greendale, the parent pays a good deal of money for their child's education with the assumption that—*quid pro quo*—the child will be guaranteed a passing grade, and in most cases a good grade. The child is also segregated from certain elements of society, usually the poorer elements. The quality of the education isn't guaranteed, though. In Adam's case, the parents' primary concern was to have Adam treated as a 'normal kid.' And even though Adam is very bright and talented, he needed more of a one-on-one educational experience. And he needed an aid or an interpreter to make certain he understood what was being taught."

"I hope you don't mind me saying this, but you seem unusually candid for someone who teaches here."

Coach Smithfield smiled. "Let's keep that between you and me. I've had it out with the school administration on more than one occasion about their lack of standards. Things've changed over the years. This used to be a great school. In fact, I attended Greendale Christian. Loved the place. That's why I'm still here."

"That would have been my next question. What did you teach Adam?"

"I was his tenth grade algebra teacher and basketball coach all the way through his senior year. I got to know him in the classroom and as an athlete. He has some pretty serious language deficits, although I think he could read and write a little. But he's good at math, and picked up on algebra immediately. Where he really excelled was on the basketball court. He's a fantastic athlete. He understood plays and even helped me diagram them. He's a pretty smart guy. He's also an artist. But, from what I can tell, he can't hear a thing."

"What have you seen?"

"Referees would blow whistles on the court, but he never heard them. He noticed their hand signals though and memorized all of the different signs for fouls, time outs, whatever. None of the other players have the signals down as well as he does. He never gets the auditory cues, but always the visual ones. If I need to get his attention I stomp my foot. I yell all the time at my players, but Adam never hears anything. But if he's not paying attention, all I have to do is stomp my foot and he's back on point."

"Would you be willing to sign an affidavit to that effect?"

"Sure. Also, my wife's an audiologist. She could help if you need it. They do a test at her clinic called the ABR. She told me about it, but I can't remember what it stands for. I wrote it down because I knew we'd be talking about this today."

Mr. Smithfield pushed his glasses up on his nose, fumbled in his pocket, and pulled out a wrinkled paper that had been folded multiple times.

"It stands for 'Auditory Brainstem Response.' They put these little electrodes on your head, and then put earphones on, I think she called them insert earphones. Then the electrodes measure whether any sounds are picked up by the brain activity. So you can objectively measure whether Adam can hear. You don't even need my affidavit, or my testimony, but I'd be happy to help if you do."

Sylvia Buchannan, Greendale's guidance counselor, stepped into the conference room and introduced herself.

"Would you mind meeting in my office? I have some records pulled for you and they're a little heavy. "

Emma gathered her belongings, relieved that the counselor was young, hoping they might see Adam and his problems similarly. Ms. Buchannan appeared to be about Emma's age, in her early thirties. Her clothes were meticulous, a scarf at her neck, perfect cut to her pants. They walked down the corridor which was quiet except for the voices of a few teachers who were lecturing. She gestured for Emma to take a seat in her small paneled office. A calendar on the wall was filled with events from the beginning of the school year and college recruiter schedules.

Emma sat down in a plastic molded chair and pushed Adam's release form toward her. "What do you remember about Adam while he was at Greendale?"

Ms. Buchanan glanced at the release briefly, checking the signature. "Mostly that his parents put him at a disadvantage because they didn't want any special accommodations for him. So he took the same tests as all of the other students, including standardized tests, with no assistance, or interpreters, even though he couldn't hear. And he scored within the upper eightieth percentile in math and a few other subjects. Obviously, in language areas, he scored lower."

"Could I see his test results?"

"Here you go." Ms. Buchannan handed her a stack of papers.

Emma flipped through the documents.

"It makes sense that his reading and reading comprehension scores are lower since he has such language deficits." Emma said, pushing her glasses up her nose.

"Yeah, reading comp was only in the sixty-fifth percentile, but that's not bad considering his disability. He picks up a lot from his environment, even without an interpreter."

"About what grade level does he read on?" Emma handed the papers back to her.

"He reads on about a third grade level. But still, with no special classes, that's pretty good. The newspaper is usually written on a fifth grade level, so he reads below what is considered literate, but he gets by." Mrs. Buchannan stacked the papers on her desk.

"Does this test also give an IQ score?"

"Yes, but since he's deaf, and not given any accommodation for that, no IQ test would be accurate. Still, they scored his IQ at 109 based on the test results."

"That's in the normal range, right?"

Mrs. Buchannan nodded. "Yes, but in Adam's circumstances, 109 is exceptional. Had he received an education that spoke to his needs, and that attempted to teach him on his level, or if someone had even explained the test-taking instructions to him, I'm sure he would have scored higher."

Ms. Buchannan paused to rest her chin on her fist as she gazed at Adam's scores.

"What would you guesstimate his real IQ at?" Emma shuffled through Adam's records.

"If I were to guess, I would put his actual IQ closer to 145 based on his math score alone. He's a smart guy."

"How much do you think he understood from his teachers' lectures in class?"

"He got by, but I'm sure he missed a lot. But he didn't cause much trouble and followed instructions in class, as much as he understood them anyway."

"Adam enrolled in a local junior college. Of course, now he's postponing his attendance. But how could he have gotten accepted there with all of his problems?"

"Adam might have had an easier time of it at a community college than at Greendale Academy. For one thing, Adam probably only needed his high school diploma to get accepted. And then, once he's there, they'd do their best to accommodate him, unlike Greendale. I know they have remedial classes. Too bad he hasn't been able to attend yet."

Ms. Buchannan leaned back in her chair and crossed her arms.

"Was Adam ever a discipline problem? I noticed you said he didn't cause *much* trouble."

"Well, there were a few occasions where Adam lost his temper. He can be pretty eruptive if he gets upset. I think he got frustrated sometimes because he had problems making himself understood."

"Do you remember anything about his outbursts?"

"It's all here in his records." She placed her fingers on the folder and slid it across the desk toward Emma.

"I'll step out of the office for a few minutes while you review them. We can discuss any questions you have when I return. Can I get you a Coke or something?"

Emma shook her head and picked up the bundle.

Emma reviewed Adam's disciplinary history at the school. There were teachers at the academy who obviously didn't like working with him. Perhaps they felt working with a deaf person "extra work." One report indicated that Adam made five attempts to answer a question in Mrs. Grayson's class during an oral quiz. She told him she didn't understand his responses and wouldn't let him write down his answer since it was an oral examination. When he yelled at her in frustration, she sent him to the principal's office. There were problems in some of Adam's other classes, but Mrs. Grayson's issues with Adam seemed personal.

Ms. Buchannan returned and said, "Mrs. Grayson made things difficult for Adam."

"Why?" Emma said, then closed the folder.

"It's hard to say. Maybe she didn't like him." She shrugged. "It happens sometimes." Ms. Buchannan cleared her throat and looked at her fingernails.

"I'm not sure why she insists he can hear. How could the school allow a teacher to treat a student like that? And why did Adam's parents tolerate it?"

"I'm not sure how involved the administration was in any of this. Unless a parent complains, the administration may not get involved at all. I don't have any record that Adam's parents called, complained, or became involved in any way. I suspect Adam didn't mention anything to them. He was written up, then called down to the office for his outbursts. But his parents were never contacted by the school. He wasn't ever suspended though, probably because his parents are big supporters of Greendale."

"Why didn't the school assign an interpreter for Adam, and require the sort of education that would have met his needs, despite what his parents requested for him?"

"Greendale doesn't receive federal or state funding, so it doesn't have to. And the government can't force the school to accommodate Adam's needs, which it could if it accepted funding. So, Adam's at the mercy of Mrs. Grayson and, even though I hate to say it, his parents."Ms. Buchannan paused. "You just met with Mrs. Grayson, right?"

"Yes," Emma said. "Sometimes people get picked on because they're different. Think that's what her problem was with Adam?"

"I have no clue. But I always thought Adam was a special guy. I like him and I'd be willing to help in any way I can."

Emma checked her watch. "Based on what you know, was Adam capable of at least occasionally controlling his temper once he was upset?"

"You know, I never saw his temper or the outbursts, so I couldn't tell you anything about that. I only heard about it from others. The outbursts were usually directed at teachers who were reluctant to work with him or who made things difficult for him, like Mrs. Grayson. So they're the ones to ask. Not me."

Emma knew that asking Mrs. Grayson about Adam's classroom behavior would serve little purpose. With the exception of Ms. Buchannan and Coach Smithfield, it was clear she wasn't going to get much support for Adam from Greendale Academy. Adam was remarkably functional considering his circumstances.

Thanks to Mrs. Smithfield, the Jonesburg Audiology Associates office was able to take Adam the next day and run the ABR test. The audiologists were able to prove, through a series of tests, that Adam was profoundly deaf. Emma was relieved since, with the audiologists' testimony, and evidence of the tests given, they had even more support for their motions.

The DA was sure to call Mrs. Grayson as a witness at the hearing. Her testimony seemed far off the mark to Emma, yet Mrs. Grayson never equivocated. Even though she was wrong about Adam being able to hear, could her testimony persuade the judge that Adam was over-reactive or unstable, or that he was so upset with Jennifer's breaking up with him that he planned and executed her murder?

12

August 23, 1990

Emma slid out of her car and stretched her legs from the thirty-minute drive. It was hot and her car's air conditioner had been leaking Freon for a while. Her skirt was stuck to the back of her thighs and her silk top wrinkled around her undergarments. She felt wilted and slightly itchy from the ragweed that wafted through the air. She scanned the circular driveway where she was scheduled to meet Robert's nephew, Ben, and only found Darcy's black Mercedes.

Emma clearly understood she hadn't been invited for another visit with the Gannons. This trip was limited to her meeting with Ben, and the meeting place had been pre-designated as Mayfair's driveway. Ben had told Darcy he wanted to take Emma by the scene of the murder. Emma wasn't sure why that was a part of his plan, but she was anxious to see the area.

Several minutes later, Emma heard a loud rumbling and looked up to see a faded red-and-white Ford pickup shimmying up the driveway. The rusted-out truck pulled up to the front of the Gannon's house and stopped, belching exhaust as its engine choked out a few more spurts. She was expecting a younger person, but the man who emerged from the vehicle appeared middle-aged. He was dressed in faded, threadbare overalls that could have come straight out of his grandfather's closet and a long-sleeved, red-plaid flannel shirt, which was so worn Emma could see the outline of his forearms through the fabric.

As the man walked toward her she noted that he was probably in his thirties, a good deal younger than she initially thought. His face was weathered and ruddy from acne and scarring.

"I'm Ben," he said with a nasal twang, extending a grimy hand.

Emma, glancing at his blackened fingernails, reluctantly accepted his handshake.

"I think we should drive on over to the Patricks' pasture," Ben drawled, looking sideways at Emma's skirt. "I'll drive since I know the way."

"I can drive," Emma said. "I'll follow behind you."

"That'll be fine if you want to risk getting your car stuck in all those ruts left by the rain. I doubt if you've got four-wheel drive on that little car neither. I think it'd be best if I do the driving. Just leave your car here. Darcy don't care."

Emma nodded, immediately wishing her skirt was at least three inches longer. Refusing his help, Emma hoisted herself into the cab and brushed off an area of the seat so she could sit down. The seat was grimy with mud and debris from what appeared to be decades of hunting and fishing trips. Emma couldn't find anything to clean her hands with and for a moment held her arm up in the air unsure of her next move. She finally sat down, resigned to keep her dirty hand away from her face and clothes. Unsuccessfully scrambling for a seat belt, Emma turned around, and accidentally knocked the glove compartment open with her knee. Stuffed inside were at least twenty small vials of a liquid substance and numerous pill bottles. Ben leaned over and slammed the compartment shut, then made certain the windows were rolled all the way down.

"A/C's been broken for years." He pointed to a smashed vent on the dashboard.

Ben wiped his nose on his sleeve, revved the engine, jammed his foot on the gas and spun out of the gravel driveway in a jarring lurch. Emma bounced about the seat as she held her hair with her clean hand, the door handle with the other, and prayed for her safety. The truck was so loud and the wind was blowing so wildly throughout the cab they couldn't talk. For all Emma knew, Nephew Ben was a sexual deviant with plans to drag her into the backwoods for an evening of torture and terror. She envisioned him chopping her up into little pieces and throwing her into a bonfire made from her bones and clothes. Emma kept her gaze fixed on the truck's open window, ready to jump at any sign of inappropriate movement from grubby Ben. And she wondered what might be in those bottles.

Fifteen minutes later, Ben pulled up to the Patrick property line and stopped just short of the fence, throwing rocks out in all directions as he screeched to a stop. Emma emerged from the truck, thankful she was in one piece and that Ben had no apparent proclivity for sexual malfeasance. Her only remaining concern was that she smelled like tobacco and dead game. She regretted her absurd choice of clothes, not realizing when she began the day that business attire would have been so inappropriate. She longed for some jeans and a pair of boots. Picking her way through the muck and knobby grass knolls next to the Patricks' pasture, she struggled to keep her balance as her three-inch heels sank in the mire. She leaned against the fence.

The pasture appeared to have been recently harvested, with bits of freshly cut hay littered about the field. Beyond the yellow crime scene tape, the ground was covered with rutted tire marks.

"Can we see the Patrick's house from here?" Emma asked.

"Yup, it's right over yonder, behind them bushes. See the white section there? That's the front of the house," Ben said.

"So it looks like about half a football field from here to the house. Is that your guess?" she asked.

"Yup, 'bout."

"Do you know the Patricks?" Emma asked.

"Yup, everyone knows the Patricks. They owned near 'bout the entire county at one time or 'nuther. But that was before my time. Lyle's daddy lost nearly all of it during the war," he explained.

"How did he lose it?"

"Story is, my grandfather, who was also Robert Gannon's daddy, bought the place from Lyle's momma when Mr. Patrick was fighting in Germany." He flicked dirt from his fingernails with his pocketknife.

"Why would she sell the land to Will Gannon?" Emma asked.

"Rumor has it that she hadn't heard from Mr. Patrick in over a year while he was away at war. She didn't have no means of support then and I guess she thought he was dead. And then there was those folks who said that my granddaddy and Mrs. Patrick had been hanging out together a lot. They say they spent nearly ever' day together while Mr. Patrick was gone."

"What do you mean by that? Who was saying that sort of thing?" Emma jotted down notes in her legal pad as she questioned Ben.

"Well, my momma, for one," Ben said. "Momma told me some of the folks in the family said something about it to her once."

"And your mother is?"

"Robert Gannon's sister, Wilma."

"Do you mean to tell me that Mrs. Patrick, Lyle's mother and Will Gannon, Robert's father had an affair?" she said.

"No ma'am. I'm not saying that straight out. I'm just tellin' you what my momma told me," he said. "I know that the Patricks lost their land because Mrs. Patrick sold it to my grandfather. That much is fact."

"Why did you want to bring me out here today?" Emma asked, looking across the field toward the Patricks' house.

"I wanted you to see something." He pointed toward the left pasture. "See where that line of trees is?"

Emma nodded as her eyes followed his finger.

"That there's the line where the Gannon property that was purchased from the Patricks starts. It's also the line that marks the best soil for raising cotton. Ever'thing over on what's left of the Patrick's land is low and holds water. You gotta raise cotton on well-drained soil. Cotton'll take to clay or sandy soils but it's gotta be well drained. This here Patrick land is boggy. Ain't good for nothing." He spat the remaining tobacco from his mouth on to the muddy road with a splat.

"So what could the Patricks do with what was left of the land they had?"

"Not much." Ben's eyes followed the outline of the Patrick tract. "Lyle's been trying to raise hay and corn on it for feed and thought he'd turn it into land for raising cattle, but he ain't never been able to do much of anything. He should'a give it up years ago."

"Why are you telling me all of this?" Emma asked.

"The Patricks are good people," Ben said. "They never asked for any of this trouble. Guess you can tell that even though my momma's Robert's Gannon's sister, they never done anything for her. In fact, my grandfather disinherited her. Robert got the bulk of the inheritance and didn't share. The Gannons don't do much for others," he said, kicking the hardened mud with the toe of his shoe.

"Do you know anyone who works for the Gannons now that also may have worked for them when Will was alive?" Emma asked.

"Sure, there's one old fellow," he said. "Name's Joe Casey."

"Where can I find Joe?"

"He lives on the Gannon's estate, Mayfair. As far as I know, he's always lived there. But he's retired now. I think he had a accident and he doesn't do much anymore."

"Think I could go by and meet him?" Emma asked.

"I couldn't tell you nothin' about that, but I don't see why not," Ben said.

13

August 24, 1990

Rounding the corner from Mayfield's grand entrance, Emma pulled up the gravel driveway just past the stables. She spied a small, weathered wooden building which she initially mistook for a tool shed. As she neared the structure, she could see a salmon pink and white fin-tailed Buick jutting into the driveway from the side of the house. Her grandfather drove the same car for at least twenty years. She'd always been fascinated by the little portholes on the side of the vehicle. She was shocked to see a car of this vintage in such good shape. Then she saw him.

Sitting on his front porch fanning himself with a straw fedora—the sort of hat Frank Sinatra might have worn on a hot, sunny day—he was elegantly attired in what must have been his Sunday best. His shirt was freshly laundered, starched, and so starkly bright in contrast to the obsidian hue of his skin that he seemed, even at a distance, cool and crisp in the extreme heat. Emma pulled up in her sputtering car and hopped out.

"Howdy! What brings you to these parts?" he said. Emma could see amusement and curiosity twinkling in his eyes as he spoke.

"Hi, I'm Emma," she said. "Are you Joe Casey?"

"Yup, that's me." He plopped his hat back on his head.

"Ben Bailey suggested that I speak with you." Emma extended her hand as she walked up the steps to his home.

"Yeah? Well, well…Ben Bailey. Hadn't heard that name in a while. What's he up to these days? Always thought he was a sorry fella, that one, but we can't all be ambitious." He grinned, revealing a twinkle of gold. "I'd be happy to talk to you for a while, anyway. Nephew's coming in a bit."

Once Emma was closer she could see that Joe's immaculate shirt was at least a size or two larger than necessary, and that the collar was frayed. Emma suspected he must have been a larger and more powerful man when the shirt fit properly. But his rose-colored tie, which was tightly secured with a gold clip, gave him a jaunty air. Although he seemed bone thin under his gray flannel trousers, which appeared to be of the same vintage as his hat, they were also clean and freshly ironed. He sported a gold ring with a scattering of small diamonds on his right hand where he clutched a freshly laundered handkerchief. A walker stood next to his beaten up chair. Emma caught the scent of Old Spice and soap when she stood next to him.

"If you don't mind my askin', how do you know Ben Bailey?" Joe said.

"Darcy Gannon suggested that I speak to him about the Gannon family history. I work for Silas Steele, a lawyer in town. He represents Adam Gannon. Did you know that Adam was arrested for murdering his former girlfriend, Jennifer Patrick?"

"Yup, Adam came to see me and told me about it." He tipped his hat back and dabbed his forehead with his handkerchief. "He's outta jail now."

"Yes, he's out on bail. But why did Adam come to see you?"

"Me and Adam been close since he was little. I don't believe Adam would do something like that, you know. He don't have it in him."

"I appreciate that, Mr. Casey. I'd like to ask you a few questions about the Gannon family. And the Patricks. I understand that you worked for the Gannons, but knew the Patricks too. Is that right?" Emma peered into Joe's front door as she asked her question. She'd never seen such a small home before, noting with a pang that the walls were covered in newspaper and that the front room was illuminated with one bare light bulb hanging from the lopsided ceiling. Joe followed Emma's gaze, and she quickly looked away.

Before she turned her head, she spotted a diminutive table and chair under the exposed light bulb, a tiny TV in the corner and what appeared to be a threadbare couch next to it. A wheelchair was folded into one corner. She guessed there was a kitchen, bathroom, and maybe a bedroom somewhere in the tiny, neat, space.

"Yep. I know'd them all. I raised Mr. Will, Mr. Robert and now Adam. I also know'd Mr. Jim Patrick, Lyle's daddy, back when he owned the back cotton fields down yonder."

"What was your job with the Gannon family?"

"I was foreman and ran the crews that worked the land. Back then it was cotton. But of course, Mr. Will bought the Patrick land and everything changed after that."

"What do you mean?"

"Will Gannon wanted to diversify. Thought he'd make more money that way. He wanted to raise peanuts, but peanuts do better in sandy soil, and we ain't got sandy soil here. I talked him into corn instead. Both crops need well-drained land, so that worked okay. We planted corn one year, cotton the next. The Patrick property was better drained than what the Gannons had before and the cotton, especially, did much better on what had been Patrick land."

Joe cleared his throat, took a gulp of lemonade from the glass sitting next to him and rubbed his knee. He gestured toward the icy drink, offering her some refreshment, and, at her refusal, continued.

"Then Will carved out a special piece to raise thoroughbreds. Race horses, you know? I worked everything but the horse farm. I don't know much about 'em. I used to ride 'em around the different pastures a little, but a rabbit spooked my horse one day and we fell with him on toppa me. I ain't walked much since. Mr. Robert lets me stay here rent-free even though I'm not really workin' any more. So, I got nothin' to complain about." His false teeth clacked as he closed his mouth.

"What did you mean when you said that you raised Will, and Robert and

Adam?"

"I took 'em out to the pastures and taught 'em about the land and how to take care of it. How to drive a tractor. How to rotate the crops so that nutrients were put back into the soil. Will understood but didn't care. Robert just didn't get it. Robert only cared about money, what he could buy, and where he could go."

"What about Adam?"

"Well, now, Adam's special. He's my favorite. Ain't no secret about that. Adam's dad didn't do a whole lot with him, and Darcy was always with the horses, so Adam would come out to the river with me sometimes and fish. Tried to take him huntin' a time or two, but he wasn't much of a hunter. Missed everything by a mile. He doesn't talk much, so I learned him to finger spell in my hand when he was about ten or so."

"What do you mean by finger spell in your hand'?"

"Well, like I said, he don't talk much, but he's been to school, and he's smart, so he learned some letters and some words and could even read a little. You know, a few simple words here and there. So, I would make a letter in his hand and then write it in the dirt. And he picked it up real quick. He started talkin' to me with finger spellin' in my hand. I think he also started to learn to read and understand things better then too."

"So you taught him to read?"

"I can't take full credit for that. He went to school, and picked up a lot there. But his parents didn't want him treated special. He was hungry to learn and he'd follow me around like a little puppy back then. I like to paint some and do stuff with clay, and he picked that up too."

"Yes, I've seen some of Adam's drawings. Sometimes he communicates by making little sketches."

"Yep, he do. He's done some right nice paintin's. I got some down in the shed." Joe inclined his head in the direction of the rough-hewn building.

"I'd love to see them sometime."

"Sure. And when you see them, you'll know he didn't hurt that Patrick girl," Joe continued, mopping his head with his cotton handkerchief. "Adam's real shy. He didn't talk at all for years. His parents never encouraged it. I get the impression they think he sounds funny. But they talk to him like he can understand everything they say. He do pick up a lot, but not all. That's why I learned him to finger spell. But his parents never did that with him. I never saw him do that with anyone but me and Jennifer. If he felt close enough to talk to her like that, I don't believe he could hurt her no how."

"So you think the Gannons wanted to limit the ways Adam communicated?" Emma turned a page of her small notepad.

"Yes, I do."

"Why?"

"I think it was Ms. Darcy. She didn't want him to get ribbed by the other kids like she was when she was little. You know, she grew up poor. I think she meant to protect him. But she ended up hurtin' him."

"I see. By the way, how old were you when you started working for the Gannons?" Emma looked at her watch.

"Well, I always been here. My daddy and momma both worked for the Gannons. My mama worked in the big house. They's always been Caseys at Mayfair. My daddy was the foreman for Mr. Joseph. Now, you gotta know that back then there weren't many black men that was foremen. Mr. Joseph was a good man, and believed in putting the best man forward, no matter his color. But he spoiled his kids. He was Mr. Will's daddy. Mr. Joseph and me were about the same age, born the same year I think."

"Mr. Casey, do you mind me asking you how old you are?"

"No, ma'am, but I'd prefer it if you called me Joe."

"And I'd prefer it if you didn't call me ma'am." Emma smiled. "Well?"

"I'm not sure how old I am, 'zactly," Joe said. "I was born sometime around the turn of the century, might-a been sometime before 1900 and might-a been sometime after. My mamma didn't get no birth certificates for any of her kids. And she had a bunch of us. But I guess I'm somewhere around ninety." He rubbed his handkerchief on his head again and grinned. "But I got to ask you why you're askin' me all these questions about the Gannons. I don't see what this has got to do with Adam or what happened to that Patrick girl.".

"That's fair. When I spoke to Ben he said that Will Gannon may have purchased the Patrick land under questionable circumstances. Do you know anything about that?"

"Questionable circumstances…" Joe repeated. "Yep, I guess I do, but I don't feel real comfortable talkin' about it to you. And I still don't see what any of this has to do with Adam."

"I'm trying to understand the relationship between the two families, the Gannons and the Patricks. Ben suggested that Will Gannon might have purchased the land from Jim Patrick's wife while Mr. Patrick was fighting in the war. Can you tell me about that?"

"Maybe. But let me see if I can follow your thinkin'," Joe said. "You're wondering if maybe the two families don't exactly get along?"

"Well, I understand that they don't, and since they've never gotten along, why did Adam ever see Jennifer in the first place?"

"I don't know nothin' about that. I think Adam and Jennifer met through some school friends or somethin'," Joe said, twisting the brim of his hat in his hands. "I don't know where you're goin' with all these questions."

"I didn't mean to make you uncomfortable, Joe. I'm just trying to do my job, which is to do everything I can to keep Adam out of jail. We want to help Adam."

"Well, why didn't you say so in the first place?" Joe said with a slow grin. "Help me get on off of this porch and I'll show you somethin'."

Emma grabbed Joe's wheelchair from inside his house, and they made their way to the porch stairs. Someone had fashioned a ramp over half of the stairs for Joe's convenience, but he still needed help since there was a significant incline.

"I'm going to show you something special. Follow the shell path here to the stables, down yonder," he said.

She followed his skeletal index finger as it pointed their way down the bumpy path to the side door of the stables. When they entered the tiny storage room, Joe held the door open for a moment so Emma could see well enough to walk in. Once her eyes adjusted to the shadowy darkness, she noticed stacks of canvases, boards, and papers along the rough-hewn wooden paneling and in front of the work bench. She stepped closer to examine the pieces, and found paintings, oils and watercolors, charcoal sketches, and pencil drawings. There were easily more than one hundred works piled up along the wall, in various heights and sizes. Joe wheeled himself in the room, searched along the paneling for the light switch and flipped it on.

"Are these yours?" Emma asked, leaning over for a closer view.

"No, ma'am. They's Adam's." Joe fanned himself with his hat.

Emma bent down to flip through the artwork, dazzled by Adam's talent. He had copied techniques of several masters in a few of the paintings. She smiled when she recognized Jennifer's soft blue eyes in a cubist portrait in the style of Picasso. Another elongated portrait, unmistakably Jennifer, reminded Emma of one of Modigliani's women. The best of the group didn't copy the style of any other artist, but instead captured the essence of Jennifer, her delicate beauty and her spirit.

"You see," Joe said. "He loved her."

"She inspired him to paint, at least. Did Adam take art courses, maybe art history? He seems to have some knowledge of other artists' styles."

"I don't know 'bout that, but when he was little he used to spend hours looking in an old book a mine. I found it in the trash one night and took it home. It's from one of them museums in France. I never been there, but I always enjoyed looking at them pictures, and Adam did too."

They closed up the stable doors. Emma pushed Joe back to his porch.

"Seems like you two are pretty close." Emma sat down in one of the metal chairs. Joe had the same porch furniture as her grandparents. Circa early fifties, constructed of metal, now mostly rust, they were painted aqua with little shell scallops along the back. The legs were one curved piece of metal tubing, perfect for rocking and bouncing, something Emma had discovered as a six year old. They would always make her think of summers in Florida. Her chair made a screeching noise as she scooted closer to Joe.

"Yes, ma'am. We are," Joe said. "I never had no kids. My wife and baby both died during childbirth, and Adam's like the son I never had. He didn't turn from me when he grew up like his daddy done. He's a good boy."

Emma smiled. "I'm glad to hear you say that. It's difficult to explain, but for purposes of Adam's defense, I believe I need to have a better understanding of the problems between the Gannons and the Patricks."

"I don't see how none a that is connected to Adam or the murder of the Patrick girl. I don't mean to be rude, Miss Emma, but that was long ago. It happened way b'fore Adam was born."

"But there's been a murder of a Patrick girl, and right now, all evidence seems to point to Adam Gannon, as the guilty party. Neither of us want that."

Joe shook his head and brought his handkerchief to his mouth.

"I have to look at all other possibilities so I can help him. I need to explore whether the family dispute could have led to Jennifer's murder. Could you take a little time, start at the beginning, and tell me what happened?"

14

Joe cleared his throat, raised one eyebrow and squinted at Emma.

"Back around World War II, I was managin' the cotton fields, runnin' the crew that did the pickin' and all a' that. Mr. Will was runnin' the place at that time since Mr. Joseph had died a few years before. Mr. Joseph, he died pretty young, about forty-five, I think. A man hits his stride around forty-five. Becomes an expert. No one can beat him at his game then, whatever it is. You can ride that long as you can stay healthy. Too bad he died so young." He shook his head.

"How old was Will at that time? Wouldn't he have been only about twenty?" Emma said.

"Yes, ma'am. Reckon he was 'bout twenty-five or so."

"Did he join the armed forces or do any fighting in the war?"

"No, ma'am. He got outta it 'cause he had to run the farm. Some said Mr. Joseph paid off some senator to keep him out afore he died, but I don't know about all a' that."

"But Jim Patrick, Lyle's father, enlisted, right?" Emma asked.

"Don't know if he enlisted, but he did go off to war. That's a fact."

"Do you know what year he left?"

"No, ma'am. I don't know no years."

"Well, the United States got into the war in 1941. Was it early on or a little later?"

"I'm not sure when he left, but I recall that he got back right after the war was over. I believe he served in Europe, somewhere in Germany. I recall he was stuck for a while in one of them prisoner a war camps, but no one knew at the time. Ever'one thought he was dead." Joe glanced down the road.

"Ben Bailey told me that Will and Jim Patrick's wife started seeing each other around that time. Do you know anything about that?"

"Well now, I don't know what you mean 'bout seein' each other," Joe said. "I recall they spent some time together 'cause I had to track down Mr. Will a few times and I was always findin' him at the Patrick place. Also, I was friends with Mr. Patrick's foreman, Cecil. We'd talk about our cotton crops sometimes at church and sometimes down at 'Rosie's'. Rosie's is a little bar along the outskirts of town where we'd get together on Saturday nights. I used to play poker there when my wife would let me." He grinned and tapped his foot a little at the memory of those times. "Them was good days."

"So, Will stayed at home during the war and Mr. Jim Patrick left to go fight, right?"

"That's right."

"And when Mr. Patrick got back, his wife had sold most of his property to Will Gannon. Is that correct?"

"Yep, that's about right."

"How did Will get Mrs. Patrick to sell the land to him, if that's what he did?"

Joe fidgeted in his seat and looked out over the stables. It was a clear day. There was hardly a cloud in the cerulean sky. The stables cast sharp shadows along the back track.

"Can you tell me what you know?"

"What I know I kinda pieced together."

"That's okay, Joe. Just tell me what you were able to put together from what you know."

"My momma always told me that it's the work of the devil to speak ill of the dead."

"Which dead are you speaking of?"

"Mr. Will and a few others, I reckon."

"Well, if you know something that might help Adam, that can only be a good thing, right?"

"That's what I can't figure. I can't figure how any of this can help Adam."

"Joe, why don't you just tell me and let me decide if it helps Adam. What can it hurt, really?"

Joe pursed his lips and sighed, then laced his fingers along the back of his neck, leaned back in his chair, and looked down his nose at Emma.

"Will Gannon was over at the Patricks near ever' day, accordin' to Cecil. I know ever' time I needed him I found him over there. The Patrick's place was the biggest in the county at that time. But there was a shortage of workers during the war, and the place had started to go down. The upper part of Patrick land was the best in the area for raising cotton. It was well drained, you know. Didn't hold water like the lower section did. The upper part was what Will wanted."

Joe sat up and adjusted the faded cushion in his seat to get more comfortable.

"Sometime after Mr. Jim been away, Cecil told me that Miz Ethel got a telegram saying that he was missin'. She took to carryin' on about that for quite a spell. Cecil said she liked to never stop cryin'. Will started showin' up over the Patricks a lot more after that. I ran up on 'em one day, Miz Ethel had her head up on his shoulder and all. Made you wonder."

"Made you wonder about what?"

"Well, made you wonder what Will was up to. One of Will's best friends ran the post office back then. Mr. Kline was his name. I don't know if they had some sort of agreement, or if Will paid him, but Miz Ethel stopped gettin' a lot of her mail after a while, even though the letters kept comin' in."

"That's a crime. How could this man get away with something like that?"

"Well, like I said, Mr. Kline ran that post office. He was there every day, during all of the working hours, which ain't that long, if you think about it. Back then there was only one other person helping him, and that was his wife. He didn't have no problems controlling the mail. No problems at all."

"How do you know letters kept coming for Mrs. Ethel?"

"Well, that's complicated," Joe said, leaning over as he dug his elbows into his knees. "Cecil's wife used to clean up at night at the post office. One night, she was cleanin' out a storage locker and knocked over a cardboard box that was up on the top shelf. Some letters spilled out. All of the letters were addressed to Ethel Patrick. She said the letters had that APO postmark that soldiers' letters had. I'm not sure if she read any of those letters then. Anyway, she finally figured out that they were from Jim to his wife, Miz Ethel, and that they were being kept from her."

"So, you think the Mr. Klein kept them and didn't deliver them to Mrs. Patrick?"

"Yes, ma'am. That's what it look like. I don't know why he kept them instead of throwin' them away, but that's what he did. Maybe he was planning on burning 'em." He shrugged. "I also know about other letters that Cecil's wife read, and they were kept from her too."

"Other letters?"

"Well, after she knocked the box over, Patsy, that's Cecil's wife, kept checkin' the box, just out of nosiness, and after a while, she noticed that a lot letters started showin' up in the box that were from places all over the country, and even places outside the country. All of the letters were addressed to Miz Ethel, but they were from New York and Massachusetts. They's even a letter from Switzerland. Patsy's curiosity finally got the better of her, because she didn't think Miz Ethel would know anyone from those places, and even though she knew she shouldn't, she started sneakin' a few letters home. She'd steam 'em open, so no one would know she looked inside."

"And?"

"She was surprised when she read that some letters were from people who had them shortwave radios, and they could tune into radio stations all the way over to Germany. Seems German stations got a hold of messages from American prisoners held in camps in the towns where stations were. One of the stations got a hold of one of Jim's messages, and his message was read over the radio. They was making fun of the prisoners, I guess. When Jim's message was read, a bunch of people on those shortwave radios heard it. At least twenty letters went out to Miz Ethel tellin' her not to worry, that

Mr. Jim was alive. The letter from Switzerland was from the Red Cross, sending Miz Ethel an actual letter directly from Jim. But Miz Ethel never got any of them. Mr. Will and Mr. Kline seen to that."

"And during this time, the war office had no information about Jim, or that he'd been captured?"

"I don't think so. I don't think she got any more telegrams. And Will made sure she didn't get any letters. So, she just thought Jim died. We all did."

"And that's what Will wanted her to think?"

"It sorta looks that way."

"And Cecil and his wife never said anything?"

"No, ma'am. Back then, it wouldn't do for anyone to interfere with Will Patrick's business, but especially a black man. Patsy and Cecil would a lost they jobs for sure. It was sad, but they had kids. They had to eat. The war was on. Food and jobs were scarce."

"So Jim Patrick must have been missing or presumed dead for quite some time."

"Reckon so."

"And that's the same time Will started staying over at the Patrick property a little more often?"

"A lot more often is more like it."

"Was Will married at the time?"

"Yes, ma'am, he was."

"Do you remember when Ethel sold the property to Will?"

"Yes, ma'am, I do."

"When was that?"

"Just a short time before Mr. Jim came home."

"Why did Ethel sell the land to Will?"

"She was having a hard time makin' ends meet. She didn't have no hands to speak of to work the land. Most of the workers who didn't sign up or who weren't drafted for some reason during the war had gone up to the big cities along the east coast to work in the factories and all she had was Cecil and a few others for pickin'. She was afraid that she was gonna lose everything and I don't doubt that Will was steady convincin' her that that was surely 'bout to happen. They'd done started a romance of sorts anyway. He'd been doin' all he could to make her think he cared about her even though he already had a wife. Brought her food, flowers, was over there fixin' things ever' day. She didn't know what to do and unfortunately, she thought she had a friend in Will. Instead he was plottin' against her."

"Do you know what she sold the land for?"

"That's the saddest part. Looks like Miz Ethel thought Mr. Will might be leavin' his wife for her, so Cecil told me she sold the land for barely nothin'. But Mr. Will planned the whole thing to get the Patrick land. He knew there were letters from Mr. Jim and that he was probably alive. He also knew that since Miz Ethel thought her husband was dead, he could get away with making romantic promises to her. He knew the land was good land and that he wanted it. Mr. Will may as well have stole that property."

"Do you remember when Jim came home?"

"Yes, ma'am, I do. Ever'one remembers that day. He stepped off the train and people in town thought they's lookin' at a ghost. Word spread like crazy that he was back. Cecil said Miz Ethel fainted dead out when she saw him. No one knew how to tell him that most of his land was gone. And I never heard no one ever speak to him about Miz Ethel and Will."

"Did everyone know about the relationship between Ethel and Will?"

"As far as I know, only those here on the two farms, and Cecil's wife. But the land that was left to the Patrick family was bad land. It broke Jim Patrick." Joe leaned back in his chair and peered at Emma. "I'd do anything to help Adam, and I'm happy to answer your questions, but like I said before, I don't see how anything that happened more than fifty years ago could have anything to do with the murder of Jennifer Patrick."

15

August 25, 1990

Ren Taylor stared at the ceiling, his feet propped on his desk. He felt much older than his thirty-two years lately. He rubbed his knee. His old football injury had been aggravated by late nights at crime scenes, and crouching with his camera and foot impression kits. He was glad that, with the exception of the recent murder, there was little crime in Greendale County. He didn't get the adrenaline rush some of the deputies did from all of the excitement.

Something else wasn't sitting right with him this morning. The arrest of Adam Gannon had been too easy. Why would the kid have left the rifle in his truck after the shooting? If he had killed the girl, wouldn't it have made more sense for him to throw the weapon away or hide it? He could have buried it. That would have made sense. Placing the rifle behind the seat of his truck was too careless. Someone who'd gone to the pains of cutting outside phone wires before they committed a midnight murder wouldn't have messed up by leaving the incriminating weapon in their truck. He rubbed his forehead, which was beginning to ache as much as his knee.

The DA told Colson that he thought Adam could hear, and that some of his teachers did too. But as far as Ren knew, the kid was deaf. That's why he brought a consent form for the search. He wanted to make sure the kid understood what was going on. Plus, he wasn't sure the judge would give him a search warrant for Adam's apartment based only on Lyle's suspicions and one incriminating letter. But now they had much more, and if the consent form didn't protect the search, all the evidence they'd seized could be thrown out.

It was such a weird case. The dad hadn't been much help. He and Adam had barely looked at each other the day of the search. They'd seemed disconnected. Ren exhaled slowly and closed his eyes, as if he was blocking out all of the problems the case might bring.

He got up to stretch his legs and wandered over to look out of his window and on to the square. He wanted to run his ideas about Adam and the rifle by Colson. He shoved on his hat and headed out of the door. It was about time for one of Lucky's milkshakes anyway.

Lucky's was the political gathering spot on the square, owned by Milton Scott, the town's pharmacist who had been the mayor for the past ten years. City council members, political hacks, judges, and lawyers frequented the drugstore during the lunch hour, so it had become one of the town's most popular spots. Recently, Milton's wife decided to place chairs and tables, café style, outside on the sidewalk lending a European air to the otherwise gothic southern town. White tablecloths completed the picture. Ladies who lunched began ordering their salad specials outside on nice days. Milton was going to rig a fan to keep them there on the hot days as well. It had become the place to be seen. Today, which was a Saturday, shouldn't be as busy. Ren hoped to find the sheriff in his usual spot.

Not seeing him outside, Ren walked into the drugstore and approached the soda fountain counter. Unmistakable grilled cheese smells changed his mind about the milkshake and locked in his lunch choice. He saw the girl who was working with Silas Steele on the Patrick case shopping in a nearby aisle. Emma? Was that her name? Nice looking. Great smile. She was in great shape too. He liked the way she wore her long blonde hair back off of her face. And there was an unmistakable intelligence behind her brown eyes. Plus, he liked a woman who dressed in athletic wear on weekends.

A few steps took him to her aisle where he rummaged for a moment in the allergy medications.

He caught Emma's eye, and extended his hand toward her. "Hi, I'm Ren Taylor. Weren't you in the office the other day looking at evidence for Silas in the Patrick murder?"

Emma nodded. "That was me." Emma moved her store items from one arm to another to meet his outstretched hand. She leaned her head back to look him square in the face and smiled, flushed cheeks betraying her surprise.

Ren returned her smile. "Let me know if there's anything we can do to help you during your investigation."

"I appreciate it. I'd like to speak to you about the ballistics identification at some point, and some of your photographs." Emma shuffled her packages.

"You'll have to get the DA's okay," Ren said, "then, sure. Anytime."

Emma blushed at his correction, and nodded her farewell. When she turned, she watched as he walked back to the counter and sat down next to an older, uniformed man she assumed was the sheriff. As she glanced at the two of them she couldn't help noticing how wide Ren's shoulders were underneath his extra-starched shirt. His waist was small for a man of his size. Realizing he must work out daily, she had to admit he was nice looking, not that she was interested. She didn't have time for men with law school, a job, and two kids. But still—she wasn't dead.

She moved back toward the soda fountain area where they were seated to continue shopping and noticed that Diane, the woman who worked behind the counter, had brought Ren and the sheriff water and was asking them for their orders.

"I couldn't help but overhear you talking to that girl about the Patrick case," Diane said as she wiped up splashes of water from the counter. "What a shame. I saw Jennifer Patrick right before she died. I think it was the day before she was killed, actually. Said she was going over to the Gannon place the very day she spoke to me."

Emma caught her breath. Darcy said that she'd never met Jennifer. Emma made a mental note to ask Adam if he'd ever introduced Jennifer to his parents or brought her to his parents' home.

"Did she say why she was going to the Gannons'?" Ren asked.

"No, she didn't say. Just said she was headed out there."

"Do you remember about when this was?"

"Like I said. I remember this pretty well because she told me she was going over there that day, and the next day I hear she's dead. So, I guess it was about a week ago. Isn't that right? She was killed about a week ago?"

"A little more than that. But thanks, Diane. We'll look into it." Colson drank from his water glass.

Emma walked to the front of the store and paid for her purchases, glancing toward Ren and the sheriff before she left. They had their backs to her and didn't see her leave.

August 27, 1990

Emma hoped it would be cooler in the smaller conference room, and had reserved that space for her Monday morning meeting with Adam. The air conditioning had been off for the weekend and the place was still musty and dank smelling, even though the receptionist had turned on the unit. Emma switched on a fan, which only stirred the moist air around a little and confused the papers on the console table that were weighed down by an old stapler.

Emma asked Adam to sit down, then pulled up a chair next to him.

"Did you ever bring Jennifer down to Mayfair to see your mother and father?" she said, carefully forming the words.

No response.

Emma noticed Adam's flushed cheeks and guessed that he understood her question. She knew that once he was familiar with a person's speech patterns, he could pick up about thirty percent of what was said. And she realized Adam tended to avoid questions about his parents or Jennifer. So she suspected he understood more than he let on.

Emma wrote:

Did Jennifer meet your parents?

"No." He shifted in his chair.

Did you ever bring Jennifer to Mayfair?

He shook his head and looked at his feet. Adam was doing everything he could to stonewall her, which meant avoiding eye contact. Did she need to stand on her head to get his attention?

Emma stomped her foot. He looked up.

To meet Joe?

"Yes," he said.

Then he wrote *Last winter.*

This year? Emma wrote.

He shook his head "No."

"Do you know why Jennifer went to Mayfair on August fourteenth?" Emma asked. She paused then wrote the question. Adam shook his head no.

"Were you and Jennifer still dating then?" Emma asked the question, and wrote it out again.

Adam shook his head.

Did you see Jennifer again after you stopped dating? she wrote.

Adam flushed and looked at his hands.

Emma reached across and touched Adam's arm. She could see a tear drop on the table.

I am sorry, but I have to ask these things, she wrote.

Adam turned away from Emma.

Why did you write that she would be sorry for breaking up with you?

Adam picked up the pen and wrote:

she not see me any more

Tears welled and spilled down his cheeks.

"Adam, is there something you aren't telling me that went on between Jennifer and your parents?"

What aren't you telling me? she wrote.

Adam didn't respond.

I can't help you if you won't talk to me.

Still no response.

"Adam, I am going to drive out to Mayfair to speak to Joe and some of the hands to see if they can tell me the last time they saw Jennifer."

Emma wrote: *travel to Mayfair, see Joe and other hands about Jennifer, OK?*

Adam nodded.

Then she wrote: *I will ask your mother and father if they saw Jennifer.*

"No!" Adam said, slamming his hand on the table.

Emma was startled by Adam's reaction, but picked up her pen and wrote: *Why not? Are you afraid of something? Are you afraid of your parents?*

Adam shrugged and turned to gaze out the window.

16

For the third time in less than two weeks, Emma drove up the curved driveway to the big house at Mayfair. Her heart pounded as she rapped on the carved door. She wished she'd spoken to Silas about her plan before she drove out. Darcy wasn't Silas's client, technically, Adam was, but Darcy and her husband had hired Silas and paid Adam's bills. And Emma was about to question her veracity. Darcy, who chaired the operations committee at First Baptist Church, didn't seem accustomed to being questioned, especially about issues that had already been discussed. But none of the others Emma had spoken to, including Joe, the groomers, or the stable hands, had seen Jennifer on August fourteenth.

Lola Mae, the Gannon's housekeeper, answered the door and ushered her into the cool hallway where she asked Emma to wait. This time Emma could see through the French doors of the library into the garden where Darcy was tending to her roses. She was wearing a white dress so ethereal and light she seemed to float through the garden. Her blonde curls were tucked under a straw hat as if she'd just stepped out of one of Monet's paintings from the gardens at Argenteuil. She knew how to make an appearance.

The housekeeper walked outside and spoke to Darcy, who waved and motioned for Emma to join them. Emma walked out onto the bright patio, blinded for a second by the sunlight.

Enchanted by the garden, Emma took in the delicate aroma of the beds of roses, and sweet jasmine lining the back trellis. That, balanced with the earthy scent of freshly dug soil and mulch, created a delicious blend of aromas that attracted birds, bees, butterflies and humans alike. The garden was a visual feast with boxwoods lining cobblestone paths, which were then separated into several sections of interlocking oval-shaped circles. Inside each section were rows of various long-stemmed roses.

"You're looking at the Crimson Bouquet," Darcy said without looking up. "Beautiful, aren't they?"

"Yes, they're lovely. Are you the one with the green thumb?"

"Well, I can't take all of the credit. My gardener and I put these in the ground a while ago, I guess maybe twelve or so years now. They've won awards at the Southeastern Horticultural Society flower show in Atlanta three years in a row." She smiled and turned. "What can I help you with today?"

"I was at Lucky's a couple of days ago. Are you familiar with the drug store in town?"

Darcy nodded. "Yes, I drive there at least once a month for our prescriptions."

"A woman named Diane, who works behind the soda fountain counter, said Jennifer Patrick told her she was going to visit Mayfair the day before she was killed. I checked with Adam and a few of the hands, and everyone said that they hadn't seen her here. Did you meet with Jennifer here at Mayfair that day?"

Darcy smiled. "Why, no, Emma. I explained that I had never met Jennifer."

"Do you think perhaps she drove out here to meet and missed you?"

"Not to my knowledge," Darcy said as she placed a rose in her basket.

"Do you think she may have met with Robert?" Emma shielded her eyes against the sun to watch Darcy as she answered.

"Robert was out of town the day before Jennifer's death, I believe. But you're welcome to check with him." Darcy smiled sweetly, then raised a rose to the sunlight, studying the saturated crimson color.

"Do you mind if I ask your housekeeper about whether she saw Jennifer at that time?"

"Not at all. In fact, I'll ask her myself. Lola Mae!"

Lola Mae walked onto the porch from the adjoining room where she'd been dusting.

"You don't recall seeing Jennifer Patrick here a couple of weeks ago, do you?" Darcy shook her head as she asked. "She's a tall young lady with long blonde hair. Isn't that correct, Miss Thornton?"

"That description would fit the photos I've seen of her."

Lola Mae shook her head. "No, ma'am, I didn't see her."

"Lola Mae, did you know Jennifer Patrick?" Emma asked.

"I know who she was," Lola Mae answered.

"And she wasn't here that day?" Emma asked.

"No, ma'am, she wasn't."

"Well, I guess that does it," Emma said.

"Is that all you needed?" Darcy asked.

"That's all I need to know for now," Emma said.

"Won't you stay for a glass of tea or something?"

"Thank you, no. I have to go pick up my boys and get dinner on."

"Lola Mae, please show Miss Emma out," Darcy said as she turned back to her roses. "Thank you for dropping by, Emma. We're so glad you're doing such a thorough job defending our Adam."

Lola Mae led Emma back into the house, through the library and hallway. She opened the heavy front door, and looked back down the corridor toward the garden at Darcy who was still preoccupied with the flowers. Lola Mae stepped outside onto the front porch and closed the door behind her.

"She was here." Lola Mae fidgeted with her sash and wiped her hands on the front of her apron.

"What?"

"The girl, Jennifer Patrick, was here."

"What do you mean she was here? Why did you—"

"Look, I got to get back in and I got no time. I didn't want to tell Miss Darcy, but Jennifer Patrick was here. I saw her. That's a fact. And I saw her speaking to someone. I couldn't make out who she was talking to 'cause they was blocked by one of them pillars in the side parlor room, and I couldn't hear what they were saying. I didn't want anyone to see me or hear me, so I didn't move. I don't know why she was here, but she was crying. That's all I know. I don't know if it was Adam that she was talking to, or who. Now, I got to go."

With that she opened the door and went back inside, closing it ever so softly behind her.

17

August 28, 1990

Emma pulled the drapes back and peered down the street. She realized she'd been holding her breath; she didn't know for how long. She started gasping in shallow, rapid bursts. Feeling dizzy, she sat down on the couch and forced herself to count to ten with each breath. She needed to keep her head together. Panic would only make things worse.

Even though the sun was now up, Deputy Taylor's car was still there, parked in the lot across from her apartment. She knew the deputy's presence should provide protection against the Peeping Tom or stalker or whoever had been outside her window last night. She should feel relieved, but she didn't.

Last night's intense moon and the streetlight on the corner had illuminated the hand that flashed across her window just before midnight. A silhouette of a head jutted into view as she was picking up the phone to call the sheriff's department. The flash of a profile wasn't clear enough to identify, but it was obviously male. Fear and adrenaline had melted Emma's fingers into quivering Jell-O until she paused, took a deep breath, and dialed 911.

"A man is looking in my living room window this very minute and he could be trying to break in. I need someone over here right away. I have two eight-year-old boys asleep in their beds, and I don't want anything to happen to them. Please get over here as fast as you can."

She gave the 911 operator her address and a deputy was dispatched.

Then she heard the sound of a truck engine turning over. By the time she looked out the window, the street was empty.

Although Deputy Taylor was quick to respond, he found nothing when he arrived. There were tiny drainage pebbles under the window outside the living room, which was where Emma saw the hand and silhouette. There were no visible footprints, and no other evidence under any of Emma's other apartment windows. Then Emma told him about the black truck.

"I haven't reported this yet but was planning to if it persisted. I've been followed this week by a person in a black pick-up truck."

"What do you mean when you say you were followed?" Ren asked.

Emma explained she thought she saw the truck following her when she went to class the previous day and again when she went to work. She didn't recognize the truck and hadn't been able to see the person inside since the windows were tinted. She didn't know the make of the vehicle but planned on taking a photograph of it and had meant to write down the license number, although she hadn't yet. The timing alone made her suspect that the two incidents—the Peeping Tom incident and the stalking incident—were connected.

Even though Emma was reluctant to tell Deputy Taylor, she suspected her ex-husband could be the culprit. Motivated purely by greed, she suspected he'd discovered she was about to graduate from law school, and knew he'd like access to an ex-wife with a decent salary. It would never occur to him she and the kids were barely scraping by. Delinquent in his child support payments, a warrant had been issued for his arrest in Savannah, but Emma didn't know where he was living now. Clandestine snooping was so like him. She shuddered.

Silas was at an out of town trial or Emma would have called him before she called the sheriff. Both incidents were criminal, and since she lived just outside the Jonesburg city limits, it was within the sheriff's jurisdiction. She had no choice but to report the crimes.

"You should have let us know about the truck earlier. If you see it again, take a photograph of it, if you have a camera, and call us as soon as you can. Do you have any idea who this person might be?" Ren wrote down his phone number and handed it to Emma.

"I don't have any definite ideas. It occurred to me it could be my ex-husband, but I'm not even sure where he's living right now. So I don't know how to check up on him."

Ren took down all of the information Emma had on her children's father. "We'll do what we can to run him down, and if you need anything else, don't hesitate to give me a call." Noticing that Emma's face was several shades paler, he reached out and touched her arm. "Don't worry. We're on top of this. It's what we do. If you hear the slightest noise or see anything remotely suspicious, remember we're only a phone call away."

"I'll start taking my camera with me so I'll be prepared if he shows up again."

"Good idea. Please know we're here for you." Ren waved as he walked down Emma's front steps.

Emma didn't want to alarm her kids, but at the same time she was afraid for them. She planned to call their friends' parents to arrange sleepovers until the situation passed. If the incidents continued, she'd have to call her parents and have them keep the boys until things were safe. She couldn't take any chances.

Emma pulled the Polaroid camera from the top shelf of her closet and walked into the bright sunlight. Pacing the perimeter of her apartment building, she scanned the ground under her windows and adjacent to walkways in case there were footprints the police had missed. Even though it was still early in the morning, it was already nearly ninety degrees. She shooed a couple of honey bees buzzing in a clover patch as she made her way around the border of the complex.

Emma lived on the first floor of one of several married student quarter apartments on campus. The building had been constructed in the 1960's in an innocuous red brick. Although the institutional metal doors were sturdy, the locks were worn and loose. Most folks knew that a good shove in the right spot was all it would take to force the door open.

Emma's street abutted a row of fraternity houses. The Sigma Pi house was directly behind hers and sat on a rolling hillside along with other similarly constructed antebellum-like mansions. Set approximately thirty feet apart, the houses were lined up, indistinguishable except for the Greek letters decorating each of the houses' tympana. They all maintained parking lots filled with German-manufactured cars in quantities sufficient to fill the Black Forest. But years of fraternity parties and pledge nights had taken a toll on the once elegant structures. Tattered drapes blew out of half-open windows through torn screens. One of the homes even had a broken window. Emma knew that none of Sigma Pi's inhabitants would have seen the truck on the night of the peeping Tom incident. She didn't even bother to ask.

She continued her search for footprints and tire tracks. Seeing none, she made her way back across to her side of the street.

Emma drove out to Mayfair after class, avoiding the path to the main house, as well as Joe's home and the stables. She wanted to ask the field hands that worked there if they knew how to find Ben Bailey, Robert Gannon's nephew. She had a hunch he might know something about the owner of the black truck. He seemed to know a lot about what went on in Greendale County.

She drove up to the farm and scanned the grounds. She spotted a small crew making repairs to a fence post, hopped out of her car, and walked toward them. They stopped digging as she approached. One of the workers took off his hat and wiped his forehead with his t-shirt.

"Hi, does anyone know Ben Bailey? I'd like to know how to get to his place from here."

"Yes, ma'am, I can tell you," one of the workers replied. "But it's bad roads.

Sure you want to try it?"

"I'm sure."

The worker pointed down the road. "If you go down a couple of miles, to where the pecan stand used to be, well it's still there, but it's empty, and hang a hard right, then down the road to where that trailer park is and make another right, you'll be there." He put his hand on his shovel and shifted his feet slightly as he cleared his throat. "But ma'am, I gotta say, I don't think it's a good idea for you to go down that road."

"Why's that?"

"Well, once you make that turn, you're committed. There's only one road in and out."

"What are you saying? Is it necessary to have multiple road access to properties around here? I'm confused." Emma smiled.

"I'm just saying that I don't think it's a good idea. Ben Bailey's known to get into his drink this time of day. It wouldn't do for a lady to travel down that road by herself. That's all I'm saying."

"I'm sure I'll be fine. I know Ben Bailey, and can't imagine that he'd do any harm to me, but thanks for your help."

Emma didn't ask the farmhand what he'd muttered under his breath as she walked back to her car and crawled in the front seat.

Emma easily found the deserted pecan stand, took a right at the trailer park. She worked her way down a long and narrow road paved with small rocks, her car kicking up dust from the pulverized pebbles. The trees canopied the road, shutting out what was left of the late afternoon sun. Emma's car sputtered, disrupting the quiet of the secluded wooded way.

As she approached a clearing she saw two small shelters, each neglected and in need of repair. One, a faded avocado-green wooden structure, seemed to be someone's living quarters. The other, a sagging cement block garage. Both buildings were surrounded by so much debris and used scrap that it was hard to tell if she'd stumbled onto an abandoned property or a private dwelling. If she had found Ben Bailey's property, it seemed deserted. There were no lights on or vehicles in the driveway. She didn't relish the thought of getting out of her car and wending her way through the bottles and stacks of bins and boxes to knock on the door. Emma winced at the thought of the rats that must be lurking behind or inside the piles.

Gritting her teeth, she slid out of the seat and picked her way through the rubble to the front door of the crumbling structure and knocked. No one answered. She knocked again.

"Hello. Anyone home?" She waited a few seconds and knocked again. "Hello?"

She stepped over to the garage and, on tiptoes, attempted to peer into one of the tiny windows near the top of the cinderblock wall facing the driveway, but she couldn't reach it. She banged on the door, but no one answered. Emma scoured the property and noticed several muddy tire prints in the driveway. Satisfied no one was there, Emma climbed back in her car and turned on the ignition.

Emma spun her car around in the pebble driveway to head home. Sensing she was being watched, she stopped and turned around, quickly scanning the house. Seeing nothing, she put the car in gear. Glancing back again as she was departing, she saw the blinds in the window of the house open ever so slightly and what appeared to be the muzzle of a rifle emerge through the slats. Emma floored the accelerator and raced down the gravel road as quickly as her car would allow.

18

It was nearly dusk when Emma reached the safety of the state road. Since the twins were spending the night with friends, she decided to drive straight to the sheriff's office in Jonesburg, pulling up to the building around six. She parked and scurried to the front door of the building, hoping Deputy Taylor was still there, stopping briefly to check her reflection in the front window. She smoothed her ponytail and pulled open the front door. A blast of cold air hit her in the face as she walked in.

She greeted the desk clerk and asked for the chief deputy.

Ren barreled through the door of the back office like a linebacker, then immediately checked his steps and slowed his pace as he drew closer. "Nice to see you again, Ms. Thornton."

Emma smiled and stepped to the side of the desk so she could speak to the deputy.

"I drove out to Ben Bailey's place this afternoon to ask him if he might know the owner of the black truck that's been following me this week," she said.

They walked over to the side of the office and sat down at one of the benches along the wall.

Ren pushed his hat back and narrowed his eyes as he looked at Emma. "Now, I wouldn't recommend that you go darting out to Ben Bailey's or anyone else's on these missions by yourself, especially since you've been followed lately. It's not safe. Plus, we're already investigating your case. And why Ben Bailey?"

"I've spoken to him before. I don't know Ben well, but he was helpful and I thought he might be again. So, I got directions and drove out to find his place. I'm not sure if I found it or not, but unless I'm mistaken, someone aimed a rifle at me through the window."

Emma smoothed her skirt over her knee. Ren followed the movement of her hands.

"Are you certain you saw a rifle?" Ren sat up in his chair and pulled a pen from his shirt pocket.

"Not really. It could have been a shotgun. I saw something move, and then there was something between the blinds. It was a muzzle of some sort, rifle or shotgun."

"Now, you know it wasn't wise to drive out there. I'd suggest you be more careful in the future," Ren said, a smile turning up one corner of his mouth. "We'll check it out. By the way, I tracked down your ex-husband."

"Really? What's he up to these days, besides peeking in my windows?"

"He's in Charleston, working for a real estate company, and last night he was at a company party. We verified it with his boss. Doesn't look like he's your Peeping Tom, and I'd bet he's not your stalker either. He's driving a new Chevy sedan."

"Interesting. Real estate. Who would have thought? Guess I'll tell the Savannah police and they can go pick him up for his back child support." She smiled. "Well, I have another idea."

"Shoot."

"I don't have the boys tonight, so I'd like to set up a plan to catch the stalker, using myself as a decoy."

"I don't like the sound of this already."

Emma pressed on. "I'll go home, go through my usual nighttime routine, and turn out the lights around eleven. But I won't go to sleep." Emma hesitated, waiting for Ren's reaction. Seeing none, she continued. "Assuming the stalker hasn't been frightened off by your patrol car which was parked out front last night, I'm guessing the truck will come by the apartment again tonight. If that happens, and if he approaches my window, I'll be ready with my camera. He could be easily apprehended at the same time by the deputy who's on duty out front. What do you think?" Emma swung her foot waiting for Ren's response.

"Sounds like you've been watching too many cop movies. I don't see why you'd need to take a photo of the guy if we apprehend him. I know you feel the need to do something, but it's not necessary. Let us do our job, Emma. I'll run your request for surveillance by the sheriff, but I'm sure he'll approve it."

Ren walked down the corridor into the sheriff's office, and threw the request for the unmarked car and deputy on the sheriff's desk.

"We have an interesting request and a developing situation with Ms. Thornton," he said.

"More of the same with the stalker?" The sheriff scanned the request.

"Yeah, what do you make of it?"

"Well, all this didn't start until she began investigating the Jennifer Patrick murder. Maybe she churned up a hornet's nest somewhere. Of course, there could be a stalker on the loose who's completely unrelated to the case. But that's unlikely. Still, it doesn't hurt to follow that black truck. See where it leads us."

"Maybe she's getting too close to what actually happened with her investigation. Someone could be trying to discourage her. Either way, we need to assign a detail to this, don't you agree?" Ren said.

The sheriff nodded. "I've agreed to send out a plain car unit," Sheriff Colson said. The sheriff signed the request and handed it back to Ren.

Emma turned out the light and prepared to wait in her living room. Before last night, she'd always felt safe there, never considering that she and the boys were only fifty feet from the street, that her apartment complex was on the edge of campus, and next to the main thoroughfare to town, or that moving into the space would ever endanger her family. The curtains were drawn tight, but she was tempted to peek outside. She glanced at her watch. It was already after eleven. She was asleep around that time most nights. She refilled her coffee cup a third time so she could stay awake. Her hands began to shake. She didn't know if it was from her nerves or the caffeine. The little band of sweat that appeared on her upper lip three seconds later told her it was nerves. But Ren was waiting outside. That steadied her a bit.

Around 11:30 she heard the rumble of a truck. She didn't dare look out of the window. The vehicle passed her apartment, paused for a few seconds, and then kept going. About five minutes later Emma sat up from the couch where she had been lying and put on her kimono. Ren knocked softly on her door.

"What was that all about?" Emma said as she opened the door.

"He obviously spotted the unmarked car."

"How can you spot an unmarked car?"

"Well, they sort of stand out."

"What do you mean they stand out?"

"They have that government-issue look about them, you know."

"No, I don't know, I just know I thought we had an opportunity, and now we don't. And I know I'm upset, and I've had ten cups of coffee, and it's midnight, and I have to go to class at eight in the morning, and I want to have my kids sleep here safely. My life is being threatened, but we didn't get anything at all tonight because of a stupid government car."

With that Emma burst into tears.

"It's just the caffeine." She sniffed, wishing she had a Kleenex. She dabbed her eyes with the sleeve of her robe.

"Well, I was able to get the make and model, as well as a pretty good shot of the truck with my camera and about half of the license plate, so all's not lost." Ren reached in his pocket and pulled out a handkerchief and handed it to Emma. "It's clean."

Emma held out her hand for the handkerchief and smiled at Ren. "Why only half of the license plate?" She wiped her eyes and nose and quickly slid the hankie in the pocket of her kimono. "I'll launder this for you."

Ren returned her smile. "Don't worry about that. I've got tons of handkerchiefs. Keep it. About half of the license plate was covered with mud, but we've still got a good part of it to go on."

"Well, I guess that's something." Emma shuffled toward the front door, pulled out the handkerchief again and mopped up the remainder of the tears from her face.

As she started to shut the door, Ren put his hand up.

"Emma, I can track all of the trucks of this make, model and year in the state. We'll find out who owns the truck. I should be able to track it down in a few days or so. The night wasn't wasted."

Emma nodded and closed the door. She didn't want to be at the mercy of anyone or anything for another second, let alone for another week.

19

August 29, 1990

Professor Anthony Beasley sat up with a start from a dead sleep, his heart pounding, his sheets drenched with sweat. He'd been waking up in a panic lately. Something in the deep recesses of his memory, something he'd forgotten about, would nag at him until he was flung into a state of near terror, awakening with a frozen image of the forgotten item emblazoned across his mind. He squinted at his bedside clock. It was 5:30 in the morning, too early to go to the office.

Jennifer Patrick's letters were on his mind when he woke that morning. He sighed. He really was getting old. Until now, he'd forgotten all about them.

He threw his legs over the side of the bed, shoved his feet into his broken down slippers, and shuffled down the stairs to the kitchen. He flipped on the coffee pot then hobbled his way back up the stairs for a shower. Might as well go to the office anyway and take a look. He'd never be able to get back to sleep now.

He peered at his image in the mirror, something he rarely did, rubbing his chin. He needed a shave. His face had grown a ghostly pale shadow overnight, the negative image of the dark beard he'd had in his youth. He squinted through his thick lenses. Nearly everything about him at this point had been traded for some sad substitute. His black hair was now white, his strong jaw had grown jowly, and his once lean physique was paunchier than he cared to admit. But the eyes that stared back at him had the same curiosity and drive he'd always known. He might forget things now and then, but give him a problem to solve and he'd make it his. Still.

An emeritus professor of law at the university, Professor Beasley's specialty was wills and estates. But the passion he'd held dearest since childhood was for history and antiquities. He especially cherished vintage letters, and believed the art of letter writing was the best chronicler of history. He considered the waning of written correspondence an indication that society was failing or at least taking a step backwards. He knew it was a sign people were becoming less civil.

Professor Beasley collected old love letters, letters between political rivals, letters from great writers, and cataloged and archived them all. At this point, with his wife deceased and his children grown, his collection gave him more pleasure than anything else in his life. His personal library included letters from several prominent people, including Theodore Roosevelt, James Joyce, Marie Curie, and a love letter from Thomas Edison to his second wife Mina Miller. His trust was directed to donate his collection to the university's library at his death.

Professor Beasley met Jennifer Patrick at First Methodist Church, when she was a very young girl. They'd sung in the choir together at Sunday morning early service until she reached an age where she was no longer interested in waking up early and singing hymns. He'd always liked her. She had a sweetness that set her apart from most kids. When she was younger, she'd visited his office at the university to see his letter collection. She'd donned a pair of white cotton gloves so she wouldn't damage the fragile pages, and had giggled when she read Edison's love letter. After that, she started writing letters to her mother throughout her mother's illness—little letters she'd tuck in her mother's blankets or dressing gowns for her to read during chemo. He'd never forget her mother's gratitude to him for sparking her daughter's interest in those tiny expressions.

About a week before Jennifer was killed she had contacted him, concerned about some letters she'd found in a hidden compartment in an old family dresser at home. She brought them by his office and told him she wouldn't speak of them to her father until Professor Beasley could authenticate the content and explain the meaning. She didn't want to alarm her dad. Then she was murdered. The professor was so upset about her death, he'd completely forgotten the letters.

He finished up his morning routine and then shuffled down the stairs to grab his coffee. He picked up his mug, lifting it a little higher than usual, a silent salute to Jennifer. He'd read her letters today.

Professor Beasley's office had been in the same wing, in the same building and located in the same hall for the past thirty years. The cleaning crew polished the floors, but had been told to never touch his desk or any of the other furniture in the space. Thirty years of papers, books, leaflets, letters, archival boxes, and odd trinkets were stacked along the floor, desk, book shelves, filing cabinets and when they fit, the window frames. He had no idea where he put Jennifer's bundle of letters, but after scrounging through his office for forty-five minutes, he was relieved to finally locate them in a file in a cabinet in his closet under the letter J.

The rubber bands holding the letters together were so dry they broke as he attempted to remove them, and he feared the brittle paper inside the envelopes would crack as he pulled the letters out. He opened a yellowed, folded page, crisp with age, dated 1945, addressed to Ethel Patrick. He read it, then read Ethel's letters to Will Gannon. He closed the letters, placed them back into their envelopes, and carefully transferred them into an archival envelope.

Professor Beasley knew that since Jennifer was dead, and particularly since she'd been murdered, the letters belonged with the sheriff. He grabbed his keys and threw the envelope onto the front seat of his car.

But faculty meetings and doctor appointments would delay his trip until the next day.

20

August 29, 1990

Emma pulled up to Silas's office building, exhausted from her trip to Augusta to drop off the boys. She'd awakened that day realizing she needed to take Billy and Bobby to her parents earlier than they'd planned.

"I've noticed a truck following me for the past few days, and then I caught someone looking in our window the other night. I thought it was better if the kids didn't stay in the apartment with me until the sheriff's department gets a better handle on what's going on. That's all there is to it." Emma paced the floor as she spoke to her mother on the phone.

"A truck's been following you? That could be anything. And whatever you saw in your window could be a reflection, especially if it was late at night."

"I'm certain I saw a hand and a head in my window."

"Oh, Emma. You could be mistaken about all of this. I don't understand why you want the kids to miss school for a week."

"Just in case there's more to it, Mom. You wanted them for the Labor Day holiday anyway and this is just a few days more." Emma didn't like the sound of her own voice.

"Of course we'll help out, but I think you need to quit law school and that awful job with that lawyer and come back to Savannah and teach school again. You'd be happier and the kids would be safer."

Emma's history with her parents, her mother especially, was a long-standing, sad, sometimes comical, but always exhausting conundrum. They had battled forever, clashing through their lives with a timeworn muscle memory. She'd moved out of the family home at age eighteen and since then it had been difficult for Emma to ask for help. But sometimes she had no choice.

Emma dropped off the kids and made it back to Jonesburg right before sunset, hoping to catch Silas before he was done for the day. It was time to tell him about the stalking and Peeping Tom incidents. She parked her car and, drained from a day of travel and fending off her mom's strafing criticisms, dragged herself up the stairs to her office.

It was nearly dusk, that time of day when the sun's rays cut through the atmosphere at just the right angle to cast the perfect blue light across the sky, so that all color deepened, and calmed the senses. It seemed the perfect end to a trying day. All of the attorneys except Silas were gone. Silas was headed up to the roof with barbecue tools in hand, a favorite end-of-the-day ritual when his schedule would allow it. He invited Emma up for a discussion of the day's events.

"We'd planned on reviewing the motion to suppress in the Patrick case this afternoon," Emma said.

"Oh, that's right. Thanks for keeping me on track," Silas said as he climbed the stairs, clanking trays of meats and barbecue sauce bottles against the metal rails. "I read your motion and brief and I think you need to beef it up a little."

Emma smiled. "How so?"

"You need to take the problems Mrs. Grayson presents head on. You've done a good job with the coach's testimony and affidavit, the ABR test results, and his reading comp levels. But you have to confront Mrs. Grayson. I know she wasn't very helpful, but don't dance around it. Use the parts of Mrs. Grayson's testimony that make her seem questionable. She didn't remember whether she gave oral tests. They never read in class, that sort of thing. How can she testify what Adam's abilities were if she has no recall or knowledge of these things? If she's a bully or prejudiced against Adam, don't be afraid to expose that."

"Okay, I'll get on it."

Emma stood up and walked over to the edge of the roof and looked out over the square just as Ren was walking out of the sheriff's office. Emma smiled as she watched him climb into his car.

"Why, Emma, I do believe you have a crush on someone. I'll keep it a secret, I promise."

"Silas, I assure you, I have no time for crushes. And it would be stupid to have one on a deputy who's investigating a case I'm now defending. That's a conflict of interest if I've ever seen one." Emma wiped her hands over her face in an attempt to disguise the warm flush that crept over her cheeks in response to Silas's comment. "With law school, work, and the kids I barely have time for sleep. Who has time for crushes?"

Embarrassed by her reaction to Ren, and shaken by the realization that Silas might be correct, Emma didn't stay for dinner and didn't think of the black truck, or any of the other things she needed to tell Silas until later that evening.

Driving home from the office, Emma couldn't help but make comparisons. Silas had such a great life. Everything was beautifully contained in the refurbished Firehouse No. 10. Built in 1917, the original design was an elegant dual-purpose structure with a residence for the fire chief on the third floor and headquarters for the fire department on the lower half. It had been transformed into a perfect law office and home. Art, music, good food and drink flowed in the residence above, and hard work cranked out one floor below.

Emma wasn't sure what she was doing wrong in her life. She worked hard but didn't feel as if she was doing anything well. There was never enough time for anything, not for her boys, or school, or work. Everything suffered. And forget about a personal life. She pulled into her assigned space in front of her apartment, parked, and adjusted her rear view mirror to examine her lipstick. She shook her head, then pushed the mirror back in place. Some habits die hard. She paused for a moment, wondering what the twins were doing, hoping they would have an opportunity to do some camping with her dad like she had when she was young. He had taught her so much about self-sufficiency and about life on those trips.

She pulled her backpack out of the back seat, and threw it over her shoulder. She grabbed her purse, locked the door, and started across the street, head down, lost again in thought.

Emma didn't see the black truck approaching. She didn't hear anything unusual at first, but raised her head when she noticed the sound of a revved engine. She screamed when she finally realized the pickup truck was hurtling toward her and that it wasn't going to stop. Leaping back, she avoided the truck's bumper by less than a foot, and fell, injuring her ankle and knee, and breaking the heel of her shoe.

She struggled to her feet, dazed by the sudden and violent attack.

The truck made a U-turn, gunned its engine, and screeched toward Emma to make another run at her. But, at the same time, a Honda Civic turned the opposite corner, headed toward Emma. Deterred by the sudden appearance of the second car, the driver of the black truck turned around and, tires squealing, sped away.

As the truck raced off Emma took inventory. She'd twisted her ankle, and banged up her knee, but she'd survived.

The driver of the second car pulled over, and ran up to Emma.

"Are you okay? Shouldn't I call an ambulance or the police?"

"I live in the apartment across the street. I'll call the sheriff's office once I get inside. Did you happen to get the license number on that truck?"

"No, I'm sorry. He left too soon, but that was a Chevy C/K. My cousin has one just like it."

Emma got the witness's information, limped to her apartment and called

Ren.

"Oh my God, Emma. I'll be right there. I've got some other information I've wanted to share with you as well. "

Emma kicked off her shoes, and splashed cold water on her face. She hobbled into the kitchen, got some ice from the freezer, made a cold pack for her ankle, and sat down on her couch to wait for Ren, thankful he'd picked up the phone.

True to his word, fifteen minutes later, Ren was standing in her apartment breezeway, holding a black notebook under his arm and clutching a bag of Krispy Kreme Donuts and two black coffees. His face was flushed, barely hiding his concern. Even though she'd been through one of the more frightening days of her life, Emma could hardly contain a smile at the sight of him.

"Donuts and coffee at eight in the evening, Deputy?" Emma said, grinning in spite of herself.

"We've got a lot to discuss tonight," Ren said, opening the door a little wider with his shoulder and making his way into the apartment. He put the donuts and coffee down on the kitchen table.

"Hungry?"

"Well, I wasn't, but I have to say, those donuts look pretty good to me," Emma said as she sat down. "But I think I'd prefer alcohol to coffee."

"No alcohol for you tonight. In fact, we need to call an ambulance and get you checked out. We can do that right away, or we can wait a few minutes, depending on how you're feeling."

"I think I'm okay for a while. My ankle hurts though."

"Okay. Let me get down the information about what happened first then I'll call the paramedics."

"I'm not sure student insurance will pay for that."

"If you're the victim of a crime, you can recover expenses for your medical bills and that sort of thing through a crime victim compensation fund. We need a record of your injuries, too. So, we'll need to get you to the hospital."

"Okay...so what's in the black notebook?"

"Well," Ren said as he pulled back a chair and sat down next to her, "I've

119

been doing some work on the types of trucks that our friend's been driving."

"You mean our friend in the black truck, the Chevy C/K?"

"Oh, so you've been doing some work too?"

"Not really. Someone told me the make of the truck today."

"Who was that?"

"The guy who saw the truck when it tried to run me down a few minutes ago." Emma handed Ren the information. "He said he'd be happy to speak to you about what he saw."

"Okay, so tell me what happened."

Fifteen minutes and two donuts later, Ren had the information he needed. He called the paramedics as well, and while they waited for the ambulance, explained what he'd been doing for the past several days.

"I felt so bad when I only got a partial license plate number the other night, Emma. I felt like I really let you down."

"I guess I thought you'd go after him." Emma propped her foot up on an ottoman by the couch.

"At that point, the driver of that black truck hadn't done anything suspicious that I'd witnessed. So I had no reason to stop him. But I also told you I had enough information to track down the truck, and I did."

"That's a relief."

"The DMV has records of seven 1989 Chevy C/K's that were sold in Greenwood and adjoining counties in 1989. Three were sold in 1990. Of all of those vehicles, three of were black. Two of those black Chevys were sold to Robert Gannon. One was sold to a man who took it out of state. One of the black Chevys sold to Robert is used by his foreman on a daily basis and is usually parked in front of the stables. We can also account for Robert's foreman today and every day since August fifteenth. But we can't account for the other black C/K Robert purchased."

"What do you mean when you say you can't account for that black truck? Do you mean it's missing?"

"Right. We can see that it was purchased, but it doesn't seem to be on the Gannon property. Although we haven't obtained a warrant for an actual search. I don't know what it all means right now. But I did want to mention that Robert also bought another Chevy C/K. It's identical to the black one in every way, except for its color. I guess you know who it belongs to, right?"

"I hadn't thought about it before, but I'll guess the truck is Adam's?"

"Yep. Same make, model and year. Just blue instead of black."

"Have you been able to match up the partial license plate numbers we have to any of the black Chevy C/Ks you found in the state?"

"Unfortunately, no."

"Why not?"

Ren shrugged. "My guess is that the license plate numbers we have from the black truck have been changed or modified in some manner."

"Why would anyone do that? Was the truck stolen?"

"Maybe, or perhaps someone wanted to disguise the numbers to hide the identity of the actual owner. But whatever the reason, the numbers we have don't show up with any of the Chevy C/Ks in the state."

"Maybe the owner's using two plates. One for criminal activity, and one for non-criminal," Emma said.

Ren nodded. "That's a possibility too."

"Adam got his truck out of the impound more than a week ago, right?"

"That's right. We released it back to him after we conducted all of our tests. I'm pretty sure he's been driving it for at least a week, week and a half, by now."

At that moment the paramedics rang the doorbell and within fifteen minutes had checked out Emma's bruises and lacerations. They treated her and recommended she come to the hospital with them to make certain her ankle wasn't broken. Ren followed.

Three hours later, Ren drove Emma back to her apartment. Diagnosed with a sprained ankle, she was exhausted, but pleased to be home. She was glad Ren was there. Not certain what to do when he helped her to the door, she invited him in. He was happy to accept. But he was a gentleman. He knew she was tired.

She invited him to sit down, and asked him if he wanted something to drink.

"No, Emma. I should go home, and you need to get some sleep."

"I agree. I've had it."

"You know you scared the heck out of me today. We need to catch this person, and I aim to. I want you to know that. I'm on him."

He reached out and touched her shoulder.

"I hope you'll be okay tonight. You've been through a lot today. Do you need anything before I leave? Is there anything at all I can do for you?"

Emma closed her eyes for a moment. She was tempted to tell him to stay. She hated to think about sleeping in her apartment by herself after what she'd been through earlier in the day.

"Thanks, Ren, but I'll be fine tonight. But since Robert Gannon could be the owner of the black truck, I'm worried about the connection between the hit-and-run and the Patrick case. I need to talk to Silas about this before I say anything else to you."

Ren nodded. "I realize that." He searched her face.

Emma looked into Ren's soft, brown eyes. His face was strong, but it was also kind. Everything about him was powerful, yet compassionate. She felt herself collapsing into him in spite of herself. The thought of that felt more natural and comforting than she cared to admit.

"I appreciate everything you've done for me." Surprising even herself, Emma reached out and wrapped her arms around Ren's neck and hugged him longer than she considered entirely professional.

Ren walked back to his car, settled down in the seat, and prepared to stay the night, keeping a sleepy eye on Emma's apartment until morning.

21

August 30, 1990

Emma sat on the edge of the sofa and moved her ankle in small circles. The ice pack Ren insisted on making before he left last night had helped. The swelling had subsided. If she was careful and wore flats, she thought she'd be okay walking short distances. She smiled, recalling the smell of Ren's aftershave when she'd hugged his neck. She didn't know many young men who used Aqua Velva.

She took several deep breaths. She wasn't looking forward to facing Silas. He wasn't going to be happy about being kept in the dark about the stalkings and Peeping Tom incident. That was an understatement. Now that Robert Gannon was implicated, he'd be furious.

Emma pulled into the office parking lot, filled with dread at the site of Silas's car. She'd do almost anything to avoid seeing him, but knew she'd have to face him eventually. She proceeded up the steps and into the building, stopping at the front desk. A note from the receptionist's told her Silas wanted to speak to her. She trudged up the stairs to her office.

The phone rang as soon as she walked in. "What's this I hear about a black truck, Emma?"

"I was going to speak to you about that today, Silas. I'll be right there." Emma hung up the phone, put her purse on her desk, and stepped down the hall to Silas's office.

He glared as she entered the room. "Instead, I had to hear about it from the sheriff at Lucky's this morning." Silas swigged his diet soda. He was finishing the last of his hamburger and fries. The odor of Lucky's grill wafted through the office. "But first things first, are you okay?"

"I'm a little banged up, but I can get around." Emma sat down in the chair across from Silas.

"Okay, good. But, why did I have to hear about all of this from the sheriff instead of from you? You should have told me about the incidents when they happened."

"I meant to mention it to you earlier, but somehow never got around to it. And I had to report what happened to the sheriff. Crimes were committed."

"I realize that. But you could have jeopardized the case by not calling me. Don't you see that?" Silas jabbed a french fry in a puddle of ketchup.

Emma felt her cheeks burn. "I don't see how I've jeopardized the case. It looks like Robert Gannon might own the truck that's been involved in some of the incidents. That's a problem for him, not Adam."

"Didn't you think it was possible that the stalking and other incidents were related to the Patrick girl's murder? Adam could have been the one driving that truck. He could be the stalker, or the hit and run driver. We'll need to follow up with him. Make certain he has an alibi for each of those incidents." Silas sighed and stared out of his window as he wiped his hands with a napkin.

"I don't think he'd do that. He isn't a psycho."

"How do you know? And why do you think it's okay to take all of this in your own hands? I'm the lawyer on the case, not you."

"I understand, Silas."

"Do you understand, Emma? We should be a team, but you don't seem to be much of a team player. You can't handle everything by yourself.

You're working on building trust with Adam, and hoping that will open up communication between the two of you. Seems to me you need to work on those same skills yourself. If you'd trusted me, you'd have called me when things started happening. But you didn't, and now we have a situation we can't control. Most of all, Emma, I don't appreciate not knowing what's going on in my own case. You've got to do better."

Emma nodded. "I'll keep you up to date from here on out."

Emma descended the stairs, holding the rail to avoid putting weight on her ankle. Silas was right. She probably wasn't much of a team player. During their marriage, her husband accused her of the same thing, saying she refused to listen to him, and that she wanted to control the checkbook. He was right, too. But he'd had no judgment, spent money they didn't have, and had a foul temper on top of that. Someone had to be the adult. After paying off the twenty thousand dollars in credit card charges he'd racked up, she divorced him, took the LSAT, rented her house, and prepared to move to Jonesburg for law school before her scores had even come in. Her choices may have seemed risky to others, but they were designed to put her family in a better place. But this was different. She never thought things could get so out of hand by keeping things to herself.

She stopped in the middle of the staircase. Was that Adam's problem? Was he keeping something about the murder to himself because he didn't know who to trust?

Still lost in thought, Emma walked out of the office, through the square, and over to Lucky's for a coffee. Caffeine always cleared her head.

Emma sat down outside, directly under the newly installed ceiling fan to enjoy the breezes wafting overhead. The café immediately transported her from the late summer heat of the Civil War era square to the sidewalks of Florence. All she needed was a gelato to complete the effect. She ordered a coffee instead and closed her eyes for a second, listening to the comforting sounds of clanking spoons on coffee cups, waiters pouring water, and birds chirping in the distance. She breathed deeply, catching the aroma of coffee and the delicate smell of asters planted in the flower boxes lining the perimeter of the café.

"Mind if I join you?" Ren Taylor dragged a chair up to her table.

"I think you just did." Emma smiled in spite of herself.

"I know you don't think we should talk, but I wanted to tell you something," Ren said, taking off his hat.

"Not really a good idea, but, since you're here," Emma looked up and smiled and waved her hand toward the seat next to her.

"I think I'm going to have a hard time staying away from you, Ms. Thornton." Ren's face flushed. He glanced down at the patio floor, pretending to watch a sparrow strutting off with a tiny crumb. "But, I'll make it quick. The maid out at the Gannons, Lola Mae? Her family called and said they haven't seen her in a few days. She went to visit her mother and she should have returned by now, but she hasn't made it back. Sort of strange—all of this stuff going on with the Gannon's, don't you think?"

"It's strange that she hasn't been home in several days. It doesn't seem right, does it? Have you started a search?" Emma's face was flushed.

Ren nodded. "I agree. Something doesn't seem right. And I thought you'd want to know, especially with everything else that's been going on. But I'll run on now. By the way, I really enjoy spending time with you." He smiled, crammed his hat back on his head, briefly touched the brim, and walked down the square toward his office.

Emma watched him go, stunned by the news. Lola Mae, the woman who had told her about Jennifer at Mayfair? Her disappearance was alarming, in light of everything else that was happening.

Emma pulled a notepad and pen out of her purse, and outlined her thoughts as she sipped her coffee. So far, she'd failed in her efforts to build a relationship with Adam. And she'd failed at gaining his trust. The wall he'd built around himself seemed impenetrable.

Adam's parents were distant and removed, probably the source of his insecurity. Robert rarely made eye contact with Adam. Emma couldn't ever recall seeing Adam and his dad speak to each other. And then there was Darcy. Darcy reminded Emma of one of the matryoshka nesting dolls she had when she was a girl—the blonde one, with tiny features, sparkling blue eyes and a perfectly sculptured nose. But inside the doll was another doll, and then another. She wasn't sure how many Darcys there were. The sweet, caring, church-going Darcy was on the outside, the person most would see, but who was on the inside? Emma suspected a childhood with an alcoholic father had left its mark. Darcy didn't want Adam to be hurt or ridiculed by others since she had suffered so much when she was young. But Adam's deafness had become a barrier. She was more interested in appearances. Adam and his feelings were never much of a consideration.

Joe was the great stability in Adam's life, the person he trusted, the one who had provided love and warmth. He'd always been there for Adam, teaching him, guiding him. If Emma could work through Joe, she might be able to break through to Adam. Perhaps she could even get him to open up about the night of the murder.

Emma paid her bill and walked through the square back to her office. As she climbed the stairs she overheard Silas on the phone.

"No, Robert, I can't represent you. Emma filed those complaints and I could have a conflict if you end up being charged. I'm sure that won't happen, though. We have no issue representing Adam, but had better leave it at that.

"...Yes, Robert, there's no problem with us representing Adam if he still wants us to...yes, Adam and Emma do seem to have a good relationship...and Emma still wants to be on the case."

Emma proceeded up the stairs to her office.

Emma glanced at her watch. It was nearing the end of the day. She'd head home after she wrapped up a few lose ends on a brief. Standing up from her desk to grab a document from the printer, she glanced out of her window in time to see Robert Gannon and his new attorney, Lamar Johnson, stepping into the sheriff's office. She knew the sheriff had requested that Robert come in for questioning about the hit-and-run incident. As Robert entered the building, she noticed for the first time that he seemed to favor his right leg.

Emma jumped up from her desk and ran down to Silas's office.

"You ever notice that Robert Gannon limps?"

"Yeah, left over injuries from his football days, probably. I even remember a game back in '68 between USG and Memphis State when Robert was tackled by a huge half back. Guy came at him sideways. Tore his ACL, I believe."

"I'd never noticed before."

"I think it's more noticeable at certain times, maybe bad weather, but it's always there." Silas pushed away the case he'd been reading and stretched his back. "Time to stop for the day. Why don't you go home too? You've been through a lot lately."

"I think I might go over to the sheriff's office and check out a couple of things first. I'll let you know what I find."

Still curious about a couple of shoe imprints, Emma had made arrangements with the DA earlier in the day for another viewing. She stepped into the square, and headed across the street. It was her favorite time of day, but she ignored the glow from the setting sun on the dome of the courthouse and the beauty of the waning light. Instead, she grabbed the Polaroid from her car and walked directly across the street to the sheriff's office, hoping to catch the clerk before she went home for the day.

"I've arranged for another viewing of the Patrick evidence. Could I get back there before the property manager leaves for the day?"

The clerk paged a deputy to escort her to the evidence room. Emma nodded her thanks as she walked through the door and followed the deputy.

The property clerk pulled the casts out of the evidence locker and placed them on one of the tables in the room. There were two casts of left shoe prints that were worn differently from other left shoe molds. Both made a greater indentation on the left side of the cast. More weight was put on the left foot, as if the person favored his right leg. The deeper indentation on one side could easily demonstrate an analytic gait, a limp. It would have to be verified by an expert, but it seemed clear to her. Robert Gannon limped, and if Emma remembered correctly, he favored the right leg. Could he have been at the scene of the murder?

Professor Anthony Beasley arrived at the Greendale County Sheriff's Department late that afternoon clutching the letters given to him by Jennifer Patrick. Accustomed to identifying documents for legal and archival purposes, he'd written his name and telephone number on the outside archival envelope, had indicated that the package was intended for Sheriff Colson, and where to call if there were questions. He'd also referenced the Patrick case in bold letters across the top of the envelope.

Professor Beasley entered the sheriff's office, paused for a second as his eyes adjusted from the bright sunlight outside, then located the front clerk.

"I have a few letters Sheriff Colson should be interested in." Professor Beasley handed the envelope to the clerk. "There's a possibility the documents have something to do with the Patrick case."

"Okay. The sheriff's in a meeting right now, but if you leave the letters with me, I'll make sure he gets them."

"You won't forget?"

"Nah," the clerk said. "Here, sign your name on this sheet. It's what we use to keep up with the people and things that come in here on a daily basis. So list the letters that you brought with you too."

The professor signed his name, listing "letters" to the side of the date.

Professor Beasley turned to leave as Robert Gannon and his attorney strode down the hall past the clerk, and toward the exit. Emma trailed the two men, her eyes glued on Robert's unsteady gait. The professor watched as the men climbed into their cars.

Emma marched up to the clerk while the professor gathered his umbrella and other belongings.

"Is the chief deputy available?" Emma clasped her hands behind her back as she waited for a response.

"Yes, ma'am. I'll get him for you."

The professor left the building and climbed into his car for the drive home, assured that the sheriff or someone from his office would call him soon about Jennifer's letters.

Ren came out to speak to Emma. The clerk watched as Ren's eyes widened and his face became red and blotchy. Emma began waving her arms and pointing toward Robert Gannon's exiting car. It was obvious they were both upset, but Emma seemed furious.

"Seems to me you have enough to hold Robert Gannon. He's the owner of the truck, right? Can he tell you where it is now? Did he report it as stolen?"

"I can't, Emma. We went over everything in detail. He's got alibis for every night something happened to you. He seems pretty solid."

Emma stormed out of the door, allowing it to slam behind her.

The letters, which were placed on the second shelf of the front desk, were forgotten in all of the chaos.

22

August 31, 1990

The telltale crack of light under Silas's door told Emma a couple of things: he was in and he was busy. She knocked anyway and waited for an invitation to enter.

Silas's tall frame was hunched over his text under one small desk lamp. He hated overhead lights, and this side of the building didn't get much of the afternoon sun.

"Got a minute or two to speak to me about the Patrick case?"

"I don't have much time today, but, sure. What's up?" Silas put down his file and peered at Emma.

"I checked out the plaster footprint casts again."

Silas nodded.

"There were two separate sets of left shoes prints at the scene of the murder."

"The killer had to have taken more than one step under the window, Emma."

"Two of the left shoe prints were worn differently and left a deeper impression in the mud, which seemed to indicate that the person limped or had an uneven gait and favored his right leg. Robert Gannon favors his right side when he walks."

"So what are you implying?"

"That Robert Gannon may have also been at the murder scene."

"I don't think you can draw a conclusion like that." Silas stacked his files on top of his desk and began flipping through the mail in his inbox. "Robert Gannon can't be a suspect in this murder solely because he has an analytic gait. Is everyone else who limps in this county a suspect? I can see why you are concerned, but is there anything else that makes him suspicious?"

"I think so. I've uncovered some information that shows Robert Gannon's dad essentially stole the Patrick property from Lyle's mom through fraud and deception. There's a chance we could prove it, and if we could we might be able to show a motive for a Gannon family member to commit murder."

"Well, that's interesting, but you'd need additional evidence to tie the sale to Jennifer's murder. First we'd have to prove the elements of false pretenses, and that wouldn't be easy. Then, we'd have to prove that the invalid sale, excluding all other theories, was the motive for the murder of Jennifer Patrick. Can you do that?"

Emma shrugged. "Right now, I don't have evidence to tie the sale to the murder."

"Exactly. Do you have anything besides rumor to prove the invalid sale? We need to raise a reasonable doubt to avoid a conviction, but this fraudulent sale idea doesn't seem to do that, does it?"

"There's an extensive family history between the Gannons and the Patricks I think you need to know about."

"I know about the land issues. Most folks around here do. They go back all the way to World War II. And how do you know about all of this? I don't mean to doubt you, Emma, but we have to be cautious about how we question issues as sensitive as these."

"Robert Gannon's nephew, Ben Bailey, and Joe, one of their former employees, told me how Will Gannon manipulated Lyle's mom."

"We'd need more than that to prove false pretenses. Plus none of that gets us anywhere. None of that proves anyone else had the motive to kill

Jennifer."

"But if we don't explore those issues, we may be doing Adam a great disservice."

"It's important to base our defenses on the evidence we have, not some half-baked story."

Silas walked over to the window by his credenza and looked out over the square. "Just remember they found direct proof of Adam's guilt. We either have to raise a reasonable doubt about Adam's culpability, or show that he shouldn't be held responsible for the crime. You've shown, in the motion to dismiss you're working on, that Adam isn't competent to stand trial because of his inability to understand language and legal proceedings. But have you found any evidence to raise a reasonable doubt about his guilt? He hasn't even said whether he has an alibi. A fraudulent sale back in the 1940's is of no consequence in this case."

"I see what you're saying. But it is strange there's so much history between the two families. I still think it has something to do with the case."

"Don't be distracted by shiny ideas that go nowhere. But if you find something that might raise a reasonable doubt about Adam's guilt, or something that might tie that sale to Jennifer's murder, don't hesitate to explore it. And don't forget to talk to me about it."

23

Emma, home early from work, missed the boys. They'd only been away for a few days, but it seemed like months. The plan had always been for the twins to come home by Labor Day. But with all that had happened since they left, she wasn't certain it was safe. Still, things were quiet. The black truck hadn't been seen for days.

She picked up the phone and dialed Ren's number.

"Think it's safe for the kids to come back by next Monday, Labor Day?"

"I'm not sure, and it's got nothing to do with your stalker."

"I guess that means you still haven't arrested Robert Gannon?" Emma sat down on the couch and grabbed her note pad and pen.

"This also has nothing to do with Robert Gannon. Or at least I don't believe it does. Remember when I told you that the Gannon's housekeeper, Lola Mae, was missing?"

"Yeah, I think you said that she'd gone to her mother's but had never returned?"

"She'd only been gone for a day when her family reported her missing, but they were so worried about her we started our search. And I understand. It wasn't like her to not check in." He sighed. "We just found her. Three days later. "

"Is she okay?"

"No, she's not. She's dead, Emma. We don't have the coroner's report back yet, so the cause of death isn't confirmed."

"Oh my God. Where'd you find her?" Emma leaned forward, elbows on knees, and rested her head on the palm of one hand, trying to take in what Ren had said.

"Can't really say yet. But looks like she's been dead about three days by the look of things. We'll know more when we get the report back."

"So, this was a murder?" Emma scribbled in her notebook as Ren spoke.

"It's not official, so don't quote me, but it looks that way."

"Do you think this is related to the Jennifer Patrick murder?"

"I don't know, but this makes two murders in Greendale County in two weeks. The same family is also involved in both cases."

"By the same family you mean the Gannons?"

"Yes. Not in the same way, but they're connected to each case." Ren cleared his throat.

"That doesn't mean the Gannons are involved in her death in any way."

"That's true." He paused. "Getting back to your original question, do you want your kids to come home now? Do you really think it's safe? There's either a serial killer on the loose or you're involved in a case where the dead keep piling up."

"I don't know what's safe anymore. I have to admit, the murders are close in time, and both of the murdered women had ties to at least one Gannon, but that could be coincidental." Emma frowned. "Getting back to the safety question—I realize it's unrealistic to put a deputy on the boys when they're leaving for school and then when they're coming home every day, but I'd sure feel better about them coming back if you could."

"We don't have that sort of manpower, Emma. We have a deputy assigned to you at night, and that's all we can spare. I'd love to have around-the-clock deputies for everyone in your family, but I can't do that."

"I understand." She paused quickly counting on her fingers. "Today's Friday. The twins will be home in a couple of days. I'd appreciate anything you could do."

"There haven't been any incidents in a few days now. I hope that means that things have quieted down. We may even have to pull the night surveillance. It's expensive and might not be justified at this point. Of course, protection for your kids isn't either." He paused. "But I want you to be able to relax about Billy and Bobby, and I'll do the best I can."

Emma smiled. "They need to get back to school before they miss too much. It would be great if you could at least continue the surveillance at night."

"I'll see what I can do. Make sure you let us know when they're back in town."

"Of course." Emma hesitated, clearing her throat. "Keeping my twins safe is the most important thing. I can't jeopardize their safety."

"I understand, but you need to be careful, too. I miss seeing you, by the way. And I've thought about you a time or two." Ren was glad Emma couldn't see the blush that was creeping up his face.

"Let's hope I'll never have to call you with another Peeping Tom report, or anything else. But, just so you know," Emma paused, "I've thought about you, too. With everything else that's going on, that's pretty remarkable." She put down her pen and smiled as she rested her chin on the phone. She enjoyed little snippets of conversation with Ren and wished they had time for more.

"We've got the whole weekend in front of us. I know we agreed not to see each other during the investigation, but we do have a few things to discuss, and I'd like to work on them in person. Could I take you to dinner? Maybe we could go up to Lake Oconee and eat at the Inn there. It's about forty-five minutes away. Chances are we won't see anyone we know."

"Let me think about it, Ren. I'll give you a call later on today."

Emma hung up the phone, then rummaged around in her closet and found her running gear. Her ankle was much better. A gentle jog would clear her head.

Emma enjoyed the rhythmic pounding of her feet on the pavement as she ran, but she'd never gotten used to the hills of Jonesburg. She loved the rich air and coastal plains of Savannah and its surrounding marshes and beaches.

Her lungs pulled and her breath caught sharply even though she hadn't run a full mile yet, but as she passed 'What's Perkin,' her first marker, she felt her body kick into her second wind.

While she ticked off the streets in rapid succession, her body settled into a comfortable rhythm, but her mind targeted festering questions.

If Jennifer's and Lola Mae's murders were connected, something, some key evidence, was missing. What, besides the Gannons, connected the two murders? Lola Mae defied Darcy by telling Emma she'd seen Jennifer at Mayfair. That was risky for any employee. Could someone have overheard her? No one was near the front door when she and Lola Mae had spoken. They'd left Darcy in the garden. Emma was certain of that.

She thought for a moment about Ren's invitation. Dinner? This weekend? It was tempting. Her children were coming back soon. And she had made plans to see Adam and Joe over the weekend. She never took time for herself. A nice dinner seemed like a relaxing thing to do before everything became hectic again.

She rounded the corner, starting mile number three and the trek back toward her apartment. She didn't notice a black truck which had pulled off on a side street, parallel to the road where she was running.

As she ran past, its driver started the engine and pulled into the street in the same direction as Emma, matching her pace, tracking her every move.

24

September 1, 1990

Ren hung up the phone. It was the ME's office verifying the time and cause of Lola Mae's death. He rubbed his neck. He knew Emma would ask questions about Lola Mae if they went out to dinner tomorrow night, and if not then, she'd be asking soon. He wasn't sure what he was going to tell her. He knew he shouldn't say anything, but recent history would prove that he might do what he shouldn't when he was with Emma.

Emma's interest in the cause of Lola Mae's death was as keen as his. He could hear her scribbling notes furiously when they spoke on the phone yesterday. He had to decide what to tell her and stick to it, or she would manage to get him to say more than he wanted to.

Ren had begun checking with Lola Mae's family and friends shortly after they'd found her, and so far, nothing about her relationships appeared out of the ordinary. She'd been married to Roosevelt for thirty-two years. They'd had the usual marital ups and downs. Roosevelt's chronic unemployment put a strain on things which resulted in several separations, but they'd been together the last six years. They had five children, all grown. Three of her children lived in the Greendale County area.

Lola Mae was a churchgoer; Roosevelt was not. Lola Mae sang in the choir, and practiced with that group every Thursday night. She was close to her mother, and visited her every week after choir practice. In good weather she would walk the half mile between the church and her mother's house, leaving her car in the church parking lot. Roosevelt usually played poker on those nights with some old friends.

All in all, Lola Mae and her husband seemed to be very different people, but, other than the fact that he was her husband, there was nothing about their situation which cast any obvious suspicion on Roosevelt. Ren couldn't find anyone who didn't like Lola Mae or who didn't have a kind word to say about her or the great coconut pie she made for the church bake-off every year. Her death had left Roosevelt grief stricken. Nearly fainting at the sight of her battered body when he was asked to identify her, it was hard to imagine he had anything to do with his wife's murder. But stranger things had happened, and Ren would include him as a suspect. Husbands always were. Ren was in the process of checking with all of Roosevelt's poker buddies to see if his story checked out the night of Lola Mae's murder.

They found her in a shallow grave right off of Highway 20, more than thirty miles from the church where she was practicing the night she was killed. That's the kind of thing Emma would want to know, Ren thought. And she'd want to know all the details. Not that she was entitled to them. But that wouldn't stop Emma, who was persistent, maybe even to a fault.

It didn't take much to kill Lola Mae. She was tiny, probably weighing no more than one hundred and ten pounds. She was older, fifty-four. Her bones were fragile. Her skull had been fractured, and her neck was broken, for good measure. But it was the blow to her head that killed her. No weapon had been found, yet. There was evidence of struggle—some bruising about the neck from a choking attempt, and skin under her fingernails, so they would be able to get a DNA sample of the murderer. They found a button from Lola Mae's overcoat on the road between the church and her mother's house which might confirm resistance or a fight. If she screamed, no one in the area had heard it.

Ren stared at the kitchen table, absentmindedly noticing a few crumbs from last night's dinner that had escaped his cleaning routine. As he wiped up the last cornmeal kernel from his catfish and hushpuppy dinner, he vowed not to tell Emma the details of the crime, especially not about the DNA. Then the phone rang.

"Hey there, it's me," Emma said.

"Fancy that. I was just thinking about you."

"I just did a short run, and when I got home I realized that Labor Day weekend on fraternity row has begun. You know that's right across the street from my apartment building."

"Yep."

"The bands are already cranked up and everyone in my building has their picnic blankets and ice chests out on the lawn listening to the music. You either have to give in to it or escape. I'm leaning toward escaping. What do you think? Want to run away with me tonight instead of tomorrow night?"

"Well, I..."

"I also remembered that I have an appointment tomorrow afternoon with some study partners. So, it would really work better for me to get together earlier rather than later."

"Well, I guess we could. I'll call the restaurant at the Inn..."

"We don't have to go there. I don't care where we go."

"Well, I still think we need to be careful where we're seen. I'll call, change reservations, and pick you up in an hour."

Ren walked up the sidewalk to Emma's apartment and knocked on her door, hoping she could hear the rapping sound over the blaring music. When she opened the door Ren stood there, dumbfounded for a moment, unable to move. Embarrassed, he stepped into the room.

Emma was dressed in a simple black dress and heels. She had let her hair down from her usual ponytail, and it was flowing, tawny-blonde and lustrous about her shoulders. She managed an extra bit of mascara and shiny red lipstick for a dash of glamour and greeted Ren with a welcoming smile.

"Emma, you look gorgeous. I've never seen you dressed up before. You look so stunning it takes my breath away." He smiled.

"Thanks, Ren. That's a sweet thing to say."

"I mean, you're a good-looking girl, but you usually have to look so professional and tonight you're not, or at least you don't look so business-like. It's nice...but now I sound like an idiot."

"No, you don't, but I'm not a girl," Emma said, laughing. "Let's get on the road before it gets too late."

As they walked down the grassy slope to the parking area, Emma pulled out her sunglasses to protect her from the setting sun as it slanted across the horizon.

"So, no official sheriff's car for the evening?" Emma smiled.

Ren laughed. "No, that wouldn't exactly help us sneak away, would it?"

"Does that mean I can't ask any questions about Lola Mae's murder?"

"You know you shouldn't."

"I'll do my best."

When they pulled out of the parking lot, the black truck waited until they were safely out of range before pulling behind them into the traffic. Staying at least two car lengths behind, the driver remained undetected for the entire forty-five minute drive to the Inn.

The restaurant at the Inn at Lake Oconee was in a charming rustic building, complete with rough-hewn timbers embedded in its twenty-foot ceilings, a roaring fire in its stone fireplace—even in September—and candlelit tables. Emma loved it. She hadn't been to a nice dinner since she'd been in law school. She nearly swooned at the sight of the place.

"Well, I'll try not to fall in love with you just for taking me here, but it's tempting. You know you're taking advantage of a starving law student and a single mother to boot," Emma said, hoping he'd realize she was teasing.

"My plan all along." Ren smiled.

They were led to a table by the bay window overlooking the lake. "This is impressive. What did you have to do to get this table?" Ren held out her seat. She sat down and gazed out the window at the lush greenery.

"Wish I could say it was something great, but all I had to do was call a few hours ahead." Ren scraped his chair against the wooden floor and sat across the table from Emma.

"Very nice, Ren. I love it. What a view. I so miss a view of the water's edge. That's the one thing I don't like about going to school here." Emma removed the flatware from her napkin. "I don't like feeling land-locked. I'm a coast person. It's hard to explain, but once you grow up next to the water, you feel as if you'll always need the sense of freedom it gives you. Being inland makes me feel confined, locked in."

"Interesting. I've always thought folks from the coast were a little strange," Ren said. "I'm kidding. I understand, I guess. Although I've always lived here. But I do like the beach."

"What I'm speaking about is more than a beach. It's the unbroken horizon from a coastline—the sense of peace you get when nothing man-made breaks your line of vision."

"You make it sound so nice. I remember feeling that way when I was a kid on a family vacation in Oklahoma. Our hotel overlooked flat plateaus there, and I imagined Indians on their horses riding over the top. The horizons there were unbroken, filled with nothing more than my imagination." He blushed, and nodded at the waiter who poured water in their glasses.

"I think you do understand, Deputy."

Emma looked over the menu and ordered a glass of wine and the sea bass. She smiled at Ren.

"You know, you were wise to get us out of town," Emma said. "I feel more relaxed here than I have in a long time. But I am a little worried about the possibility of liking you more than I'd planned. That wouldn't be prudent."

"Guess not. This isn't exactly a good career move for me."

"I don't imagine. But, just to remind you, this dinner was your idea. But you and the sheriff are pretty close, right?"

"Yes, but fraternizing with the enemy won't sit well with him, believe me."

"I'm not exactly an enemy, now, am I?"

"You are definitely the other side."

"I suppose so." Emma said. "Well, what are we going to do about all that?"

"I suggest we proceed, with caution," Ren said.

"We could wait until the case is over. I haven't meant to put you in an awkward position."

Ren slowly swirled the water in his glass.

"Emma, sometimes you do. Like when you asked me about Lola Mae's murder."

"I don't think it hurts for me to ask. But I don't mean to pressure you."

"You're persistent, Emma. And sometimes you do pressure me."

"I see." She smiled. "I guess I think you shouldn't have a problem telling me what you could tell the press. That way I'd only get the information I'd be entitled to anyway. I'd just like to hear it before it hits the papers."

"Entitled? I don't think you're entitled to anything."

"You don't tell the press about anything that might jeopardize your investigations, right?"

"Right."

"I'm not entitled to know any more than what you'd tell them."

"There's that word again. We probably shouldn't be talking about this at all. You are working for the defense in the Patrick case, Emma."

"Okay. Sorry." Emma squeezed Ren's hand.

A waiter appeared and hovered over their table with his tray.

"Well, just so you know, we don't know much more than what we've already told the newspaper."

"Where was she found?"

"In Jones County. That was in the paper."

"I didn't see the paper today. That's pretty far away. Any weapon yet?"

"No."

"Cause of death?"

"Blunt force trauma to the head."

"Oooh. Tough. Any other evidence?"

"Just the usual."

"Usual?"

"You know. Usual."

"That's pretty cryptic."

"It's got to be that way for a while, Emma."

Emma sighed. "The sea bass is great. How's your chicken?"

Emma allowed herself a brief snuggle next to Ren on the way home. Traffic was light that time of night and the highway was unlit. They didn't run a realistic risk of being seen by anyone from Jonesburg on the way back from Lake Oconee. Ren turned on the radio and Emma placed her head on his shoulder. She was asleep within seconds.

The first bump woke her up instantly.

"What was that?"

"Some idiot just rammed the back of my car!" Ren said. "Get over on your side of the seat and put your seat belt back on. I wish I had the squad car now." Ren pushed the car up to seventy miles per hour.

As they approached a curve in the road, they were struck again, this time with greater force, throwing them into the opposite lane. Emma screamed. Ren immediately over-corrected, veering onto the right shoulder, and then back on course. Emma turned around to look at the vehicle in pursuit.

"It's a truck. A large pick-up truck. Dark, it looks black, but it's hard to see. It might have the same headlights as the truck that tried to run me down. He's right on our tail!"

Ren floored the accelerator again, pushing the car up to eighty-five miles per hour. The truck stayed close behind, and began gaining speed.

It struck again as Ren's car was approaching a small bridge, hitting the left bumper at the precise angle required to send the car flying toward an abutment, flipping it over onto its roof. It slid in slow motion, down a fifteen-foot concrete embankment to the empty river bottom below.

The driver of the truck stopped to survey the damage, which in his estimation was extensive. It was a fifteen foot drop, after all. Satisfied, he climbed back in the cab and lit a cigarette for the long drive home.

25

September 2, 1990

Emma woke up and stared at the key-lime-pie-green walls, not knowing where she was. She panicked, blinking. *Think. Think.* What was this place? What had happened? Finally realizing she was in a hospital room, she began fitting the pieces together.

She remembered the battering Ren's car took and the horror of the ensuing plunge from the bridge. Everything seemed to have slowed down as she descended. An image of the twins when they were babies floated through her mind. Filled with an overwhelming sadness, she didn't believe she'd see her boys again.

She sat up in bed, shaken, but relieved to have survived. Her head began pounding with the precision of a metronome, a sledgehammer its pendulum. She checked out the rest of her body. No apparent broken bones. Arms, legs, feet, all okay.

But what about Ren? She looked around the room, seeing for the first time an officer, Sheriff Colson, sitting in a chair in the corner, asleep. She rang her buzzer.

A young RN appeared.

"Can I help you?"

"Yes. Can you tell me where I am, why I'm here, and why that man is sitting in the corner over there?" Emma said nodding toward Sheriff Colson.

"You are in Putnam County Hospital. You were in a bad car wreck, but even though you were shaken up and banged your head, you seem to be okay, no concussion, no broken bones. We kept you overnight for observation to make certain there was no internal bleeding. The man in the chair said he was a friend, and he's also the sheriff of Greendale County, so he might have some questions about the accident."

"Do you know what happened to the driver of the car?"

"He wasn't as lucky as you. I can't really discuss his condition unless you're an immediate family member, and I don't think you are, are you?"

"No. Can't you take me to see him?"

"I'll have to check with his doctors to see if he can have visitors right now. Visiting hours are later in the afternoon."

"I can tell you a little more," Sheriff Colson said, standing up and stretching his legs.

"Good morning. Hope you slept well." Emma attempted a smile.

"You guys had us pretty scared."

"We were pretty scared as well. Can you tell me how Ren is?"

"Looks like he's got a broken leg and may have torn a ligament in his shoulder, but he's lucky. It could have been much worse. That car saved your lives. That and the fact that the river bed was made of pure sand."

"How did the car save our lives?"

"Ren got it at a government auction. It was an old cop car, and it had a roll bar built into the roof, so when you slid down the embankment, the roof didn't cave in. That car's built like a tank."

"I'm afraid I don't pay attention to cars, but I'm certainly thankful for that now."

"So, what can you tell me about what happened?"

Emma took a deep breath and paused for a moment before continuing. "We were knocked off of the road by a pick-up truck, and I believe it's the same truck that's been stalking me."

"Emma, I hate to ask, but why were you and Ren together?"

Emma felt as if she were a third-grader brought to the principal's office for misbehaving in class. She looked down at her hands, and then back at the sheriff before answering.

"We had dinner plans last night, Sheriff. We thought it was better to meet out of town, which is what we did. On our way back we were rammed by a truck. It wasn't an accident. When do you think I'll be able to see Ren?"

"Emma, did you or I should say do you and Ren, discuss the Jennifer Patrick murder?"

"No, Sheriff. We have a policy that he can't tell me anything he can't tell a newspaper reporter. And I don't speak to him about the defense of the case."

"I see."

"I know it looks bad, and we really haven't seen each other that often. We usually only speak to each other about the run ins with the black truck or how to protect my kids. This was our first official date."

"Well, it was a doozy of a first date."

"Yes, it was." Emma gingerly rubbed a hand over her head. "I'd like to get out of here and go see Ren to make sure he's okay. Also, I expect my children back tomorrow. Ren was planning on arranging protection for them. Is that something someone else in your office can help me with?"

"We should be able to, Emma. Just give us a call and we'll see what's available. There have been a number of incidents now. Last night's was just one. Then there's the death of Lola Mae Robinson. It would be hard not to link all of the incidents to the Patrick girl's murder. At the very least, they all seem to be connected in some way to the Gannons, wouldn't you agree?"

"We don't have any information on the truck that rammed us yet, so we can't connect that incident to the Gannons. Also, Lola Mae was the Gannon's housekeeper so, I guess there's some kind of connection between her death and the Gannon family. But if you discover anything else that links Lola Mae's murder to the Gannons I'd like to know about it as soon as possible. I just don't think that's going to happen."

"You'll be the first to know of any relevant information we feel we can share, Emma."

Emma was discharged that afternoon. Sheriff Colson promised to drive her home.

"I have to go see Ren first, though. I'll only be a minute. I'm sure they're limiting his visitors." Emma checked her hair in the mirror.

The nurse allowed her to walk down the hall for the visit with Ren. She dreaded what she might see.

"Hey there, lawyer," Ren said as she entered the room.

"Well, aren't you a sight for sore eyes. You don't look as awful as I expected," Emma said, leaning over to give Ren a kiss on his cheek.

Emma was shocked by the extent of Ren's injuries, even though the sheriff had described them to her. His leg was raised in traction and his arm was in a sling. She knew surgery was scheduled for the shoulder later in the day.

"Can't you do better than that?" Ren said.

"Your boss is probably lurking around the door, and has already cornered me about what we were doing together last night."

"Oh. What'd you say?"

"The truth."

"Ouch."

"No use lying at this point, Ren. He would have figured it out anyway. All he had to do was go back to the restaurant at the Inn and that would have been it. I'd rather have him find out from one of us. Anyway, it was our first real date. Nothing has ever really happened between us."

"Well, that's not actually true, Emma."

"It was our first official date. That much is true."

"I can grant you that one, at least."

"Will you lose your job?" Emma said.

"I don't know."

"I'm sorry, Ren. I didn't mean for things to get so complicated."

"I've been a full participant, Emma. I asked you out, remember? I wanted to see you more than anything last night. I'm just glad we're okay."

"Are you okay?"

"I will be. I may have to be in a wheelchair for a while, mostly because my shoulder is messed up, and I won't be able to handle crutches, but I should be okay in about six weeks. I ought to get out of here in a couple of days."

Emma walked out of the hospital with the sheriff several minutes later. She and Ren had agreed that she wouldn't contact Ren for a while, even though he obviously needed help during his convalescence. He had family that could help. She knew she'd miss him.

26

September 3, 1990

Emma pulled into the square. At ten in the morning it was already crowded. The parade wasn't scheduled to begin until one that afternoon, but she'd made plans with her parents to meet the boys in the square before it started.

Labor Day was one of two holidays celebrated by a parade in Jonesburg, and was, with the exception of the Christmas celebration, the most popular event of the year. Years ago, someone started a picnic in the square after the parade. The number and range of spectacular desserts prompted a pie contest the following year. The annual Labor Day parade, picnic, and pie contest attracted more people to Jonesburg on that one day than would drive through the tiny town the remainder of the year.

Emma's kids were excited about the celebration. Her parents had made the unusually helpful decision to drive all the way to Jonesburg this time. She was thrilled to finally see the twins, so excited she forgot about how achy she was from yesterday's incident.

Emma parked behind Silas's office. She had some work to do, and also wanted to call the sheriff's office before the parade. She enjoyed watching people moving through the square from her office window while she worked, and hoped she might catch a glimpse of the boys as they approached in the next hour or so. She loved watching them, especially if they didn't realize she could see them. When they were all together, they vied for her attention and could snipe at each other, but on their own, they banded together like little pirates.

Staring out of the window and watching the parade festivities get underway, Emma saw Robert Gannon saunter by dressed for the parade in cowboy boots with spurs, a plaid shirt with silver tips on the collar, and a bolo tie. He topped off the look with a black straw cowboy hat.

Emma noticed Robert make a sharp turn down Maple Street and then another turn behind the McFarland law office. He was walking slowly but deliberately, his limp less obvious at this speed, his eyes straight ahead. From Emma's vantage, she could see a corner of the McFarland's back parking lot, where she spotted a rusted out old pick-up truck that looked vaguely familiar to her. As Robert rounded the corner of the McFarland's back lot, Ben Bailey emerged from his truck. Emma's curiosity got the better of her and she headed down the stairs toward the back door of Silas's building, which had a view of McFarland's parking lot. Emma knew if she hid behind the back stairs, she should be protected by the enclosure Silas had built to conceal the garbage cans along the rear of the building. If she was lucky, she might even be able to hear what was being said between Robert and Ben.

"This should be enough to cover it. And I don't want to hear from you again unless it's to say that everything has gone the way we had it planned." Robert, frowning into the sunlight, handed what looked to be a roll of bills to Ben.

"If that's what you want, then this had better be plenty," Ben said, flipping through the wad. "We'd agreed on another ten thousand."

Robert grabbed Ben's t-shirt and shoved him up against the back of the building, causing the wooden structure where Emma was hiding to shudder.

"Don't push it Bailey. I don't care if you are my sister's kid."

"All right, all right. But from now on, why don't you get someone else to do your dirty work?"

"I don't want to see your face again."

Robert turned and left abruptly. Ben stood there for several minutes, counting the money Robert had given him. Ben tucked the wad in his pocket, got in his truck, and quickly exited the parking lot.

Emma was tempted to call Ren, but knew she needed to speak to Silas first, plus, she didn't have enough information. Ben could have done a million things for Robert that would have required payment. But if it was completely legitimate Ben wouldn't have called it 'dirty work.' And what did Ben do for a living anyway? She'd never even asked him. She recalled seeing the vials of drugs in Ben's glove compartment. What was that all about? She'd heard that drugs and horseracing were linked, but she wasn't sure how.

She sprinted back up the stairs. Her investigation of Robert's dealings with Ben Bailey would have to wait. Before she could begin to work on that or any other problem in Adam's case, she had to secure surveillance for her kids at the apartment, starting tonight.

Once she was in her office, she dialed the number to the sheriff's office and asked to speak to Sheriff Colson.

"Sheriff Colson's not in at this time, but I can put you in touch with Deputy Glass. He's serving as the chief deputy while Deputy Taylor's on sick leave. I'll put you on hold for a few minutes until I can locate him. He's in this morning."

As Emma waited, she looked out over the crowd. The parade was still two hours away. She was beginning to question her decision to meet her children in the square. There weren't many deputies visible at the parade site. She only saw one, whom she didn't recognize. A voice came on the line.

"Hello? This is Chief Deputy Glass."

"I'm Emma Thornton, a law clerk working with Silas Steele on the Jennifer Patrick murder. The sheriff has agreed that I could get a surveillance unit out to my apartment. I've been assaulted recently by someone in a black truck and will need help tonight and in the foreseeable future. My eight year old twins are coming home from their grandparents' today, so they'll need protection and I'll need to set up someone to watch my apartment until the person is found and arrested. The sheriff said I'd just need to call and arrange it. I think surveillance has already been secured for tonight."

"I'll check on that for you, Miss Thompson. But I'm certain you're going to be just fine and there's no need to worry. I'm familiar with your situation and from the notes I reviewed earlier, most of the attacks have occurred while the truck was moving. I wouldn't think you'd be in much danger at home."

"The name is Thornton, not Thompson. If you look a little closer you'll see that there was a Peeping Tom violation at my apartment, which was followed by the more violent attacks from the moving truck. I'm worried that once we're all home, especially after dark, we'll be even more vulnerable. The sheriff has essentially agreed to make arrangements for us."

"Miss Thornton, if you're so concerned about your children, why are you allowing them to come home at all? Why didn't they just stay with their grandparents? Why are you allowing them to come back into an environment where they might be in danger?"

"I don't owe you an explanation, Deputy, but my parents have had both of my children for over a week, and neither is in good health. And my kids need to get back to school. This protection is particularly important right now."

"I'm sure you know your children aren't entitled to any more protection than any other citizen of this county and it's not my duty or the duty of the sheriff's department to provide security for them or you. I understand you're a law student. So I assume you already knew that."

Emma drummed her fingers on her desk. She was on edge, jumpy from the car accident, and found it more difficult to focus. She also had a pounding headache and didn't need grief from Deputy Glass.

"Where's Sheriff Colson?"

"I'm not sure. He may be out at the parade site. But I don't really keep up with him unless he tells me where he's going. Today he didn't."

"Thanks for all of your help." Emma slammed the receiver down. "Son of a bitch ...," she muttered.

Emma opened her window and scanned the crowd for the sheriff's hat. He was taller than most, so she didn't think he should be a difficult person to spot. Finally spying the sheriff's distinctive tan cowboy fedora, she found him next to a hot dog cart. Emma bounded down the stairs.

When Emma reached the stand, the sheriff had wandered off.

"Wasn't Sheriff Colson here a few seconds ago?" she asked the hot dog vendor.

"Yes, ma'am. He was here talking to the bank president. Not sure where they went but I think the sheriff may have gone off that-a-way." He pointed toward the high school marching band lining up farther down the street.

Emma headed off at a half trot, keeping her eyes peeled for the sheriff, trying not to panic. Finally, she spotted him walking along the parade line-up.

"Sheriff! Wait!"

Colson turned, smiled and waited for Emma to catch up with him.

"How are things, Miss Emma?"

"Not so good, Sheriff," Emma said, trying to catch her breath. "My children are coming in, in about thirty minutes to be exact, and I've just met some resistance from Deputy Glass about the surveillance at my apartment for tonight. I'm really worried about the kids before and after school too."

"Now hold on, Emma. We already have someone scheduled to be at your apartment tonight, but we never agreed to have someone follow your kids to school. That's entirely unnecessary. They'll be fine in school. They'll be in a protected environment and they'll take the bus home."

"Ren and I had discussed all of that earlier. He didn't think it was necessary either, but with this recent murder, I'm concerned."

Sheriff Colson shook his head. "We can't afford to accommodate every aspect of your schedule, Emma. You're going to have to make other arrangements. Maybe you'll need to stop working late. We'll be there after nine in the evening since you've had someone approach your apartment after dark. I want to do what we can to make sure that you're protected during those late hours."

"I appreciate whatever you can do, but now that Ren is laid up, I'm terrified none of the other deputies will take an interest in our situation. The acting chief deputy doesn't seem very concerned."

"Hey, Mom!"

"Billy! Bobby!"

The twins ran up to Emma, their arms extended. Emma wrapped her arms around both of them.

"Sheriff, let me introduce you to my kids, and my parents, who are probably done in at this point."

The sheriff shook hands all around.

"Deputy Glass will be there tonight, Emma. Don't worry."

"Great. That's all I need."

27

September 4, 1990

By six the next morning the deputy's car was gone. Emma wasn't surprised, but she hoped he would have stayed at least another hour, through sunrise.

The last two nights had been uneventful. Deputy Glass had been correct. The black truck hadn't shown up again, and if things stayed quiet, she'd be happy to admit to him or anyone else that her worries were needless.

Adam drove up the road to the family's stables. He had plans to meet Emma at Joe's place later in the afternoon. Driving behind the barn he pulled to a stop and checked his surroundings. No workers were in the area. The door to the storage shed scraped the ground as he tugged it open. Even though no horses were kept in this small building, he was immediately struck by the unmistakably strong odor of the stables—the earthy smell of horse sweat, hay and manure. His eyes widened as they adjusted to the darkness. A light bulb hanging from the center of the room caught a flash of the early-afternoon sun through a south-west window. He flipped the light switch on, illuminating the dust that danced about his head.

The space was dank, but unchanged since his last visit. He scanned the small room and walked over to a shelf where he gathered a box of paints, a can of mineral spirits, and a handful of rags. He placed these next to a stack of frames leaning against the wall, covered by a large sheet of canvas, pulled a painting from the back of the stack and examined it in the scant light. Taking one of the rags, he soaked it in mineral spirits, and began wiping the corner of the piece. Slowly the color began rub off, leaving the residue on the cloth.

He hesitated for several minutes, unable to continue, gazing at the painting and the damages he'd done to it. Then, he placed the painting back in the stack with the others and covered it again with the canvas cloth.

He walked to a corner of the shed, moved several boxes, and found two small holes in the floorboards. Grabbing a screwdriver from the work bench, he inserted it into one of the holes and pulled upwards to reveal a hidden space. Looking inside, he could see an empty magazine from the AR-15. His dad's shoes were still there too. He shut the trap door and put the boxes back on top, making certain they were in the exact same spot as before.

He sat for a while on the floor, his head in his hands, sobbing.

It was a beautiful day. Emma had made arrangements before she was hospitalized to see both Joe and Adam to discuss the upcoming hearings. And even though she wasn't feeling well, she was looking forward to seeing Joe Casey. Something about him was grounding, even soothing. A natural teacher, he exuded common sense and decency. Emma had come to rely on his moral compass.

She pulled up the drive to his tiny home. Joe was sitting out on the front porch as usual, his straw fedora tilted to the back of his head. Adam was next to him. His face was flushed.

"When are you goin' to get a car that'll get you places on time, Miss Emma?" Joe smiled and removed the remnants of his lunch from his teeth with a wooden toothpick.

"Don't you worry about that. This old car is just fine." Emma walked up the steps, then sat down in the rusted chair opposite Joe and Adam.

"Today, Joe, I need for you to act as my agent, to facilitate communication between Adam and me. That way, the conversation we three are about to have will not waive the attorney-client privilege. Does that make sense to you?"

Joe nodded.

"Of course, you will be expected to keep whatever is said here today to yourself. And, we'll need Adam's permission to proceed. I'll explain what the waiver means."

"I would never say nothing to hurt Adam." Joe mopped his forehead with his handkerchief and patted Adam's knee with his free hand.

After receiving Adam's approval, Emma explained the motions she and Silas were filing.

"I need to know what Adam understands about everything that's happening to him. I also need Adam to clear up a couple of things for me. If we aren't successful with our motions, we'll have to go forward with a full-blown trial. Adam should be prepared to show where he was at the time of the murder, even if we keep him off of the stand. If he doesn't, his guilt will be presumed by the jury. It's just human nature."

Adam re-tied his shoes, then stared off toward the stables, pretending to watch the horses run.

Emma wrote:

You said a man shot Jennifer. How do you know that? Were you there?

Adam looked down at his shoes.

"Adam," Emma said, moving into Adam's line of sight, "we can't help you if you won't help us."

Adam took the legal pad and the pen from Emma's hands and wrote:

I at house that night but left before she killed

Emma read this and felt her pulse increase. Although Adam had never admitted he was at the Patrick house on the night of the murder, she and Silas had always suspected he was.

She wrote: *Why were you at the Patrick home that night?*

She handed the legal pad back to Adam. He read and responded: *I want to talk about why she break with me. She let me in window. Then I go home.*

That would explain his boot prints at the scene, Emma thought. No one would believe he left before the shooting.

Emma scribbled: *Did you see the person who shot Jennifer?*

Adam paused, and stepped over to the edge of the porch. He put his hands behind his back, his thumb immediately finding the same place on his finger Emma had seen him nervously dig at before. Hoping for a response, she touched his shoulder. He turned toward her, his face collapsed in despair.

Eager to avoid another breakdown, Emma sat down and scribbled out another question for Adam.

Why do you think the deputy took your boots and jeans and the other things from your apartment? She passed the pen and paper to Adam, who sat down next to her.

"Joe, can you help Adam?"

Joe began tracing letters in the palm of Adam's hand and pointing to the question on the paper. Adam nodded and picked up the pen.

It is not good. It is a bad thing.

Emma asked him why it was a bad thing. Adam turned his back to Emma and refused to participate in her questions, written or spoken.

"Joe, I need to know who besides Adam has a key to his truck. Can you get his attention? I need to know why the gun was in his truck in the first place. Did he put it there? Also, the magazine is missing. I need to know if he knows anything about that, too. If he didn't put the rifle in his truck that night, whether anyone else had a key to it becomes a very important issue." She hesitated. "And Joe, if you can, get him to talk about the man who shot Jennifer, please."

"Can you give us a second to talk, Miss Emma? Why don't you step in the kitchen and grab some of that lemonade I made earlier? It's a hot day. It ought to taste good to you about now."

Emma stepped into Joe's modest but immaculate living room. Although it seemed designed for one person, this was Joe's family home, and once was stretched to its capacity with five Caseys of various ages. This and several

160

of the other smaller houses at Mayfair were a part of the original plantation, and pre-dated the Civil War.

The kitchen was along the opposite side of the room from the television. A circa 1950s refrigerator stood in the corner, whirring peacefully. Emma peeked inside and spied the lemonade. It looked frosty cold. She reached for a glass from Joe's tidy cupboards.

As she sipped her drink she wondered what Joe and Adam were discussing. It must have something to do with Adam's parents. They had to have a key to his truck. She caught Joe's eye. He nodded for her to come out.

"So, who has keys to your truck, Adam?"

"His parents do. There might be another spare. One of the hands could have access, too. All of the extra keys are usually kept on the back wall of the kitchen, by the door." Joe nodded.

Adam folded his hands and rested his wrists on his knees, staring at his feet. Recognizing this as his method of cutting off any exchange of communication, Emma stomped her heels on the wooden porch. Adam looked up at her, startled.

Emma picked up the pen again.

Are you helping someone, Adam? Is that why you won't answer my questions?

Adam looked at Emma for several seconds before responding, then slowly shook his head. Then he wrote: *Someone take keys.*

"Then they'd have to steal the rifle from you, too. Who could get to your rifle and then put it into your truck? Where did you keep the rifle before the shooting?"

He stood up and pointed to the shed down the road, next to the stables.

"Can we take a walk together down to the shed so you could show me where you kept the rifle?"

"Don't see why not," Joe said.

The three of them moved slowly toward the shed, Adam pushing Joe in his wheelchair, Emma walking alongside, all careful to avoid the red clay mud holes and rocky pits as they picked their way down the road.

28

September 5, 1990

Emma walked into the quiet, empty courtroom and headed toward the table on the far right. The defense side. She was the first one there, which she preferred. It gave her time to collect her thoughts. She also wanted to be there when the interpreter arrived.

The courthouse in Greendale County was partially re-built in 1865 following Sherman's March to the Sea, in the same footprint as its predecessor. Although a significant portion was gutted, much of the building was left untouched during the Civil War since Union soldiers were too interested in scavenging what they could from local shopkeepers and farms to worry much about courthouses. Emma enjoyed sorting out which parts of the structure were original and which were not, particularly during calendar call or other more mundane courtroom procedures.

It was a fine old structure, solidly built, with leaded glass windows in the bell tower and a lovely clock on the face of the building. Constructed of ubiquitous Georgian red brick, the courthouse rotunda was flanked by Grecian columns. The floor of its main courtroom was recessed by nearly a foot, and the judge's bench was elevated, so that lawyers were required to gaze upwards as they made their arguments. There was no doubt about the judge's command of the room. Soaring twenty-foot ceilings were supported by majestic pink Etowah marble columns, mined from north Georgia quarries. The sheer height of the ceilings and the use of the elegant stone gave an air of solemnity and near reverence to the space. Newcomers to the area often confused the lofty edifice with the local Baptist church, and to a few of the citizens of Greendale County, it was even more sacred.

At 9:55 Silas and the prosecutor headed over from their offices on the square, as if they had synchronized their watches. Adam was with Silas and followed him into the courtroom. All of the prosecutor's witnesses remained sequestered outside the courtroom on benches. Silas noticed Adam visibly stiffen at the sight of one poufy-haired woman sitting with the group. He made a mental note to ask Emma to take a bathroom run to see if she was familiar with the DA's line up, particularly the woman with the strange hair. He needed a little intelligence on each of them.

The prosecutor, Assistant District Attorney Chester Manville, was the DA's right hand man. Manville was about forty and had been with the DA since he graduated from law school. He was a no-nonsense, slow talking but quick-witted fellow who could tell a good joke when he needed to. People liked him. Silas had known him for years. He could be found at Lucky's counter every day at 12:15 sharp. Folks often gathered around to speak with him or exchange jokes well after they had finished lunch. Some predicted Manville would be in political office within the next five years. Silas suspected he had his eye on the DA's spot.

Silas knew they'd drawn Judge Lamar R. Baggett for the case. "Sleepy" Baggett—a man who often fell asleep during hearings, and who'd even been seen clipping his fingernails at trial. He often favored the loudest argument, not the best, but Silas wasn't concerned. He'd been before Sleepy for more than twenty years and had no problem keeping his attention.

Five minutes earlier than expected, the officer announced the judge's entrance into the courtroom as the assembly rose from their seats. Judge

Baggett was an older fellow, but his sandy blonde hair showed only the faintest hints of gray. Freckles were sprinkled across his face and the bridge of his nose, and were deeply embedded in little crinkles around his eyes, making him appear like a dried out, over-grown ten-year-old. He nodded, indicating that people should be seated and the proceedings could begin. With a shake of his head Silas indicated that Emma had to forget the bathroom run. He would take his chances with the prosecutor's witnesses.

The interpreter, a young woman hired by the court from the state school for the deaf, was sworn in. She stepped down from the podium and sat down next to Adam.

Silas stood up, introduced himself and explained their position.

"Our Motion asks the court to dismiss the case based on the fact that Adam, a deaf man, isn't competent to stand trial. He doesn't understand language on a level that will allow him to assist in his own defense; he didn't understand why he was arrested, or why certain evidence was taken from his apartment. No interpreter was present when he was arrested as required by Georgia law. We'll show he didn't understand the nature of his arrest, that he has difficulty understanding abstract concepts, and that he does not possess the present ability to consult with his attorney with a reasonable degree of rational understanding. Thus, Adam is not competent to stand trial, and the case against him must be dismissed.

"Secondly, we've filed a motion requesting that the court suppress certain items from evidence which were removed from Adam's apartment and truck. These things were wrongfully seized, without Adam's full understanding or permission. Even though Adam signed a consent order, we'll show the court that he didn't understand its content, again noting that there was no interpreter present at the time of the seizure, as required by law. We'll show he reads at a third grade level. We'll also show the court that Adam has a profound hearing loss, which means that Adam cannot hear conversation or spoken language, which we will also prove. Also, Adam never learned sign language, and although Adam is a lip reader, we will show that he only understands about thirty percent of what's said. So, Adam didn't fully understand what took place the morning the evidence was taken from his apartment. We'll show that all of the evidence seized that day including the tires, the boots, the trousers and the rifle, must be suppressed from the evidence in this case, and that any and all charges against Adam must be dismissed.

"We'd like to call our first witness, Dr. Ellis Griffin, an ear, nose and throat specialist who is also an expert in Auditory Brainstem Response testing."

Silas glanced up at Judge Baggett, who seemed to be staring at his shoes. Could he be asleep already? Not a good sign. Emma, who apparently noticed the judge's slack-jawed pose, elbowed one of her files to the edge of the defense table. It dropped to the floor with a repercussive bang. Silas scowled, but Sleepy responded with a start and seemed to have been awakened, at least momentarily, from his stupor. Emma coughed for good measure. Silas made a mental note to remind Emma to keep such trickery less obvious in the future. Theatrics like that wouldn't work in front of a jury.

Silas called his first witness.

"Yes," Dr. Griffin responded to Silas's question about his technique. "During testing the subject is placed in a reclining position and is asked to close his eyes. Sticker electrodes are placed on his head and behind his ears. Auditory brainstem response audiometry typically uses a click stimulus that generates a response from the basilar region of the cochlea. The positive peaks of the waveforms reflect combined afferent and likely efferent activity from axonal pathways in the auditory brain stem."

Silas glanced at the court reporter to make certain that she was keeping up with the testimony, and checked out the judge's attentiveness again.

"Can you explain your findings in a language we can all understand, Doctor?"

"I found that Adam Gannon had very little response to the stimuli. In other words, he had very little brain wave activity in response to the sound stimuli. Specifically, he only heard sounds above ninety-five decibels. Adam had a profound, genetic sensorineural hearing loss."

"Can Adam hear or understand human speech at any level or decibel?"

"No."

"Objection, Your Honor." Manville stood up. "The doctor can't testify about what Mr. Gannon can understand. He may be able to testify about what he allegedly believes Mr. Gannon can hear based on the test he gave him, but the good doctor can't testify about what Mr. Gannon can understand regarding human speech because he didn't test for that. Calls for speculation."

Judge Baggett looked uncomfortable with the objection, but showed no sign of ruling.

"I'll rephrase my question."

"Dr. Griffin, can Adam Gannon hear human speech at any decibel?"

"No, he cannot."

"If it's true that Adam can't hear speech at any level, isn't it also true that he can't understand speech when it's spoken at any decibel?"

"Yes, that's my opinion."

A.D.A. Manville stood up. "Objection, Your Honor. This testimony continues to call for speculation. There are any number of ways a deaf person has of understanding human speech other than at decibel levels."

"Your Honor, counsel is misrepresenting testimony. The testimony was that Adam Gannon couldn't understand the spoken word. It's an essential fact in this case."

"I'll reserve my ruling on this. Let's move on." Sleepy looked down at his court reporter. "Please mark this objection. We'll go back to it."

Silas wasn't surprised that the judge didn't rule. Sleepy was known for putting off evidentiary decisions until the day of trial, and then letting everything in. But this ruling was important, and had constitutional implications.

"Dr. Griffin, would a person with this level of hearing loss, who was a lip reader exclusively, have a difficult time understanding abstract concepts such as his constitutional rights?"

"Objection, Your Honor. Again, I object to this witness testifying as to what the defendant is able to understand."

"I'll let him testify, and mark this objection for a later ruling as well. You may respond, Dr. Griffin. I'd like to hear your answer."

"Abstract concepts are very difficult for the deaf, in general. It's easier to teach a concrete fact. For instance, you can teach the word apple, by handing them an apple. But how do you teach an idea such as the right to an attorney, or the right to certain protections under the law? It's difficult, and it's a lost concept on many deaf individuals, especially those who haven't had training in a rigorous deaf education program. And Adam hasn't. His communication skills are poor. His records show he reads on a third grade level. It's no reflection on his intelligence. It's a consequence of his handicap and education."

"We have no further questions, and tender the witness, Your Honor."

Manville's cross of Dr. Griffin was far less insightful than his objections.

They progressed through the other witnesses. First they put Evelyn Miller, the speech and language expert from the Georgia School of the Deaf, on the stand. She testified that deaf individuals who rely exclusively on lip reading only understand about thirty percent of what is spoken. Then they put on Jerry Smithfield.

"Good afternoon, Mr. Smithfield. Please tell the court how you know Adam Gannon."

"I was Adam's high school basketball coach."

"What is it about Adam that stands out in your memory?"

"I guess the way I used to get his attention on the basketball court."

"And how was that?"

"Well, yelling at Adam didn't work. So, to get his attention, I stomped my foot at him or I waved my arms. Things like that. That's the only way I was able to get him to pay attention sometimes."

"Why was that, Mr. Smithfield?"

"Adam couldn't hear a thing. 'Deaf as a post,' I used to say. I used to tease him about it but he didn't mind. He was a pretty good student, but an outstanding athlete. Sports were important to him. We had to learn how to communicate when he was on the court, and we did, so he could do his best. When I stomped my foot, he responded to the vibrations he felt on the floor."

Silas tendered the witness and noticed the judge seemed to be paying attention for the time being. Silas was pleased with Smithfield's testimony.

Manville stepped up to the podium.

"Coach Smithfield, do you recall ever having problems with Adam while he was at Greendale?"

"None. He was a good student."

"Do you recall any problems on the basketball court?"

"I'm not sure what you mean."

"Do you recall one game where you had to intervene, and finally pull Adam off of a player in a fight?"

Silas jumped in. "Objection, Your Honor. Relevancy. Also, we haven't opened the door to character evidence. I don't see how this line of questioning is tied in any way to the direct examination or the subject of the motion."

"I can show how it is connected, Your Honor."

Sleepy overruled the objection. "You can continue, Mr. Smithfield."

"That was a situation where a kid had elbowed Adam in the throat during a game. Adam thought he'd done it on purpose, and maybe he had, so Adam hit him back. I stepped in to break up the fight." Coach Smithfield removed his glasses and cleaned them on the elbow of his jacket.

"How did you get Adam's attention that night? Did you stomp your foot—wave your arms—something like that?"

"I tried, but it didn't seem to work that night."

"Why not?"

"Adam didn't pay attention to much of anything that night."

"Why not?"

"I guess he was angry about getting jabbed in the throat."

"Would you agree that Adam has a bad temper?"

"Objection, Your Honor, irrelevant. Calls for character testimony and speculation."

"Overruled. You can answer, Mr. Smithfield."

"That night he thought someone deliberately punched him. It must have hurt, and it could have been dangerous, too. That would make anyone angry. Adam can have a bit of a temper, sometimes, but most high school boys do. Adam also has the added frustration of being deaf. So he has more problems than most students. But he's a good kid."

"I'd like to re-state my objection, Your Honor, and object to the responsiveness of Coach Smithfield's answer. He doesn't have the expertise to make this sort of commentary."

"Overruled. You're the one who called him to testify about what the defendant could understand and how he got along at school, Mr. Steele." The judge checked his notes.

The DA continued. "But didn't you have a great deal of trouble getting Adam to stop fighting that night?" The assistant DA paced back and forth behind the podium waiting for a response.

"Objection, relevancy."

"Mr. Steele, I'm going to allow this line of questioning. You're welcome to continue to make your objections, but I'd like to hear everything the witnesses have to say about these issues."

"Yes, it took a while to stop the fight."

"And was the other kid hurt?"

"You mean the kid that hit Adam in the throat?"

"Yes, that kid."

"He wasn't doing so well by the time we pulled Adam off of him."

"Did you need to call the ambulance?"

"I seem to recall doing that."

"Did you need to call the ambulance for Adam?"

"I think he was okay."

"Do you know what sort of injuries the other boy had?"

"I'm not sure. Maybe a broken nose and a broken rib or two."

"Thank you, Coach Smithfield. No further questions"

Silas stood up.

"Coach, do you agree that Adam was acting defensively and merely finished a fight another boy started?"

"Yes."

The defense rests, Your Honor."

"The state calls its first witness, Mrs. Mabel Grayson."

Silas looked at Adam. Adam's reaction to Mrs. Grayson as she walked into the courtroom was visceral and immediate. His nostrils flared. His face reddened and his eyes narrowed. Silas glanced over at Emma as she scribbled furiously in her notepad. This must be the teacher Emma had been telling him about. The one who insisted Adam could hear.

Mabel, stuffed into her navy polyester dress with scalloped hem and string-cinched waist, bounced up to the witness stand like an over-filled balloon animal about to burst. Her recently coiffed hair had been shellacked into a tortoise-like shell. Smug with self-righteousness, she hoisted her stout body into the chair and sat down, raising a puffy hand for the swearing in.

"Mrs. Grayson, please tell the court how you know the defendant."

"I was Adam's tenth grade history teacher."

"What sort of student was Adam?"

"I'd say he was a poor student."

"Do you have an opinion on Adam's ability to hear?"

"Objection, Your Honor. Mrs. Grayson is not an expert in the field of audiology or speech pathology. She's not qualified to testify regarding Adam's ability to hear."

"She's as qualified as your witness, Coach Smithfield, Mr. Steele. She can testify as to what she has observed. Overruled."

"Adam could hear. He always did ever'thing the other kids in the room did. He got up when the bell rang. He read his homework assignments from the board. He took tests just like ever'one else."

Mabel reached up to pat an imaginary piece of hair in place and rubbed her nose.

Silas glanced up at the judge. He was leaning toward Mrs. Grayson, obviously attentive to her testimony.

"Was Adam able to follow your instructions in class?" Manville asked.

"Not always, but he didn't always pay attention. He was even belligerent sometimes."

"Please explain."

"Sometimes we'd have tests in class and he'd get angry and wad up his test paper and throw it in the trash b'fore he was done."

"Why would he do that?"

"I don't know. He had a bad temper."

"What would you do when he behaved that way?"

"I'd give him a zero on his test. So he'd usually make a bad grade for the term as well. When he'd get real mad, I'd send him to the principal's office."

"How often did something like that happen in your classroom?"

"It happened several times."

Silas was relieved to see that Emma finally passed her note down the table to him. Emma wrote that the tests Mabel was referring to were oral pop quizzes. Adam couldn't understand the questions, so he threw his test paper in the trash can.

"Do you have any other memories of Adam in your classroom which stand out in any way?"

"I recall that he got into a fist fight once in my class with another student. I don't know what started it, but I sent them both down to the principal's office. Like I said, Adam's got a temper."

"What was the other student's name?"

"I don't remember." Mabel squirmed to adjust the position in her seat.

Assistant DA Manville walked back to his seat. "Tender the witness."

Glancing over his shoulder, Silas noticed Adam growing more and more agitated as the oral interpreter mouthed the courtroom dialogue. Trained to enhance her interpretations with facial expressions, Adam scanned her gestures and grimaces for clues. With a clearer understanding of Mrs. Grayson's message, Adam's face flushed. He glared at Mabel, gritting his teeth so tight his jaw muscles rippled across his temples. Adam kept his clenched hands in his lap, his nails digging into his palms. Silas was relieved the judge was focused on Mrs. Grayson, not Adam.

Silas stepped up to the podium for his cross of the witness. With the exception of Emma's brief visits to the school, they didn't know anything about Mabel. Why would she insist Adam could hear? Could she possibly believe that or did she have something against him? There were so many questions he'd like to ask, but he couldn't. Not in the middle of a hearing. If they didn't win today, he'd have to ask Emma to investigate Mabel.

"Mrs. Grayson, isn't it true that the tests which Adam refused to take in

171

your class were oral pop quizzes that he couldn't understand because he's deaf?"

"I don't remember if the tests were oral pop quizzes or not, and I don't believe that Adam Gannon is deaf. If you were to ask me, I'd say Adam Gannon can hear."

"And you're basing your assessment that Adam can hear on the fact that he got up with the other kids when the bell rang indicating that class was over?"

"That's right. When the bell rang, he'd get up like the other kids."

"But don't you agree that the fact that the other kids were getting up would easily signal that class was over?"

"All I know is that when the bell rang, he got up. So, as far as I'm concerned, he can hear."

"Do you have any background or expertise in auditory training or deaf education?"

"No, I don't."

"Do you recall giving oral pop quizzes in class?"

"I may have, but I don't have a specific recollection, no."

"Do you have any recollection of Adam refusing to take oral tests in your class because he couldn't hear or understand the test questions?"

"No, I do not."

"Did you ever have students read out loud in your classroom?"

"No I didn't."

"So you wouldn't know the reading levels of any of your students, correct?"

"I'd assume that if they were in the tenth grade they could read at a tenth grade level."

"No further questions, Your Honor."

When Mabel stepped down from the stand she was required to walk in between the two parties' tables to exit the courtroom. In doing so, she had to walk by Adam, who was sitting next to Emma. As she neared the defense table she paused, glanced at Adam from the corner of her eye, and for reasons known only to Mabel, smiled. No one but Adam and those at the defense table could see it. The gesture, more of a smirk, or even a sneer, was finished off with a self-satisfied tilt of the head.

Unable to constrain himself any longer, Adam exploded. He rose up from his seat, threw out his arms and yelled, "Ooo bidd!" He shook his fists in her face. His eyes bulged as did the veins in his neck. His nostrils flared and he lunged for her. He was immediately restrained by the deputies in the courtroom, and taken away in handcuffs.

As she watched Adam being led from the courtroom, Emma realized the feeling she had in the pit of her stomach was dread brought on by the dawning realization that Adam's case had taken a fatal turn. And that "Ooo bidd" sounded a lot like "you bitch."

Following Adam's outburst, Judge Baggett decided to take the entire matter under advisement, which meant he was not sure how he was going to rule on the motions, with one exception. He ruled that Adam should undergo an exam for competency to stand trial, stating that he'd appoint a forensic psychiatrist from the state hospital. Silas was sure Sleepy would let his decision on the outstanding motions ride until the first day of trial.

But first, he had to get Adam out of jail.

Shaken by Adam's behavior in the courtroom, Emma was just as shocked by Mabel Grayson's gloating smile. Why would a grown woman, a teacher, have such a grudge against a former student?

As they were gathering their belongings to leave the courtroom, Emma noticed a few spectators walking out of the double doors in the back. She bent down to pick up her briefcase, and as she stood up, saw a man resembling Ben Bailey dart out from behind a column, push through the double doors, and enter the elevator directly across the hall. Emma flew after him, anxious to confront him, curious about his interest in the case. The elevator was occupied, so she took the stairs, tripping in her haste. When she got to the street, Ben Bailey, or his doppelganger, had disappeared.

29

September 6, 1990

Emma pulled her bistro chair up to the wobbly metal table, and sat down directly under the overhead fan. She'd scheduled a meeting with Robert Gannon to discuss yesterday's hearing. She'd asked him to meet her at Lucky's since it was possible to have a private conversation there. And, she felt safe in the middle of the open patio. She didn't trust Robert, even though the sheriff had verified his alibis for each of her attacks. She still couldn't shake the suspicion that he'd killed Jennifer Patrick.

Part of Emma's distrust stemmed from her prejudice against privileged men, men who were accustomed to demanding and getting what they wanted. She was certain Robert assumed that either his family name or position would keep Adam from serving time for Jennifer's murder. But he was wrong. In fact, Adam would be lucky to get out of jail after yesterday's self-destructive outburst.

She was also glad Silas had asked Robert not to attend the hearing yesterday. His feeble stabs at helping Adam understand what was going on during the search and seizures at his apartment weren't very helpful.

Robert's presence in the courtroom could have muddied their argument that Adam didn't understand why the items were taken. Plus, Silas was afraid the DA could have made a last ditch attempt to put Robert on the stand to explain his role that day. Since Robert hadn't been subpoenaed, Silas didn't want him anywhere near the courtroom. But as it turned out, Adam was handcuffed and jailed before they even got to the suppression argument.

Jonesburg was a small town. The folks who were in the courtroom yesterday would talk and soon everyone at Lucky's would know what happened. News of Adam's short fuse would spread to larger groups, churches, and the Lions Club, until eventually someone in the jury pool would know that Adam balled his fists up at Mabel Grayson and was taken out of the courtroom in handcuffs. They'd probably need to change venue, which could delay the trial. They had only a few days to get that done.

Robert walked into the café right on time. Emma noticed his gait immediately, scrutinizing him as he crossed the patio to her table. Dressed in his usual jeans, blazer and cowboy boots, he definitely favored the right leg. Emma didn't find him attractive, but she noticed several other women watching him as he walked past. He exuded wealth and, even though he limped, he still had the confidence of an athlete.

"Howdy, Ms. Thornton." Robert nodded his head toward Emma as he grabbed a chair to sit down. "I'm assuming you want to speak to me about Adam. I'm hopin' Silas can get him out of jail right away. He explained what happened in the courtroom. Guess Adam's got my temper."

Emma shook Robert's hand and nodded. "I won't lie—Adam's outburst hurt his case. But Silas could get him released today, if Adam's lucky. If so, another bail will be set. Silas will need you over at the courthouse in about an hour."

"What happened to set him off?"

"Mabel Grayson testified against Adam, then looked right at him and smirked on the way out of the courtroom. Adam lost it and ended up in handcuffs. But even scarier, he lunged for her. I can't imagine anything much worse at a hearing in a murder case. Also, it seemed as if Mrs. Grayson baited him. Do you know if she has something against Adam?"

"Silas told me about Mabel's testimony. I know who she is. I went to high school with her. She was one of those ultra-religious weirdos back then. Lived way out in the country. We used to call her 'Pioneer Woman' because she wore one of those strange poufy hair-dos with longer dresses. She looked like she just stepped out of a covered wagon. I think we might have made her cry a time or two, but we didn't mean to. We were young." He shrugged.

"Did you know that Mabel has also been insensitive to Adam?"

"Adam never mentioned anything to me about it."

"I don't think Adam tells others much about his troubles, Mr. Gannon."

"Up 'til now, he hasn't had any troubles, Ms. Thornton."

"Do you really believe that?"

"Well, I know Adam lost his temper in the courtroom, and that's not good. But it also seems as if this lady deserved everything she got from him." Gannon rested his ankle across his knee.

"The problem with Adam's outburst, Mr. Gannon, is that since he's been charged with murder, the judge will now associate the fact that he lost his temper with that crime. And you're correct that it's not good. It makes Adam seem more capable of a crime of that nature."

"Well, Adam's not capable of any crime."

"It may not look like that now to the judge. But Adam's rage and issues related to how he treats others shouldn't come up at trial, unless we raise it first, and we won't. Still, his lunge toward Mrs. Grayson was a threat. I'm glad there wasn't a jury to observe what he did. That sort of behavior's got to be kept in check. Have you ever seen Adam react like that before?"

"Not really. But if I was honest, I'd have to admit that I don't spend that much time with him. He sort of keeps to himself, or goes off with Joe. Always has."

"Would Mabel Grayson have any other reason to retaliate against Adam, other than you and your friends calling her 'Pioneer Woman' and making her cry?"

Gannon crossed his arms and put his head down as he thought about

Emma's question.

"Once we thought it might be fun to nominate her for homecoming queen, so we did. She didn't get it."

"What happened to her when she was nominated?"

"She got dressed up and came to the dance. They called out the name of the winner. It wasn't her. That's all."

"Did you see her that night? Did you notice whether she was hurt or crying or upset? "

"I remember seeing her, but I don't remember if she was upset. She really looked awful. I guess some of the kids laughed at her. Maybe some of the guys I was with laughed. Maybe I did, too. I hate to admit it, but we were just dumb kids, you know."

"You nominated her so you could make fun of her?"

"Maybe. Probably."

"Do you think she figured that out?"

"That's a possibility."

"Do you think she's taking that out against Adam now?"

"Well, if she is, it's ridiculous since she's an adult, and he's a kid."

"I agree, but do you think it's a possibility?"

He shrugged and nodded in agreement. Then he folded his hands and looked at them in his lap, appearing to cocoon himself in a protective outer layer, as if he wanted to avoid Emma's questions. The waiter appeared and saved him by taking their order.

"There's one other thing, but I don't think this is really anything," Robert said.

"Please continue."

"Mable is my sister's sister-in-law. In other words, my sister is married to Mable's brother."

"Well, that is something. Do the two families get along now? Your family and Mable's, that is."

"We never see them. Ever."

"What about you and your family and your sister's family?"

"Same. We never see each other, except I occasionally have Ben, that's my sister's son, do odd chores for me. But that's rare, and I've decided not to use him anymore."

"Why don't you want to use Ben?"

"It's just not a good idea to hire family."

"What's your sister's name?"

"Wilma."

"Why don't you and Wilma see each other?"

"My parents disowned Wilma when she married Ben's dad, George. George Bailey. Now that's a worthless one if there ever was one."

"And she didn't inherit anything after your parents died?"

"Nope."

"I see."

"Do you know whether Wilma harbors any resentment since she didn't inherit any of the family wealth?"

"I have no idea and I don't see why any of this is relevant."

"I'm sorry to bombard you with all of these questions, Mr. Gannon, but Mrs. Grayson's open hostility toward Adam should be explored and I thought there was a possibility it could be connected to Mrs. Bailey's disinheritance."

"I don't see how, but even if it was, what does it really matter?"

"The more I know, the better I can plan Adam's defense. Also, we've never gotten together one-on-one to discuss the case, and so many things have happened lately I wanted to ask you about. Adam's situation is even more serious now, and we need to step up our investigation. For instance, before the shooting, did you know where Adam kept his rifle?"

"No, ma'am, I didn't then and I don't now."

"Do you or Mrs. Gannon have a key to Adam's truck?"

"I believe we have a spare key somewhere at our house in the event Adam loses his key or needs help." Robert Gannon's knee began bouncing up and down like a needle in an old-fashioned sewing machine.

"I see. Did you ever use it?"

"No, ma'am, not that I recall." Robert Gannon pushed his chair back from the table and looked out over the remnants of the lunch crowd. "Sure is hot today." His face flushed beet red and little beads of perspiration began forming along his hairline. His eyes drifted toward the sun baked town square as if he wanted to make a run for it.

"I've always wanted to ask you why you gave your permission for the deputy to take the evidence the morning they came to Adam's apartment. What were you thinking?"

"Well, Adam also said it was okay and signed a consent form. And then, I also figured the sheriff was entitled to it. He could have come back with a warrant later anyway. I understood what was going on, and let them have it."

"Did you believe Adam understood what was happening?"

"I thought I could explain it to him later."

"Why did you think that was good enough?"

"That's the way we've always done things with Adam."

"How do you think Adam felt about that, Mr. Gannon?"

"I've never thought much about it. We've always done what we thought was best. I think Adam appreciates that."

"Did you ever meet any other of Adam's teachers at Greendale Academy beside Mabel Grayson?"

"No. But I knew a few of them. Went to school with them."

"Who do you know?"

"I went to high school there, with Adam's Coach, Jerry Smithfield. We were both on the football team. I was the quarterback. He was my receiver. Good player."

"Did he also know Mabel back then?"

"I really don't know. Look, it's hot and I'd like to find out what's going on down at the courthouse. I'm not sure what more you might need, but you know how to reach me."

Robert pushed his chair back even further and stood up. He extended his hand to Emma.

"Let me know if you need anything else."

Robert made his way to the courthouse, his unsteady gait betraying his pain.

Emma watched until him was out of sight. Estranged from his sister, detached from his son, and disconnected from his cruelties, Robert wasn't a kind and loving man. But was he a murderer? Until today, he'd never considered the consequences of the tricks he and his friends played on Mable Grayson. Emma couldn't blame Mabel for resenting Robert. But she didn't know why Mabel would allow her anger to spill over to Adam, or how far her hatred could go.

30

Adam sat on the corner of his bunk, his back flush against the wall of the cell, knees drawn to his chin, eyes closed. A fine line of perspiration had broken out above his upper lip. Although he appeared calm, meditative almost, he wasn't. His mind was racing. He'd allowed himself to get too upset, too angry, and he knew it. And he hated his cell. What had Joe told him to do when he was afraid? Breathe….

Adam began to inhale slowly and count to ten. His head started to clear and his hands stopped shaking. He felt his heart rate slow down. He gripped his head with his hands. Mrs. Grayson taunted him, and he knew she was trying to hurt him. She'd always hated him. He just didn't know why.

Adam's felt his pulse increase and his neck muscles tighten. He began to pace the length of the cell. He didn't want to have another panic attack. Falling to his knees he put his head down against the concrete floor and stretched out. The cool, smoothness of the polished floor calmed him, and he stayed there, until at last he closed his eyes and slept. He was found in that position several hours later by a guard who came by to tell him that he was being released and that Silas was waiting for him.

Silas was shocked by Adam's appearance. The once tanned and fit athlete had become gaunt and haggard overnight. But Silas was concerned with more than the dark circles under Adam's eyes. Something had disturbed him on a deeper level. Silas called Emma.

"Can you get down to the office this afternoon? I'm concerned about Adam. I'd like you to take a look at him."

"I guess so. What's up?"

"I know he doesn't like being jailed, but I've never seen a transformation like this. Everything about his demeanor and appearance has changed. I think we should get a psychiatric evaluation in addition to the competency evaluation. I'd like your insight, especially since you've been working with him more than I have."

Thirty minutes later Emma stepped into the conference room where Adam was waiting, and could see, instantly, that Silas was correct. In the last twenty-four hours Adam had undergone more than a physical change. He was defeated, detached and unresponsive. His eyes were flat, lifeless, as if he were in a daze. It was as if he'd checked out—given up.

She sat in front of him with a pencil and a pad of paper.

Adam, I'm sorry things went so badly in the courtroom yesterday, she wrote.

Adam looked at her notepad and nodded. She was relieved he had responded.

We are working on the problem with Mabel Grayson.

When Adam read this, his face flushed and the veins along his forehead became noticeable, but he didn't respond.

We spoke to your father about her to see what he might know about it.

Upon reading this, Adam pounded his fist on the conference room table, stood up and began pacing the room. He stopped suddenly and shouted at Emma. "No!"

He resumed pacing, and then, grabbing Emma's pencil wrote, *She is bad. Not me. My father does not no. You do not no.*

He stood up, quickly turned, and strode toward the door.

As Adam began to leave, both Emma and Silas attempted to block his exit. Emma reached out to him and Silas threw his body in Adam's path.

182

After the hearing, Silas had convinced the judge that Adam could be released on his own recognizance since he was not a flight risk. But the judge put a condition on the release, which required Adam to check in with pretrial services every week. Adam's first week began the day of his release. Adam's interpreter had explained this to Adam in court, but he hadn't understood. Unfortunately, neither Silas nor Emma had had the opportunity to show Adam where to report, and they knew he didn't understand what was required of him.

As soon as they tried to stop him, Adam's athletic instincts kicked in and he dodged their grasp by darting in the opposite direction. He bolted out of the conference room, and was out of the front door and in his truck, which was parked in front of Silas's office, in a matter of seconds. Before they knew what was happening, and could go after him, he was down the street.

Emma looked at Silas. "My ex-husband always told me I could mess up a soup sandwich. I never understood what he meant until now."

Emma was certain she knew where Adam was headed. Joe was Adam's teacher and guide, the one person in his world he could trust, and the person he knew he could rely on without criticism or judgment.

Fifteen minutes later, Emma arrived at Joe's. She walked up to the porch and knocked. Joe opened the screen door.

Emma explained what had happened over the course of the past two days. Joe shook his head as he motioned her inside his home, offering her one of his ever-present glasses of lemonade.

"So, you haven't seen Adam?"

"No, ma'am. Not today. Things aren't lookin' too good, are they?" Joe motioned for Emma to sit down.

"Well, it could be better. Any idea where Adam would go if he didn't come here?" Joe had been putting together a jigsaw puzzle on the coffee table. A picture of a racehorse. Five hundred pieces.

"He could be anywhere. I got a few ideas. But it'd be like looking for a needle in a haystack. You may as well wait for him to show up at this point.

He will, I'm sure of it."

"Well, I'm not. He didn't seem to be himself after he got out of jail. Have you ever known Adam to be...um...a little irrational?"

"Adam can get upset sometimes."

"Well, the situation I told you about yesterday in the courtroom would have been tough for anyone, but Adam couldn't control his reaction to it and it could harm him a lot. If he doesn't stop this sort of thing, it could cost him the trial."

Joe sighed and shook his head.

"Have you ever seen anything like that before in Adam?"

"He do have some of those problems, but you be asking a lot of the boy." Joe rubbed his head with his hand as if he were trying to soothe a deep pain.

"What do you mean?"

"Well for one thing, Adam get all panicky in small, dark spaces and a jail cell is small and dark, so that's one thing that got him upset. We found that out when he was a kid playin' hide and seek. He just can't be enclosed in places. I guess he loses too much of his other senses that a way. He panics. Starts losin' his breath. So, I understand why he got upset when he was in jail. I know he done it the first time he was in there too. He just didn't run from you guys then."

"Well, he chose a bad time to run. And a panic attack doesn't explain what happened to him in the courtroom. By the way, do you know anything about Mabel Grayson?"

"Can't say that I do."

Emma shook her head. "We've got to do something about that woman. I can't believe Silas got him out of jail after the second arrest. Silas convinced the judge Adam wasn't a flight risk. But it appears Silas was wrong."

"I know Adam's done nothin' wrong. Adam couldn't have done nothin' wrong." Joe's eyes began to well with tears.

Emma reached out and touched Joe's arm.

"I'm sorry, Joe. I believe you. But unless we find Adam soon, he'll be in a lot of trouble with pretrial services which means he'll be in trouble with the judge again.."

"I know of a couple of fishin' camps where we can start."

"Tell me where they are and if he doesn't show up tonight, we'll start there in the morning."

31

Emma pulled into the parking space in front of her apartment.

"Mommy, are we gonna have pizza tonight?"

Friday nights were the nights the kids got to choose what to eat, within reason.

"I think that's what Billy wanted. What about you?"

"Yeah!"

"Well, then it's decided!"

"What topping do you want, Bobby? Billy wants pepperoni." This was a decision that Bobby could ponder for quite some time, but Billy could always be counted on for the same choice. Following nearly five minutes of deliberation, Bobby made his call for meatball topping, and, finally, everything was ordered.

The delivery of the pizza was a time for celebration. Then it was dinner, a little homework, TV, and bath time for the kids. To Emma, there was nothing quite as wonderful as the transformation of a squirrely smelling little boy to a squeaky clean one, with shiny cheeks, wet hair and sweet smells. The twins were still cuddly at bedtime too, but she knew that wouldn't last much longer. They were already all elbows and lanky angles, outgrowing clothes and shoes at an alarming rate. She read them a story and put them to bed at a reasonable hour.

At 8:30 the twins were sound asleep. Emma picked up her Federal

Jurisdiction casebook and began reading the next day's assigned cases. After reading for nearly an hour, she dozed off.

Around 11:00 Emma woke up, and prepared for bed. Since she slept in the living room, she faced the street, and all of the lights and noise that accompanied that. It was often difficult for her to drift off to sleep. But tonight, after she turned off the last light, she was out in a matter of minutes.

Emma wasn't certain what woke her up, whether she had a dream, whether she heard a noise, or sensed something was wrong. When she opened her eyes, she also opened her mouth to scream, but a strong, bony hand was instantly on her throat clutching it tightly, digging into the flesh of her neck so forcefully she couldn't make a sound, and could hardly breathe.

"You're gonna come along with me, little miss smarty-pants."

His breath was hot and nasty smelling. Cigarettes. His voice was familiar too, nasal, with an unmistakable twang. He was nothing but a silhouette, a shape, but it was a recognizable form, a thin, loose, lanky profile. One she'd seen before. Ben Bailey. At least she knew whom she was dealing with.

"Make any sound at all and I'll just kill ya right here. You understand?"

Emma nodded.

He pulled something out of a back pocket. Duct tape. He grabbed one of her arms and flipped her over so that she was face down on the couch and then roughly pulled both arms behind her and taped her wrists together. Grabbing her by her hair, he pulled her off of the couch and on to her feet.

Even though the house was dark, the streetlights illuminated the living room well enough to see certain features, but Emma didn't want Ben to know that she recognized him. She also didn't want to alert him to the fact that she heard Billy's bedroom door open.

"What are you going to do?"

"That's for me to know and you to find out, which isn't too far off from now. Let's see, ain't you got some kids in here?"

"Leave them out of this!"

"Now, you know I can't do that."

"They have nothing to do with anything."

"Well, it just wouldn't be complete without the kids."

"What wouldn't be complete? I don't get what you're talking about. What are you doing? Who are you working for?"

"Now, aren't we getting chatty? Shut up!" He hissed. "I told you not to make any noise."

Ben turned toward the hallway and the children's bedrooms. Emma threw her body against him and knocked him off balance. She butted her head into the small of his back, which pitched him to the ground. As he was struggling to his feet, she kneed him in the groin. Taking advantage of his momentary pain, she ran to the kitchen for a knife. By that time, Ben was on his feet, and right behind her. He took out a knife from his back pocket, grabbed her around her throat with one wiry arm and placed the tip of the dagger under her chin.

"Don't think I don't want to finish you off, 'cause I do. I just been told not to leave a mess. So I'm gonna wait to kill you. And getting the kids is a part 'a not leaving a mess too. So I'm getting 'em."

Ben pulled Emma down the hallway with him to the kids' bedrooms. He opened Billy's door first. Emma peered around Ben's shoulder. The bed was empty. Ben walked inside the room and looked under the bed and inside the closet, pulling Emma along with him. He then turned around and walked down the hallway to Bobby's room and opened his door. Bobby's room was empty as well. Ben flung back the covers of Bobby's bed and stabbed first under the bed and then throughout Bobby's closet with his knife in a frenzied attempt to find him.

"How do you explain this?" he said, turning toward Emma and pointing toward the empty room with the knife still dangling loosely in his hand.

"My kids spent the night at a friend's house."

"Then why didn't you say that earlier? Why didn't you just say they weren't here when I said I wanted to take them?"

"I was upset."

"Somehow I don't believe you, Ms. Thornton."

Ben swung around and punched Emma in the face, causing her to lose her balance and fall to the floor. He pulled out a black canvas bag he had had folded in his jacket pocket, slipped it over her head, tied it securely around her neck, and opened the front door. Looking around for any neighbors, he picked Emma up, flung her over his shoulder, and left the apartment, closing the door behind him. He threw Emma in the back of the black Chevy pick-up truck and drove off just as she was beginning to rouse. It was 3:20 in the morning.

32

September 8, 1990

Emma was dazed and disoriented as she bumped down the road in the truck bed. But even so, she was proud of her children. Their plan had worked. She wasn't sure how they had awakened, especially at 3:00 in the morning. They must have heard Ben Bailey break in or perhaps they heard him speaking. It didn't really matter since they did what they were supposed to do. Emma and her children had a system worked out in the event the Peeping Tom, stalker, or any other person who wished them harm showed up at their apartment again. As quietly as possible, Billy, who was the lighter sleeper of the two, was to go to Bobby's room, wake him up, and open his window. Then Emma had instructed them to climb out, which was easy since they were on the first floor, close the window, which was nearly as important, and run to the apartment next door. They even did a pretend walk through of the escape plan as if was a game one day. Bobby thought it was fun. The neighbors had agreed to help out in advance. She was shocked that it worked so well when it came down to the real-life event. Her kids had been so brave and didn't make a sound. She shuddered to think of what would have happened to them if they hadn't prepared for this.

Emma started picking at the tape on her wrist until it had peeled about halfway off. When they first headed out, even though she couldn't see, she thought she could keep up with where they were headed by the turns in the road. But after they turned off of the main highway onto a gravel road, she realized she had no idea where they were. She knew that her children and the neighbors had already told the authorities what had happened, but Ben had pulled off of the main roads and highways so soon after leaving her parking lot, she wasn't sure she would be found. She didn't have much time.

Who would be behind this? How did they think they could murder the law clerk for Adam's attorney and get away with it? Emma paused for a moment and took in her circumstances. Her face hurt. And, with her hands taped behind her back, her shoulders ached. She couldn't see a thing and could hardly breathe. Perhaps they were getting away with it. But why did they want to kill her?

Emma nearly had the tape undone from her wrist. Once that was done, she had to tackle the canvas bag. As she pulled the final piece of tape off of her wrist, the truck slowed to a stop. She heard cussing from the cab as a truck drove by.

"Who the fuck's that? Who would be driving around here tonight?"

Emma, blinded by the canvas bag, sat up in the back of the truck, hoping the truck driver, whoever he was, could see her.

Ben put the truck in park, grabbed his shotgun from the back of his window, and slid out of the seat.

"Get down, stupid bitch."

He hit Emma in the head with the butt of the gun. Then he grabbed some rope from the back of the cab and trussed her up, hooking the rope into the eyelets along the bed of the truck, crisscrossing it down the length of the canvas bag and wrapping it around her body so she couldn't move, much as a pig about to be pit roasted.

Sheriff Colson got the call around 3:30 in the morning from his night clerk.

Emma's neighbor had called in to say she had Emma's children and had informed him of the abduction. Three days earlier, at the recommendation of Deputy Glass, the department had called off the overnight deputy who'd been watching Emma's house. Deputy Glass had convinced the sheriff and everyone else that there was no reason to waste county money on the extra manpower.

The sheriff dreaded the call to Ren.

A groggy voice answered the phone, but it didn't take him long to wake up. "What do you mean Emma's been abducted? Wasn't there a deputy on duty at her house?"

The sheriff explained the situation with the acting chief deputy to Ren.

"That arrogant son-of-a-bitch. I ought to come down there and kick his ass. I always thought that guy was a jerk. What were you doing making him the acting chief deputy anyway?"

"Look, Ren, I know you're upset, but there's really nothing you can do. We've got all cars but yours out looking for Emma right now. All highways as well as back roads are covered. We'll find her. We're looking for the truck. The neighbors said that a dark-colored truck took off from the parking lot right after the kids got to their place. We have to assume that was him. It was a little after three in the morning, so they couldn't be certain it was black, but it was dark."

"Nah, I'm coming down there."

"How are you going to do that? Can you drive with your leg in a cast?"

"It's a soft cast. I can figure it out."

"I'm asking you to stay put. You're off duty. You can't come in. You're upset. It would be a mistake, Ren. I just wanted to tell you before you saw it on the news."

"I hear you, but I'm not making any promises."

"Just so you know, there's something else. There was a problem during a hearing and Adam was arrested. The judge let him out but put him on probation. Then Adam didn't report in like he was supposed to, and now there's a warrant out for his arrest. I don't know if any of that is related to Emma's kidnapping or not."

Ren hung up the phone. There was no way he was staying at home while Emma was out there at the mercy of that man, whoever he was. And what was going on with Adam? Could he be the stalker and now the kidnapper? If only he didn't have this stupid cast. He'd have to risk it. It was his left foot, and his shoulder was much better now. He should be able to drive. He grabbed his keys.

Joe thought he heard something and sat up in the cot. He was at the fishing camp he and Adam liked to visit years ago. He had his nephew drop him off earlier hoping that Adam might come by. He wanted to speak to him about the hearing, and that Mrs. Grayson, and everything that had him upset. Maybe that noise was Adam driving up right now.

He pushed himself up from the cot, put his slippers on, and peeked out of the curtains. He could see lights approaching, and could tell that they were from a truck. He put on his pants, grabbed his walker and stepped out on the porch.

As the truck drove up the gravel entrance of the camp, Joe inched forward, waving as it approached. The truck stopped, slammed into reverse and careened backward down the driveway at a considerable speed until Joe couldn't see it any longer.

Joe went back inside shaking his head. "I could 'a sworn that was Adam. Sure looked like his truck."

Emma's body slammed against the ropes as the truck was thrown into reverse. She heard loud cussing from the cab again, this time louder than the last.

"What the fuck are all of these people doing in the woods tonight? It's a regular convention. Let's all meet in the mother fucking woods!" Ben banged his hand against the steering wheel. "FUCK! Fucking Joe doesn't even drive! How'd he even get there?" He swerved the truck, turning it in the opposite direction and barreled down the road at break neck speed.

By this time Emma had figured out two things. Ben was seeking out a camp or a location where he could not only kill her but use the site to hide the means of disposing of her body, or his technique for not making a mess. She didn't know if he would chop her up, or use chemicals, but he needed a structure to hide the processing of whatever method he chose. Otherwise, he'd shoot her and be done with it. Ben must be acting at the instruction of someone else. She couldn't imagine he was capable of thinking through so many possibilities. She knew she held all the clues and had triggered this entire debacle by uncovering something during the investigation of Jennifer Patrick's murder. If she could resolve that, she'd know who was behind her kidnapping, and would know who Jennifer's killer was. But the way things were going, she'd be dead before she figured it all out.

33

Emma was vain, but had little money to keep up appearances. She couldn't afford manicures, but discovered that she could make up for the lack of one by applying a protein enriched polish to her fingernails every night. This stuff made her nails look great and had the added benefit of turning them into oval-shaped daggers. Her nails had become her handiest tool. She'd repaired Bobby's model airplane with her right index fingernail the day before yesterday.

When Ben pulled up to what Emma thought might be the final stop, she was prepared for him. She had managed to free her arms from the duct tape and even though they were sore and her body ached from the long ride, she was poised and ready to defend herself. Ben began untying the complicated roping system he had secured around Emma's body. Once it was undone, and he'd removed the hood from her head, Emma sprang toward Ben, aimed for his eyes with her thumbnails, and dug into his sockets with as much force as she could muster. She ripped her fingernails all the way down his face. She felt his flesh give way under her fingertips. Ben howled in agony. She blinded him long enough to escape the truck.

Emma hadn't thought beyond that point. She was in her pajamas, barefooted and in the woods at four in the morning. She wasn't familiar with the area and she was pretty sure Ben Bailey was, although she hoped that for a while, at least, he wouldn't be able to see her or anything else. She started running as fast as she could into the inky black woods. Even though she had substantial calluses on her feet from her daily runs, the twigs on the floor of the forest were painful. She hoped there weren't snakes. And she knew Ben wouldn't be far behind.

Ren knew that Emma could be anywhere. Even though he didn't want to think about it, she could already be dead, lying in a dump or in the lake. He felt his pulse quickening. Or, if she was alive, she could be headed across the state line by now. The possibilities were endless. But he didn't think Emma's kidnapper would chose an interstate highway crowded with law enforcement as their escape route. If Emma was still alive, she'd be on a back road somewhere. So, that was where he was. Even though driving randomly through the back thoroughfares of the county might be useless, it made him feel better. There were a few abandoned fishing and hunting camps along the lake in the outskirts of Greendale County. He thought he'd check those out, plus the old state roads out by the lake could provide an alternate access across state lines.

Ren realized Emma's kidnapper had to be someone who was involved in the Jennifer Patrick murder, and that Emma must have uncovered something significant during her investigation. All of the troubles in the case began with the Peeping Tom incident, about two weeks after Jennifer's murder. Lola Mae was killed right afterwards, but he didn't know what could have triggered either event.

Ren had concluded that Lola Mae's husband, Roosevelt, was not a suspect in her murder. All of his alibis checked out. Even though he thought Lola Mae's homicide had to be linked to the Gannons, he didn't know why they'd want her dead. Who would want all three women, Lola Mae, Jennifer, and Emma dead?

Ren's headlights highlighted the cluster of trees that lined the narrow road. He could only see ten feet or so in front of his truck. Beyond that was a cave-like velvety blackness. Occasionally, a small creature would be captured for a moment, frozen in time by the beam of white light. He thought he might have seen a rabbit or perhaps it was a fox. He was creeping along well below the speed limit, eyes peeled for anything unusual.

He rounded a bend and saw in the near distance a flicker of a light glowing in what he knew was one of the fishing camps facing the lake. He drove down the gravel drive leading to the camp house and was surprised to see there wasn't a vehicle in the driveway or one parked close to the camp. With some difficulty, he got out of his truck, making certain he had his gun visibly exposed in its holster, and knocked on the door.

Joe answered, and looked down at Ren's badge and gun. "Can I help you, Officer?"

"Maybe. First, can you identify yourself? I presume you're the owner of this cabin, or have authority to be here. I don't see a truck or any other vehicle, and I'm a little curious about how you got here. Also, it's not exactly hunting season and they say the fish haven't been biting since June."

"I'm Joe Casey. I asked my nephew to drop me off last night. Is there some kind of trouble or somethin'? This here is the old Gannon camp, and ain't no one been here for years. The Gannons don't care if I stay here. You can ask. I used to be their foreman, and still live on Gannon property down by the stables. You want to see some ID?" Joe opened the door wider. "You're welcome to come inside." Joe turned with his walker and gestured toward the camp's interior. "I can fix you a cup of coffee if you'd like."

"That's fine. You don't need to show me your identification. I believe I've heard Emma Thornton speak of you before. I don't have much time, but I need to know if you noticed anything unusual since you've been here tonight."

"Well, there was one thing. A truck. Not that it was all that unusual, but the time it drove down here was, and then the driver backed down the driveway kind of crazy."

"What kind of truck? What happened?" Ren stepped inside.

"Well, at first I thought it was Adam's truck, that'd be Adam Gannon, since I was hopin' to see him tonight." Joe maneuvered his walker closer to Ren. "But I didn't get a good look at anythin' 'cause as soon as the truck neared the cabin, it slammed into reverse and started to back outta here, fast as it could go."

"How do you know it was a truck then?"

"Well, I saw that much. And the lights looked like the lights on Adam's truck, too. But I don't know why he'd act like that if he saw me, 'cause I stepped out and waved to him. So, I'm sure it wasn't Adam."

"Could you see the color of the truck?"

"It was a dark color, maybe black. Hard to tell."

"I hate to tell you this, but it looks like Emma Thornton has been taken, kidnapped, actually, from her apartment, at around three this morning. We think the person who took her is in a dark colored truck. Do you think Adam could have done this or do you think he might know something about it?"

"No way! I sure am sorry to hear about Miss Emma, but ain't no way Adam had anything to do with no kidnappin'. Emma's been trying to help him. He knows that."

"Maybe Emma uncovered something about the Jennifer Patrick murder that Adam didn't want her to know about."

"No, sir, that can't be true. I know Adam. He had nothin' to do with murdering Jennifer Patrick and he would never harm Miss Emma."

"Well, things aren't looking so good for Adam right now. He's violated a court order for failure to report to pretrial services, so if I see him, I'll have to arrest him."

Joe stared down at the floor.

"It may not look so good for Adam, but I know what I know. Adam wouldn't have no cause to kidnap or hurt Ms. Emma."

"I hope you're right, and I hope I didn't upset you. I'm headed down to the next camp. Thought I'd look around a little."

"Be careful there, now. There's a bog down close to the lake that has a little patch of quicksand in it that catches a deer nearly every year. Nothing can be done with anything once it gets caught in that mud."

Ren nodded his thanks to Joe and climbed back in his truck.

34

Emma's eyes had adjusted to the near total darkness of the woods. She could see the outline of the trees and could differentiate between the scrub bushes so that she could avoid them as she ran, but her feet were gouged by twigs and debris from the floor of the forest. She knew they had to be bleeding by now. On a good day, Emma could run a seven-minute mile, but this was not a good day. By her calculations, she had about a five-minute advance on Ben Bailey. She was certain that he had started after her by now.

As she ran, she could see the moon sparkling on the lake to the west, and instinctively took a turn in that direction, since the path was more clearly illuminated along the body of water. Within seconds, she found herself up to her knees in a swampy, muddy silt that seemed to suck her down further every time she moved. She squinted at what appeared to be the path to the lake and realized that even though it was filled with vegetation, it was actually a bog of some sort, which was why it reflected light. She'd heard of these places. It looked solid, but it wasn't. She needed to find a tree branch or a bush, or something to hold onto so she could pull herself out of the quagmire. But the only vegetation within reach were marsh grasses and reeds. When she tried to pull her legs out of the bog, she sank deeper. But, when she moved her body backwards, her toes, then her legs were able to inch out, ever so gradually.

The smell of the place made her dizzy. It reminded her of rotting carcasses, swampy rotten vegetation and, it was unmistakable—sewage. She shuddered, remembering something she had learned about septic tanks and cracked terra cotta piping, and how rural areas often allowed sewage to drain into lakes and rivers. She wondered about the content of the slippery, sticky mud she found herself sinking in. She was also absolutely certain a dead animal was nearby. Even though it was still early fall and the temperature was relatively warm, Emma was chilled to the bone. Her clothes were damp with the oily mud-like substance and were stuck to her skin. A slight breeze had kicked up from the north, and she was beginning to shake uncontrollably from exposure and adrenaline. She hadn't made much progress at removing herself from the bog before she heard stumbling and shuffling noises. Suddenly, Ben Bailey emerged from the nearby thicket.

Emma had no choice but to recline on her back, grabbing protective long grasses for support. To her relief, in doing so, her feet were released even more from the gripping mud. At this angle, she was also able to see Ben's face, which was illuminated by the moon. The light captured certain features and deepened the shadows of others so that, along with the damage she had done to his eyes, his face took on a ghostly distortion. There had been substantial bleeding from the wounds of her earlier attack, which had dripped down his face and onto his shirt. But most of the bleeding was in and around his eyes. From the way he was stumbling around, it was obvious he was only able to see shadows and faint images. She was horrified with what she had done, but hoped with all her heart he couldn't see her.

Ben moved uncomfortably close to Emma and started poking the ground with his rifle.

"Bog's here somewhere." He stuck his leg out and patted the ground with the toe of his boot. "Yep, ground's wet," he said after hearing tiny splashes made by the contact.

Ben turned and began to make his way back through the underbrush. As he did, a figure appeared from behind Emma and hit Ben on the back of the head with what looked to be a large stick or branch. Ben fell to the ground.

As the person turned, Emma could see that her rescuer was Adam. Adam!

Shocked, but thankful to see him, she had no time to question his sudden appearance. Keeping her body on a horizontal plane, her feet continued to release, slowly, from the muck. With Adam's help she was free within a few minutes.

Emma grabbed a twig and tried to scrape off the wet mud from her legs. Then, hoping to avoid waking the unconscious Ben, she grabbed Adam's arm and motioned to him, indicating they needed to run. Adam nodded. At that moment, Ben shook his head and pulled himself up to his knees.

Adam grabbed Emma by the arm and, running past Ben, began pulling her through the woods as fast as he could go. She was limping, and Adam was half dragging her through the woods, but even if Adam had to pick her up and carry her, they could still run faster than a half-blind Ben. And even though Ben had a rifle, the possibilities of him hitting them were pretty slim.

As if on cue, shots rang out and zipped through the trees around them, hitting several nearby branches. Emma pantomimed a gun with her hands to let Adam know.

Adam zigzagged randomly around trees and boulders, dragging Emma behind him as if they were on a basketball court, dodging bullets instead of guards. The odds weren't great, but they didn't have a choice. Adam was making as straight a path as possible to the clearing and his truck.

Ren pulled up to the third and last campsite along the lake, and was surprised to see a black truck parked there in full view. He could see that a struggle had taken place. The door of the truck was open; the cab was empty. There was a black hood on the floor of the bed. Ropes that had been laced in the eyelets along the truck bed had been undone, as if someone had either escaped or had been released. And there was blood. Blood was found on the tailgate, pooled under the truck, and trickled along the driveway, towards the woods. There was no rifle in the truck, although there was an empty shotgun rack along the back window.

Ren peered into the windows of the cabin. The lights weren't on, but there were signs someone might have been there earlier. A coffee pot light was on, glowing red in the distance. He tried the front door, but it was locked. He walked around to the back and found a screen door which was ajar.

He drew his gun as he entered a small kitchen through the back door. He checked the sink. It was clean with the exception of one recently used cup, the dregs of fresh grounds still clinging to the bottom. Feeling his way along the side of the wall into the den, he checked the room for signs of occupancy. It was also empty, as were the bedroom and bathroom. Whoever had been there was gone. And the bed hadn't been slept in. He checked the refrigerator for provisions. None. It didn't seem as if the occupant had planned to stay.

Ren got back in his truck and took a slow drive back down the gravel driveway to look for clues. Spying a small clearing he hadn't noticed earlier, he shone his flashlight inside, and noticed, for the first time, another vehicle hidden within the brambles. He parked his truck along the side of the road, and got out to inspect.

As he approached the covered vehicle, he could tell by its shape that it was a truck. It was still dark, so its color and make was difficult to discern. He shined his flashlight on the surface of the truck so its bright blue color was revealed through the vines and leaves. He knew he had found Adam's truck. He radioed the sheriff.

Emma had stepped on a sharp stone and had bruised one of her heels. This slowed them down considerably and, even though they knew he couldn't see very well, Ben Bailey was gaining on them. Emma was in pain. Once they could see the outline of the old state road, Adam turned, scooped Emma up and began running. At the same time, one of Ben's stray bullets grazed her shoulder.

A thicket of trees surrounding a large boulder lay ahead, and Adam sped with Emma toward the sheltered area. He placed her on the ground, on the side of the rock protected by a large pine tree, until he could get his bearings and check on Emma's shoulder. Scanning the area for Ben, he checked with Emma, pantomiming, to see if she was able to run. She nodded and they emerged from behind the rock and ran, with all the strength they had, toward the clearing.

As they neared the open area, Adam guided her toward the road. He was in front when they approached the clearing and continued to stay ahead of Emma, holding on to her arm.

When they stepped out on to the road, the sheriff and his men surrounded Adam.

"Put your hands behind your head and get down on your knees." They motioned with their guns toward Adam, pointing to the ground. One deputy walked over and put handcuffs on Adam's wrist.

"Wait!" Emma screamed. "Don't do that! Adam saved my life. He rescued me! Ben Bailey is the kidnapper and he's still out there. Don't waste your time here! He's not far away! He's right back there, probably in that thicket." She pointed toward a clump of trees. "He's got a rifle, too. Didn't you hear it? He just shot at us!"

"Emma, you're shot!" Ren rushed to Emma's side.

"With everything else going on I didn't even notice until it started bleeding." She collapsed, sitting down on the road. She put her head on her knees for a moment, then looked up. "Please, Ren. Get your men to go out there and find Ben Bailey. Adam shouldn't be handcuffed."

"They've gone after Ben."

"What about Adam?"

"They've got him in the squad car."

"Ren, certainly you're not going to arrest him. I would think he's had enough of jail for one week. You shouldn't have put him in the squad car after he saved my life."

"Well, we'll get to the bottom of all of this. You can tell us all about it. Let's take a look at your shoulder. We're calling an ambulance for you right now."

"I don't want you to get too close to me. I got stuck in a bog and I'm covered in disgusting stuff. You can't believe how awful that was. I can only imagine what was in there. I'm probably toxic."

"Bogs are mostly rotting vegetation unless an animal also fell in and its carcass added an additional scent to the festering mess." Ren smiled, but seeing no response from Emma, continued. "But you shouldn't have been exposed to anything toxic."

"I'm more concerned about Adam. You shouldn't be detaining him right now."

"There's an issue with a violation of a court order. I'm sure you know about the pre-trial services thing. It should be able to be dealt with quickly. Don't worry."

"Just so you know, there was a screw up when Adam was released. He never understood anything about that court order. It was our fault, really, not Adam's."

"Okay, Emma. You may not realize it, but you've got to be in shock or something close to it. Adam will be dealt with fairly, I promise. We need to take you to the hospital, get your shoulder taken care of, and get you cleaned up. You've been through a terrible experience."

Emma heard the ambulance approaching and walked up to the squad car. She looked through the window at Adam. He refused to turn his head in her direction, but she saw a tear tracing the outline of his cheek.

35

"You shouldn't be here. I'm not sure what you think you can do. Adam's locked up at least until I can get another hearing date." Silas stood up and walked over to the door where Emma was standing and gave her a hug. "You can serve the case and yourself better by going home and resting. You've been through a lot. How are you feeling, anyway?"

"Okay. A little shaken. They patched me up at the hospital. My arm looks worse than it is. But I've got a bad bruise from a rock on my heel. They said I bruised the bone. The doctors told me to stay home, but I wanted to talk to you about Adam."

"Well, come on in for a minute, then you need to get back home. Follow your doctor's orders." Silas strode back to his desk. "Can I get you anything, coffee, water?"

"I'm really fine, Silas. You know they've got no business putting Adam in jail this time," Emma said.

"He's in on a technicality—violation of a court order. I'll file a motion today for an expedited hearing on the motion for his release."

"Glad to hear that."

"By the way, someone was in that cabin where Ben stopped the night you were kidnapped. Deputy Taylor apparently inspected the place about the time you and Ben were running through the woods, then, after they found you and all the excitement died down, the deputies went back. They found evidence and fingerprints proving that Adam had been inside the cabin. So, now they suspect, especially Acting Chief Deputy Glass, that Adam may be involved somehow with Ben Bailey."

"Well, that's ridiculous. The fact that he was at the cabin proves nothing. By the way, I never really heard. Did they arrest Ben?"

"Yes, but he's not talking. I thought he'd sing like a canary, but so far he hasn't. Boy, from what I heard, you did a number on his eyes. I doubt if the man will ever have his full vision again."

"I did what I had to, to escape." Emma looked down at her hands.

"Of course. And what's this I hear about you falling in a bog? You've really been through it, Emma. You're lucky to be alive."

"That's the understatement of the year." Emma pursed her lips.

"And, you're right, the sheriff's position is pretty weak. They found Adam's truck hidden in the brambles down the road. They put that together with the fact that he was at the camp and came up with the theory that Adam and Ben acted in concert. But Adam saved you from Ben, so it's counter-intuitive if you ask me. Deputy Glass thinks Adam couldn't go through with the plan and changed his mind at the last minute. He also thinks there's a connection between Adam and Ben because both trucks are owned by Adam's dad. But I don't think any of it makes sense."

"So, why does he think Adam and Ben would want to kill me?" Emma asked.

"He thinks you've uncovered something Adam, in particular, doesn't want you to know."

"It's my job to investigate. Adam's never been upset about that. Where's Deputy Glass coming from?"

"It's not really been your job to investigate. It's your job to prepare motions, and review evidence. I always thought you went a little overboard with the investigation. You're aggressive and thorough, which I like. But sometimes you're too aggressive and too thorough, which has had a few bad consequences. Still, I don't know of anything you've uncovered in all of your digging around that could connect Adam to your kidnapping."

"Do you know whether there will be any charges brought against Adam for the breaking and entering and the fact they found his fingerprints at the cabin?"

"No, the owners don't want to press charges. They've known Adam for years. They didn't have a problem with him spending some time at their camp. They never use it, apparently."

"Ren said Joe was at the Gannon camp. Think that's why Adam broke into their friend's place?"

Silas shrugged. "Looks like a possibility."

"So, do you think the sheriff will let Adam go?"

"The only valid reason to keep him in jail would be his failure to check in with pre-trial services. So let's hope we can get the expedited hearing, and that the judge is lenient with him. I don't know what good it does anyone for Adam to sit in jail. I should know soon."

"Jail seems like a cruel sentence for Adam because it makes him so anxious. Maybe it's even an Eighth Amendment violation, cruel and unusual punishment."

"Jail isn't unusual punishment. And I don't think it rises to the level of cruelty, even for a person with an anxiety disorder triggered by small dark spaces. If it did, everyone would fabricate a phobia about incarceration and no one would ever serve time. But it might be worth looking into," Silas said. "First we'd have to prove he has an anxiety disorder."

Emma nodded. "I've not been able to get in touch with that forensic psychiatrist, but I'll try again. You wanted to get him tested anyway."

Silas peered at Emma over the case he'd been reading earlier. "Yes. The court will appoint someone to test him for competency purposes too. And the judge will have to arrange that before the trial. I think I'd rather keep it simple at this hearing. It isn't necessary to get into Adam's emotional and anxiety issues. We should just set out that Adam took off before we could explain that he was required to pre-trial services. And we need to emphasize he didn't understand the interpreter's translation in court that day either."

"Shouldn't the judge know that Adam loses it when he's confined in a cell?

You know the longer Adam stays in that cell, the worse he'll get. If we get him tested, then the doctor will be able to tell if treatment or medication for his anxiety might be necessary, at least."

"We should get him tested for competency issues since the court is. The evaluation could be used to counter the court's expert. So move forward. And we could also find additional support for our competency argument, which was what I was looking for in the first place," Silas said.

Ren pulled out the chair, and sat down next to Emma. The waiter walked over to see if he wanted anything to drink, but he waved him off. He'd only come to see Emma. He wasn't interested in lunch. He knew he'd find her at Lucky's. She was there every time her schedule would allow an end-of-the-week treat. He was concerned about her. She'd always been a small person, but now she seemed tiny, fragile even. She'd been through a terrible ordeal, even though she tended to play down her problems. She hadn't said much of anything about what she'd been through to anyone yet, that he knew of.

"Feeling better, I hope?"

"The key lime pie I get after lunch every Friday always helps."

"Feel like talking about your run-in in the woods?"

"Nope."

"You've got to give us a little more than you did at four this morning. I know you're tired."

"I can't. And I can't sleep. Can't stand being in my apartment either." The wind blew the hair away from Emma's face and blouse, revealing bruises along her cheek and upper arm. Her eyelid was swollen and was beginning to darken into a considerable black eye. Her left arm was bandaged and in a sling and her left foot was wrapped as well.

"Looks like you're working on quite the shiner."

"Yep. Never had one of those. Never thought I would either. Now I'm wondering why I was so eager to continue working on this case after the first sign of trouble. Things have gotten much worse since then."

"I'm so sorry, Emma."

"Me too. I'm just so thankful my kids are okay, though. I don't know what I'm going to tell them." A tear started down her cheek. She covered her eyes. "I didn't want to start this. I may not be able to stop." Tears streamed down her face. "I'm just so proud of the boys. What if they hadn't escaped?" She kept her hands over her eyes hiding her tears, then, taking a deep breath, dug in her purse for a tissue, wiped the mascara from under her eyes, and her nose. "It's really okay, and they got him. They got Ben Bailey."

Ren squeezed her hand. "If we weren't in a public place I'd give you a big hug, Emma. I think you need one. And I don't believe this would have happened if I'd been there. I can't believe that jerk wad acting chief deputy pulled your night duty protection. I feel just awful for you and the kids. But we need you to come down and give us your statement pretty soon. Think you can do that?"

Emma nodded.

"I don't want you to forget any of the details."

"That would be impossible. But I'll walk down to the sheriff's office once I've had lunch. Don't you want to order something too?"

"Guess so."

"By the way, I thought you were on sick leave for six weeks. What's up with your involvement in my case?"

"I got my doc's okay to return to light duty just this morning. I've got to be careful, but I wanted to. It's important to me. I care about you and the kids, Emma." He squeezed her arm. "I'm not going to leave you alone again."

Emma smiled as the waiter approached. Ren placed his usual lunch request—the special of the day—which on Fridays was meatloaf, mashed potatoes and green beans, and Emma ordered her usual Cobb salad. They were both creatures of habit. It gave them a sense of continuity and stability.

"And what do you think about getting off of the case now? Think it might be a good idea?" Ren scrutinized Emma's face as he took a sip from his water glass.

"If you can make certain my boys are protected, there's no chance I'm quitting now. Ben Bailey isn't going to get away with my kidnapping, and I'm more convinced than ever that Adam is innocent."

About an hour later, Emma and Ren walked into to the sheriff's office. Emma sat by Ren's desk while he looked for the proper form for Emma's statement. Just then, she heard a familiar jangling sound and looked up. Sure enough, it was Frankie, the lanky deputy she had met the day she reviewed the evidence. It seemed like a year ago, but it hadn't even been a month.

"I sure am sorry to hear about what happened to you, Miss Emma, but I'm glad it turned out so good. You gave ole Ben Bailey a run for his money. Bet he wished he'd never met you! Man! You did a number on his eyes! Ooo wheee!"

Emma tried to smile.

"They're bringing ol' Ben down to the interrogation room right now. I think the sheriff's going to take a crack at him."

Frankie sauntered off, the cacophony of his keys noisily banging down the hall as he walked.

"Do you want to watch the sheriff interrogate Ben through the two-way?"

"I can do that?"

"I don't see why not, unless you'll find it too upsetting."

"No, in fact, I'd be happier if I could do it myself."

"You know that can't be arranged," Ren smiled. "You'll have to be satisfied with looking in."

The interrogation room was tiny, only ten-by-ten or so, the size of a small bedroom. It contained nothing more than a long government-issue metal table and two metal chairs.

Ben was there, seated at the table. He was alone. Gauze had been wrapped around his head, covering both eyes, which were further obscured by bloody patches. There was no doubt that Ben's vision would be affected by the wounds Emma inflicted.

Ben was a chain smoker, a drinker, and by all accounts, had a drug habit. He reminded Emma of some of the inmates at the drug rehab facility where she'd once done some volunteer work. He had the same yellow skin tone and constant sniffle. Emma remembered beer on his breath at their first meeting, which had been early in the day, and he reeked of cigarettes. He hadn't had beer, cigarettes or drugs since he had been in the custody of the sheriff's department for the past nine hours and was looking shaky. He was beginning to sweat. That, in conjunction with the wounds she'd inflicted, could push him over the edge.

Sheriff Colson entered the interrogation room and turned on the overhead lamp. Ben raised a hand to protect his covered eyes from the light.

"Mr. Bailey, can you tell me what it is you have against Emma Thornton?"

Ben compressed his lips and turned his head away from the sheriff.

"We're about to get Emma's statement detailing each and every thing you did to her last night and early this morning. We know you kidnapped her and it seems obvious that you had a plan to kill her. Georgia's sentencing laws are tough. You've been convicted of other crimes, and lucky for you, they've all been related to drugs. This is your first violent crime. You'll be charged with kidnapping at the initial hearing tomorrow morning, at the very least, which carries a sentence of between ten and twenty years. But you could also get brought up for attempted murder and aggravated assault on top of kidnapping. And aggravated assault carries a penalty of up to twenty years. We got your DNA now and we're running it with some samples from another crime that happened recently in the county. If there's a positive result, it's even more in your interest to cooperate with us. So, we need to know a few things." The sheriff paused. "Feel like talking?"

Ben didn't budge, but sweat started trickling down his forehead.

"Ben, we know you're not acting alone. Why would you want to kidnap and kill Emma Thornton? What's she ever done to you? It just doesn't make sense. Who put you up to it? Was it Adam? Did Adam Gannon pay you to kill Emma Thornton?"

Ben jerked his head up with a sudden movement, looking toward the direction of the sheriff's voice.

"I need to see my lawyer. I need to see my lawyer, now."

"And who would that be, Ben?"

"Lamar Johnson"

"Isn't that the lawyer I saw here with Robert Gannon a couple of weeks ago about that black-truck-stalking incident? The same black truck that you were using when you kidnapped Emma Thornton? Doesn't that confirm the connection between you and the Gannons? Are the Gannons paying your legal fees too, Ben?"

"In case you haven't figured it out by now, I ain't saying nothing and you can't make me say nothing. I'm entitled to whatever lawyer I want and it ain't no business of yours who pays my bills or if they're even paid." Ben's hands were shaking and his face was flushed and glistening with sweat.

"This isn't looking very good for you Ben. We've definitely got you on kidnapping and aggravated assault. We may even have you on the murder of the Gannon's housekeeper Lola Mae, depending on the results of the DNA test. If that comes through like I think it will, looks like the death penalty for you, unless you can find something to bargain with here."

Ben turned his head toward the sheriff.

"No, we hadn't forgotten about her. The DNA results will be back soon. Things are closing in on you, Ben. You need to start talking and help yourself out."

Emma motioned to Ren.

"DNA results? In Lola Mae's case?"

"They sent off Ben's for comparison to the sample we have from under Lola Mae's fingernails. It might take up to two weeks before we get the results, but we're hoping for a shorter return since we're right here at the university, and they have a lab that does that sort of work."

"That's encouraging. Also, the sheriff's correct. Lamar Johnson represents Robert Gannon. What do you make of that?"

"Could be a coincidence."

"No way. Ben Bailey can't afford an attorney like Lamar Johnson. He charges upwards of two hundred dollars an hour. Ben just doesn't seem to have that kind of money from what I've seen. I would think someone else is paying his attorneys fees. It could be the Gannons. Robert said he employs Ben occasionally, but even though Ben is also Robert's nephew, I'm pretty sure they're not close. I saw them in an argument once about money. Robert was paying Ben then, and he said something about not ever doing it again. So, I'd think it would be weird if Robert covered his legal fees."

"That's a good question. I've been thinking, Emma. I know you're really banged up, and you've got to be feeling a little shaky too. I wondered if you'd like me to stay over tonight so you and the boys wouldn't be all alone."

"That's sweet of you to sacrifice yourself to our worthy cause, Ren, but I don't think so."

"I didn't mean to offend you, Emma. I thought you might like some company, that's all."

"I'm sorry. I'm not sure why I snapped at you except I'm feeling a little overwhelmed. I don't think it's a good idea. I'd rather be with my boys. They need to feel safe tonight with me and I need to be with them. I know you only meant well though, so thanks." Emma reached over and touched Ren's arm.

"I understand."

"Ben meant to harm my boys too, and that's what's really bothering me. Keeping them protected is the most important thing in my life. If you can help me with that, you have done more than you can ever know."

36

September 10, 1990

D r. Winnifred H. Whittley, M.D., a forensic psychiatrist who had previously worked with deaf patients, was a rare find. She taught at the university and had a private practice on the side, but had been out of town for nearly two weeks due to a death in the family. Overwhelmed with the details of funeral arrangements, the collection of life insurance proceeds, even the probation of her stepmother's will, she was thrilled to be back at work and far away from the pitfalls of estate management. She told Emma she'd be happy to evaluate Adam. She'd also bring along a lip-reading specialist. By the end of the day, Emma was on her way to the jail to explain what she could about the testing to Adam.

Emma showed her identification to the deputy at the jail and was led into a small chamber off the main waiting room. Except for two chairs and a dirty florescent light fixture, the room was empty. Another deputy brought in an orange-suited Adam in shackles who shuffled through a side door. The deputy stood by the entrance as Emma motioned for Adam to take a seat.

Emma took out a tablet and a pen. She quickly wrote:

We are working on getting you out of here.

He nodded.

She asked him how he was, but her question wasn't necessary. He looked awful. He was thinner. His skin had taken on an icy-blue cast and the circles under his eyes had darkened.

Not good, he wrote.

She asked him whether he'd slept.

He shook his head.

She noticed his hands were trembling. Emma explained that she and Silas had asked a doctor to give him tests that week, assuring him that all he had to do was answer to the best of his ability.

What tests?

"Tests that may help us see what you understand and how you feel."

What kind of test? Read?

Emma shook her head.

Ear test?

"No, Adam. Not a hearing test." She pointed to her ear and shook her head.

What? Adam's eyes darted around the room as if he was in search of something.

Emma wrote: *A lady will ask you questions. Your answers will help us help you.*

Do I get out of jail?

"We'll see. This test might help with that."

What if I do not understand? Adam wrote, touching his forehead.

"We will have an interpreter there for you."

You there too?

"Why?" Emma wrote.

Adam shrugged. *I want you to.*

September 11, 1990

The next day, Dr. Whittley stomped up the steps to the entrance of the jail, her Birkenstocks slapping against the concrete as she climbed. Emma recognized her immediately from their phone conversations, even though they'd never met.

"Dr. Whittley, I presume?" Emma smiled, and reached out to shake the doctor's hand.

Dr. Whittley stopped mid-step, changed her satchel and books from one side to the other, shoved her glasses up her nose, and extended her hand to Emma.

"Ms. Thornton? I'm hoping you've pre-arranged for the testing with the jail. We'll need an additional room." Her voice echoed down the steps to the landing.

"Yes, it's all been arranged. I believe we're still waiting for the interpreter, though. It shouldn't be long. We're a little early." Emma couldn't help but notice the coffee stains on Dr. Whittley's white shirt, which was only partially tucked in her long, flowing skirt. Her hair, which was a mass of curls, looked as if it couldn't be tamed and bounced around her head as she spoke, accenting her speech with pointed jabs.

"Here's the interpreter now," Dr. Whittley said, nodding toward a young man walking toward them from the entrance. Johnny Webb, who didn't appear much older than Adam, introduced himself.

Emma took the doctor and the interpreter through security. They were shown into a small room; the testing was to take place in an adjoining space.

Dr. Whittley planned to evaluate Adam by asking him narrative questions structured around the DSM III-R, a psychiatric assessment instrument that established guidelines for anxiety and other disorders. She'd also use the Georgia Court Competency Test to determine whether Adam had the ability to consult with Silas with a reasonable degree of rational understanding, and the MMPI to determine veracity and whether Adam had a tendency toward malingering. Emma knew it was important for the doctor to establish a rapport with Adam. She hoped that was possible.

Dr. Whittley's examination, a series of meticulously constructed questions, took five hours. Johnny Webb, the interpreter, slowed down the process considerably. Whittley began by asking general questions and Johnny wrote each question down for Adam. Earlier Johnny had explained that even though Adam was a lip reader, certain words look identical to others when spoken, such as "hope" and "cope." Johnny showed each question to Adam and ensured that he understood the context of the query and each word. Usually, an oral interpreter would silently mouth-speak, then use facial expressions and gestures to help a lip reader understand. Johnny did this, and then went several steps beyond.

"Adam, when did you first learn about the murder of Jennifer Patrick?" Dr. Whittley said.

Johnny wrote down the question and read it as he showed it to Adam. Adam's hands began to tremble as he read the question. His face flushed a deep red and he shook his head.

"I'd like to speak to you outside in the hallway, Dr. Whittley," Emma said. Emma and Dr. Whittley stepped outside.

"It isn't good to interfere with the testing process, Ms. Thornton." Dr. Whittley crossed her arms in front of her chest. "Disruptions can cause inconsistencies and inaccurate results." Her voice bounced off of the walls and down the hall, and grabbed the attention of the guard who stood in the doorway of the room used for testing. He turned his head toward them.

"I wanted to stop you before you went any further just to remind you not to go beyond the scope of what we asked you to do. We asked you to limit your examination to issues related to Adam's time in jail, anxiety related to that confinement, and competency issues. The question you asked is designed to explore his knowledge of the murder itself. That goes beyond what we asked you to do."

"I'm entitled to explore any issues related to Adam's anxiety, not only anxiety related to his confinement, as well as the competency issue. Certainly, his reaction to my question would indicate he's experiencing a good deal of anxiety related to the night of the murder. So, I may not be able to say that the confinement is the sole cause of his problems. That question was just the first in a series of questions designed to test just what he understands. The fact that he's deaf will mean he'll miss a percentage of spoken language, but I still need to explore his ability to understand, factually, the legal proceedings, and whether he can communicate with you and Silas about it. And, although this is not related to the competency issue, from where I'm sitting, it seems Adam might also have an impulse control disorder. But that won't be a part of my report, at this point anyway."

Emma didn't have the authority to stop the testing. Silas was in a hearing in another case and she couldn't get him on the phone. And the doctor was correct. Silas had asked Dr. Whittley to take a look at Adam for all of the reasons she mentioned. Emma wanted to narrow the questions to the issues they'd need at the hearing or at trial. Dr. Whittley's approach was broader than Emma had anticipated. If the doctor explored Adam's knowledge of the murder itself, his mental state at the time of the murder, or drew any conclusion typically left for the jury, they couldn't request a report from her. It was better not to put certain opinions in writing.

From the corner of her eye, Emma noticed the guard at the doorway pulling out a notepad and jotting down notes.

"The evaluation can go forward, but please avoid asking direct questions about the murder."

"That's where you and I disagree again, Ms. Thornton. I need to see his reaction to those questions. He's in jail because someone was killed. How can I judge his reaction to being jailed unless I can also see his reaction to the underlying crime? And it's the same with the competency issue. I've got to see whether he understands the charge against him. How could I do that unless I ask him about the murder?"

"The problem Adam is having is akin to claustrophobia. He can't hear, and when he's confined he panics. This is true, especially in the dark, because he can't see and can't anticipate what's about to happen to him. And I'm not so sure you need to get into Adam's specific case to test his competency."

"With all due respect, Ms. Thornton, that is something I need to assess."

The guard continued to jot down notes. Emma wanted to punch both the guard and the doctor in the nose. She walked around to the doorway where the guard was standing.

Noticing his name tag, she said, "Oliver, why are you standing guard here in the hallway?"

"I'm to stay here with the prisoner during the testing. It's for your safety, ma'am."

"Adam is my client. I don't feel unsafe with him. Please do not eavesdrop on our conversation. Could I see your notes?"

"It's just my grocery list. I'm running by the store after work. I meant no offense, miss." The guard tucked his notepad in his back pocket.

"Nonetheless, I'd appreciate it if you'd respect our privacy." Emma watched the guard walk down the hall. Dr. Whittley followed Emma back into the evaluation room.

The doctor sat down and picked up her pad of paper and pen to begin her questioning again.

"Adam, what do you expect from Mr. Steele, your attorney? Do you understand what he does for you?"

Adam read Johnny's handwritten replica of the doctor's question and shrugged.

"Do you understand that your attorney represents you and what that means?"

Adam barely nodded.

"Can you tell me what that means?"

Adam shook his head.

"Why were you arrested, Adam, do you know?"

Adam shook his head again.

"Do you know what a trial is?"

Adam read Johnny's notes, then shook his head.

"Can you tell me why you went to court last week?"

Adam shrugged.

"Can you tell us how you feel about Jennifer Patrick's death?"

Adam looked at Emma. His face and neck were deep red and his hands were trembling. He picked up a pencil.

Bad.

"Do you live with your parents now?"

Adam looked down for a minute.

After J. died.

"Are you happy living with them?"

Adam looked at the question and paused. He looked at Dr. Whittley and ever so slightly shrugged.

"Do you and your father spend any time together?"

Adam shook his head. "No."

"Do you see your mother, or spend any time with her?"

Adam read the question and put the paper down, trembling. "No."

"Did your parents, your mother or your father, know Jennifer Patrick?"

Adam covered his face after reading the question. Emma thought she saw tears when he put his hands down. He shook his head. "No."

"Do you understand the word 'trust,' Adam?"

Johnny Webb wrote down the question for Adam and handed it to him. He nodded. "Yes."

"What does it mean to you?"

He read the question, and wrote, *truth.*

"Who do you trust?"

Joe.

And then he looked at Emma and pointed. "And her."

Emma blinked back tears. She hadn't expected that. She'd doubted Adam so many times. She'd defended him, she'd worked hard for him, but she hadn't always been sure of him. But he trusted her. All of her misgivings about him vanished the second he pointed at her. That was how it worked. If he trusted her, she'd trust him. So much for legal objectivity.

"Who's Joe?"

A friend.

"Does Joe always tell you the truth?'

Adam nodded in agreement.

"Do you trust your mom?"

Adam read the question and looked away. He stood up and began pacing about the room, then stopped abruptly and shrugged, handing the question back to Johnny. When Dr. Whittley asked him about his father, Adam merely shrugged again.

More than five hours later, the evaluation was concluded and all parties in the room were exhausted. As much as she hated to admit it, Emma was impressed with Dr. Whittley's thoroughness. But she wasn't sure whether Silas would be able to use the results.

Two days later, Emma received a call from Dr. Whittley. She was ready to write her report, but as Emma had requested, she called to give her verbal opinions first. Certain aspects of the evaluation merely confirmed what Emma had known all along. Adam had a panic disorder brought on by his confinement. And the disorder was linked to his disability, which was even better news. But Dr. Whittley also revealed other findings, which were more troubling.

"Ms. Thornton, it's my opinion that Adam is hiding something about Jennifer Patrick's murder," Dr. Whittley said.

"What do you mean hiding something?" Emma said.

"I asked questions that were designed to detect truth-telling as much as they were designed to illicit information about his competency to stand trial. He isn't telling the truth about the night of the murder."

"Why did you ask questions designed to detect truth-telling? Is that a common testing technique?"

"It's important for a psychiatrist to assess the subject regarding truth-telling or malingering. It's typically done in every examination. I needed to determine whether Adam was exaggerating his anxiety, whether he really understood the legal proceedings, and whether he was telling the truth."

"Was he exaggerating his anxiety, or was he telling the truth?"

"He wasn't exaggerating his anxiety, but, as I said, it appears he is hiding something about the murder. I'm not sure what. So he's not telling the truth, in the purest sense of the word."

"What else did you look at?"

"I also wanted to determine whether there was any underlying anxiety which may have exacerbated the panic attack at the jail. In other words, was there something else, such as the murder, that he was reacting to? So, many of my questions were germane to the issue of anxiety."

"I explained earlier that you cannot include anything at all about the murder in your report. But Mr. Steele may not even want you to prepare a report at this point. I'll need to confirm our next step and get back with you," Emma said.

Dr. Whittley made shuffling sounds on the line, but didn't speak.

"I'd like you to explain your complete findings so I can explain them to Mr. Steele, if you would." Emma readied her pencil in anticipation of Dr. Whittley's response.

"If the proper protections are in place and his interpreter is present, Adam can understand a good percentage of language, but I don't think he understands the legal process. He knows something is going on that is bad, but he can't truly assist in his defense. He didn't understand the hearing he participated in last week, and still doesn't know what a trial is. I'm certain he has no understanding of the role of an attorney. So, when you put all of those factors together, it's clear that he's not competent to stand trial. Also, even though the biggest part of his angst is about Jennifer's murder, it doesn't mean that he is or isn't the murderer, necessarily." She paused. "He also shows some signs that are classic of childhood abuse—lack of confidence, and that sort of thing. Of course, that could be related to his disability as well," Dr. Whittley said. "And there's something else."

"What's that?"

"He also has intermittent explosive disorder, which is a part of the impulsive control issue. I believe Adam could lose control of his emotions and could be fully capable of committing a crime, even murder. Needless to say, none of this, or any diagnosis, is going in my report."

"I'm not sure why you're telling me this, Dr. Whittley. What do you mean by fully capable of committing a crime. Do you think he killed Jennifer Patrick?"

"I'm not saying that, nor can I. I'm only saying that Adam, who is largely isolated and has symptoms of childhood abuse, if pushed to extremes, could go there. Some of us wouldn't tend to lose control to that extent. Some of us could. But people with these diagnoses are capable of criminal behavior, and that includes Adam. That's what I'm saying."

"The intermittent explosive disorder isn't a psychosis, right? But could it affect his ability to form the intent to commit a crime? In other words, if Adam explodes in a rage, does he have any control over his behavior?"

"People with the disorder react without thinking, and I'm pretty sure a few courts have recognized that intermittent explosive disorder can impair a defendant's capacity to act with malice. That affects criminal responsibility. But, frankly, that argument is a stretch."

"Because it's not a true psychosis?"

"Pretty much. Like I said, it's a personality disorder. But no diagnosis will be in the report. I just wanted you to know, mainly because the court's expert could reach a similar conclusion about Adam."

"That's all we need."

"His impulse control disorder could have been triggered by the fact that his parents never provided much emotional comfort or support. I think they tried, but they didn't know how. They still don't know how to communicate with him. They apparently provide plenty of material or physical comforts, but Adam is lonely. He hasn't learned many coping skills. So, emotions have stayed bottled up in him, and sometimes they explode. You've seen that, right?"

"Yep. On more than one occasion. That's not a defense to murder though. You're saying Adam understands the difference between right and wrong even though he has this problem?"

"Yes. He just can't seem to control his reactions in extreme circumstances. And this problem, in certain situations, could lead to extreme violence. You need to at least consider that it may already have."

"You're not going to want to put Dr. Whittley on the stand, Silas." Emma limped into Silas's office and sat down in his over-stuffed chair, looping her foot over the ottoman in an attempt to quell its ever-increasing swelling. The damn thing was becoming a distraction.

"Part of Dr. Whittley's testimony could be helpful. She'd be able to state

Adam wasn't competent to stand trial, and she could explain why. But she conducted a more complete analysis of Adam's personality, and a good prosecutor could draw that out. If that happened, she'd probably testify about his impulse control disorder and other problems, all of which would be far too damaging. She could prescribe an anti-anxiety medication for him though."

"Okay. I agree. It would be too risky to put her on the stand." It was Silas's turn to pace the room. "Guess I'd better argue what I'd planned on from the beginning."

"That the pre-trial services debacle was all our fault?" Emma said.

"Something like that, along with a few other pleas for his well-being. I'm hoping if I'm persuasive enough, the judge may release him."

"Do you think it'll work?"

"It might, if for no other reason his parents are well-known and have paid out a lot in bail already. It wouldn't work in a larger city, but we aren't in Atlanta."

"I meant to ask you earlier, what do you make of the guard taking down notes as Dr. Whittley and I were speaking in the hallway? He said he was writing out a grocery list, but I got the sense he was interested in what we were saying."

"I wouldn't worry about it. We haven't seen a request for a copy of the test, so the guard wasn't a spy for the DA. It's important no one discovers that we had testing done in case we want to get another psychiatrist to test Adam when we re-urge the motion to dismiss."

September 12, 1990

The next day, Silas and Emma walked up the steps of the courthouse for the hearing. The deputies had brought Adam from the jail earlier. They allowed him to dress in a suit for the occasion, but he was still in handcuffs, sitting on a bench along the side of the courtroom with the other prisoners, who were all dressed in their orange prison suits.

Silas and Emma didn't have a witness. They filed a brief that made no mention of Adam's anxiety issues, and had petitioned the court to allow Jimmy Webb to serve as Adam's interpreter. No one from the DA's office raised the issue of Adam's evaluation by Dr. Whittley earlier in the week.

Judge Baggett entered the courtroom, and asked Silas and the DA for a brief statement of their positions.

"Here's how I'm looking at this, Mr. Manville, and please correct me if I'm wrong about the order of events. Adam's family could afford a substantial bail following his arrest, and I initially released Adam to his family. They've always been upstanding members of our community, and still are by all accounts." The judge nodded toward Robert Gannon who was sitting in the courtroom. "Then, in Adam's suppression hearing, he lost his temper during what I recall was difficult testimony from a former teacher. Adam served time in jail after that, and then failed to check in with pretrial services after he was released. Have I got it right so far?"

"You have, Your Honor."

"It appears Adam didn't quite understand what to do at pretrial services, although it also seems he may have been in hiding at the time he was found in the woods by the deputy. Do you consider that a fair statement, Mr. Steele?"

"I'm not certain I would consider him in hiding since he'd rescued Ms. Thornton right before he was taken into custody, Your Honor," Silas said.

"I'll get to that. Following his second arrest, he was placed into custody again. I don't think we need to go into any more legal argument on this. I think he's served enough time. So, I'm going to release him again. He also helped save Ms. Thornton, and helped bring in Ben Bailey, her alleged kidnapper.

"But let me tell you Mr. Gannon...and Mr. Webb, make sure this is clear to him," he said, waving his arms toward Adam and the interpreter which caused his robes to flap about his desk, nearly knocking over the pile of cases his law clerk had carefully stacked on his ledge. "You need to realize you are on trial for murder and your outbursts work against you. You look bad to the court and it would be shocking to a jury if you had angry outbursts in front of them. It makes you appear temperamental which is not good in a murder trial. Am I making myself clear? Mr. Webb, please make certain he understands this."

Johnny wrote down the gist of the judge's statements and handed them to Adam. Adam read Jimmy's notes, looked at the judge and nodded, acknowledging his understanding.

"Things are not looking good for you, Mr. Gannon. Even though you helped rescue Ms. Thornton, you need to be careful. Mind your temper and your ways. You are released again, back to the custody of your parents. But you must report to pre-trial services on a weekly basis. Your lawyers are charged with the responsibility of explaining the importance of that to you." The judge paused to glare at Silas. "One more misstep and you are in jail for the duration of your case."

37

September 13, 1990

The next day Emma drove out to the Gannons', unannounced. She liked the thought of surprising them. Emma took the back roads to Mayfair which were tree lined and shady. Oaks covered the old lanes most of the way, bending to gracefully cover the bumpy roads. The drive helped her think.

Dr. Whittley's findings about Adam played repeatedly in her mind like an old forty-five with a scratch on the first track. Although she didn't know whether Adam was hiding information to protect himself or someone else, she found it easy to dismiss Deputy Glass's allegation that Adam and Ben Bailey planned Emma's kidnapping together. Deputy Glass had the instincts of a slug. But Dr. Whittley's assessment carried far more weight.

Emma pulled up to Mayfair. The last time she drove out to the big house, Lola Mae was alive. She'd been murdered only a few days after that meeting.

Emma got out of her car and knocked at Mayfair's massive door. A new housekeeper greeted her. Emma introduced herself and explained that she'd like to speak to the Gannons about Adam's recent hearing. She was shown inside and led into the front parlor. She watched through the back window as the gardener carefully deadheaded roses in the garden. She was amazed at his speed. He removed dozens of dead blooms before she realized nearly ten minutes had passed. She checked her watch and stood up in search of the housekeeper. Suddenly, she heard a familiar voice.

"It's so nice to see you again, Ms. Thornton."

Emma turned around to see Darcy enter the parlor, hand extended, looking as if she'd just stepped out of a *Town and Country* magazine. Emma wondered if Darcy woke up like a Disney princess every day, each hair in place, dewy complexion glowing as she gazed at the world through her glistening cornflower blue eyes. She was the very picture of perfection.

"Care to join me? I'm indulging in one of my favorites, a mocha espresso. I'll have Cook make one for you. It's a great morning pick-me-up, you know." Darcy rang the bell on the tea cart which was standing in the corner of the room. "Monica, please tell Cook to make one of these for Ms. Thornton."

"Oh, no thank you. I've already had my usual two cups this morning," Emma said.

"You don't know what you're missing. The first time I had one was when Robert and I traveled to Venice for our honeymoon. They've been my special treat ever since."

Emma smiled. "I drove out here today to talk about the hearing yesterday. I know Mr. Gannon was there, but I didn't have an opportunity to speak to him afterwards. I also wanted to ask you a few questions if you've got the time."

"Of course. Please have a seat and make yourself comfortable. Adam came home last night. Everything seemed okay, but we didn't really talk much about it. Of course, Robert knew the judge would let him out of jail." Darcy took another sip of her espresso. "Can I get you something to eat?" She made another move toward the bell on the teacart again, but Emma stopped her before she picked it up.

"No, I'm not hungry." Emma sat down and pulled out her notepad and pen. "I'd like to make sure you understand a couple of things, too."

"You go right ahead."

Emma noticed the pad of paper Adam carried with him to communicate was on the coffee table.

"You said Adam came home after the hearing?"

"Yes, he came by."

"Is he still here?"

"No." Darcy put her espresso on the coffee table.

"Is everything okay, Mrs. Gannon?"

Darcy lifted her head. "Well, not really. We had a little tiff."

"Where's Adam?"

"I'm not sure."

"Do you know why he left?"

"No. Yes. Well, apparently he's upset with his father and me."

"What happened?"

"Let's just say he was pretty angry when he walked out. I'm not exactly sure why, but I got the impression he didn't want to come back anytime soon." She stood, walked over to the teacart and grabbed a napkin to dry her eyes.

"If you do see Adam, could you tell him that he has to check in with pre-trial services on a weekly basis? If he doesn't, he could end up in jail again, this time for the duration of his case. We've told him, but if you tell him too, it would be helpful. We need to do what we can to make sure Adam avoids jail again."

"I understand. Don't worry. But I don't think I can promise anything at this point, Ms. Thornton. He said he didn't want to see us again."

"Did he say why?"

"He didn't need to."

"What do you mean?"

Robert Gannon entered the parlor from the side hall.

"Darcy, we need to get on down to the stables this morning. I wanted you to look in on that new foal. You may not know this, Ms. Thornton, but Darcy works magic with newborns, especially the sicklier ones. She has a special touch. We'd best get going now, Darcy."

"I have one other question, if I may," Emma said.

"Yes?"

"The last time I was here, I spoke to you about Jennifer Patrick."

"I don't recall that," Darcy said.

"At the time, you said that you'd never met her."

"That's correct."

"But as I was leaving, Lola Mae, your housekeeper, told me that Jennifer had been to your house right before her death. Do you know who Jennifer saw that day?"

"No. I have no idea. Like I said, I didn't see Jennifer, and I'm pretty sure Robert was out of town around that time. Isn't that right, Robert?"

"I think you're right." Robert put his hand on his wife's shoulder.

"So, if she came by I don't know who she spoke to."

"I'm not sure why you think this is significant, Ms. Thornton," Robert said. "But I do think you need to concentrate on the important facts in the case."

"Has the sheriff spoken to you about Lola Mae's death?"

"We know about her death, obviously, but no, we haven't talked to the sheriff about it."

Darcy rose from the couch and stood next to Robert who put his arm around her.

"Let's go, Darcy." He gestured toward Monica. "Please see to it that Mrs. Gannon has what she needs for an afternoon in the stables." Turning toward Emma, he said, "You'll have to excuse us, Ms. Thornton, this may take a while. I hope you don't mind finding your way out." He began his way up the stairs behind Darcy and the new housekeeper.

Emma grabbed her keys and started out, and then, noticing Adam's notepad, put it in her purse as she walked out of the house.

Emma pulled out of the Gannon's driveway knowing that she might pass them on her way to see Joe. He was home, as usual, sitting on his front porch, watching the horses run. He waved as she approached.

"Hey, Joe, been a while." Emma climbed up to the stoop. "Seen Adam in the last few days?"

"Yep, he came here last night, and I 'spect he'll be stayin' here 'til the trial. He don't much like to stay at the big house, even though he's only got a couch at my place." He nodded toward the lime green sofa that was visible from the front door.

"Do you know anything about an argument he got into with his parents?"

"Well, I'm not really sure. What I do know is Wednesday night I was woke up by a lot of loud noises and shoutin' at the big house. About five minutes later, Adam came rappin' at my door. He was upset and wanted to stay at my place, which was okay by me. It was pretty clear that there was some sort of problem at home."

"What time do you think it was?"

"It was probably around ten or so, not too late."

"Do you know where Adam is now?"

"Don't reckon I do, but I'm sure he'll be back before dark. He knows he's got to watch it now."

"Could you help keep an eye on him? And call us at this number if there is the first sign of any trouble?" Emma scribbled her number on a piece of paper for Joe and handed it to him. "Also, do you know what Adam does all day? He doesn't have a job, he's not in school, and no one seems to know where he is."

"Can't say I do. And I haven't made it my business to ask."

"I need you to make it your business, if you would. I'm going to have to keep up with him, and it looks like I'll need your help. By the way, Joe, did you know Lola Mae, the Gannons' housekeeper?"

"Yes, ma'am. Everyone knew Lola Mae around here. I'd known her for years, the whole time she'd been at the Gannons, anyway."

"Did you know whether the Gannons let her go before she died?"

"I never heard nothin' like that and I think I would have."

"Also, I know that Ben Bailey is Robert's nephew, but is there any other connection to the family? Can you tell me anything about what he does for a living or anything that would give me insight into him?"

"Even though Ben is Robert's nephew, they really have more of an employee - employer relationship, you know? Robert's main thing in life is his horses. Ben was his horse handler for a while. He was their stall cleaner, groomer, stable hand, and all around gofer out at the stables for a long time. He'd accompany Robert to all of their shows and the races. Darcy did some of the shows too. Darcy rides, you know. And then all of a sudden Ben stopped showing up."

"You don't know why?"

"Well, I got my suspicions."

"What's that?"

"Juice."

"What's juice?"

"Drugs. Ben does 'em, sells them, and juices up the horses. Gets horse tranquilizers from crooked vets. Sells 'em to jockeys at the tracks. Then he juices horses with several different kinds of things. Like the milkshake. That's a mix made with baking soda, sugar, and electrolytes. You get a tube, shove it up the horse's nose and it gives him a high for a while, makes him run a little faster. Ben sells cocaine to jockeys and to trainers for the horses. They also shove cocaine up a horse's nose just like a man's. Steroids are used too. Even cobra venom is shot up in those beauties by some of the crazier trainers. Can you believe it?"

"Not really. That is crazy. So, you think Robert fired Ben because he discovered he was committing crimes?"

"No, I think he got rid of him because he was afraid his stables might be connected to illegal activity. There were rumors all over the tracks about Ben. Robert was afraid of an investigation. The activity continues, but Ben's no longer an employee. That's the only difference."

"Ben doesn't have any other job, does he?"

"Not that I know of."

"And Ben still does drugs?"

"That's the rumor."

"Do you know if Robert does drugs?"

Joe folded his hands and looked down at the floor. "Nah. I don't think so. He likes his drink, but I really don't think he'd take no drugs."

"Has one of the Gannon horses won a race after being given drugs, or do you know?"

"I have my suspicions. That's all I'll say."

Joe agreed to stay in touch, and promised to call Emma if Adam failed to come back to his place at night. On her way back down the drive, Emma saw the Gannons' truck at the stables. It was identical to the truck that had stalked her.

At least a mile and a half of the road that led back to Jonesburg from Mayfair was private. Originally constructed solely for the owners, the road had been isolated from the public for years. Today, it was connected to a state road, but a smaller section of the passageway was still private. The Gannons kept their thoroughfare in excellent condition, although it was heavily wooded and rarely traveled on by anyone other than Gannon employees. Emma could always tell when she hit the state road by the bumpiness of the surface.

Emma had driven about ten minutes when she heard a sharp ping, and the sound of something hitting her rear bumper. Startled, she kept an eye out for loose rocks and potholes, and continued down the road. When she heard two additional pops, she realized her car was being pelted by something metallic. She pulled to the side of the road and got out to see whether a loose part had caused the popping noise. Instead she found two holes in the side of her car, and two holes in the trunk. The holes were perfectly round. Hands shaking, she opened the trunk and found brass bullets inside. With adrenaline now on overload, she moved in slow, jerky motions, and took a few steps back toward the driver's side door. She then heard another crack as a bullet whizzed by her ear and into the bush, about twenty feet ahead. Jumping back in her vehicle, she put it in gear and pushed the pedal to the floor, propelling the car down the road fast as it could go.

Emma didn't stop until she reached the sheriff's office. She showed Ren the bullet holes along the side of her car and trunk.

"Well, you're lucky to be alive, Emma. Those are from a rifle. Looks like a .22. We'll need to put another unit in your apartment parking lot tonight."

"I don't know what this is all about, but I'd just left Joe Casey's place when this happened. I've obviously upset someone by my work on the Patrick case, but I haven't got a clue about what it might be."

"Did you get a sense of where the shots were coming from?"

"Not really. It seemed like they were coming from behind because I was hit in the rear. But I didn't see anything. It's wooded along that stretch of road. The trees could have provided a cover."

Ren nodded. "You said you saw the Gannons, too?"

"Yeah. Mrs. Gannon was a upset about the last time she saw Adam, but other than that, there was nothing unusual when I saw her or Mr. Gannon."

"Why was she upset?"

"You know I can't discuss our conversation, Ren."

"Okay. Sorry." He paused. "This is starting to feel like a serial murder case."

"I wouldn't think you'd have to worry about a serial murderer because everything seems connected somehow. Aren't serial murders more random in nature?"

"Not all of them. Some may lack an obvious motive, but then others have a theme to the killing. I think the only real requirement for a serial killing is that they murder three or more people. The killing is usually done in service of an abnormal psychological gratification too, and there's usually a pretty significant time between the killings. We don't have enough information in yet to determine whether all of the elements are met here."

The kids were finally asleep, the dishes were done, and the house was quiet. Emma got ready for bed and turned off all the lights but one. She grabbed her purse and pulled out Adam's notepad.

One thing was clear, Ben Bailey was in jail and couldn't have been the person who took shots at her car. But Emma had a few suspicions about who it might have been. Robert hadn't threatened her but he made it clear that in his opinion she was on the wrong path in her investigation, especially when she asked about Jennifer's visit. Silas would argue that Robert's comment was innocent. But Emma didn't think anything about Robert Gannon was benign. And if what Joe said was true, he drugged his horses. If he could do that, he had no conscience.

Emma opened Adam's notepad. She half-heartedly flipped through the pages, then stopped suddenly when she saw the word "hate." She flipped back to read for content. The writing was hard to follow, and was scribbled across the pages randomly.

"*I could kill you,*" was written in a script Emma recognized as Adam's.

Then someone had written "*Tell your mother you are sorry.*"

This was followed by Adam's handwritten comment, "*I hate you bitch.*" And, "*I hate both of you.*"

Emma knew Adam had a temper but she'd never seen him direct it at his parents. She wasn't surprised there were problems in the Gannon household, but things must be worse than she thought or Adam wouldn't have lashed out like that. No wonder Darcy was upset. Adam's notebook and the threat against his parents weren't relevant to Jennifer Patrick's case and it was a good thing. The DA would love to see proof that Adam was capable of making brutal threats.

38

September 14, 1990

Ren received the call from the sheriff's office at about five in the morning, and told them he'd come down. He called Emma before he left.

"Robert Gannon's body was found a few minutes ago. He was shot while in his stables. I'm driving out there shortly to check it out."

Emma gasped. "What happened?"

"I don't know yet."

She rubbed her forehead. "If Silas okays it, I'd like to come on out there."

"I'm not sure what you think you could do, Emma."

"I'd look around. See what I can see, you know."

Emma hung up the phone and got dressed. Once she was ready, she called Silas and they both agreed she should drive out to Mayfair. She arranged for her neighbor to get her kids on the bus, and took off.

Emma floored the accelerator, her engine straining under the pressure of its worn pistons. She didn't slow down until she pulled onto the Gannon property. Bypassing the gathering of county vehicles surrounding the stables, she rounded the curve by the barn and continued on. She decided to run by Joe's place first, hoping to catch Adam. If Robert Gannon was murdered, Adam would be a suspect.

Her brakes squealed slightly as she came to a stop in front of Joe's house. Emma bounded up the steps and rapped on the door. She heard a muffled shuffling coming from inside and, in a few seconds, Joe's sleepy head appeared.

"Sorry if I woke you Joe, but I need to speak to Adam. It's important. Can you get him up?"

"I'm sorry, Miss Emma. He never made it in last night. I haven't seen him since yesterday mornin.'"

Scanning the road, she expected to see Adam come running up at any minute. "Is this usual for Adam? Does he do this sort of thing regularly?"

"No, ma'am, can't say he do."

"Just to let you know, Joe, Robert Gannon's been shot. He's dead."

"Oh, no. That's not good news." Joe leaned against his cane and put his shoulder against the doorframe. "That's real, real bad."

"Did Adam ever talk to you about the reason he left his parents' house last night? Yesterday you said there might have been a problem at home. Do you know if Adam and his dad had an argument?"

"Adam didn't say anything to me about an argument or anything else. But I know Adam would never hurt his father." Joe shook his head again. "No, ma'am."

"Thank you, Joe. I didn't mean to upset you."

"Adam is a good boy. He's been dealt a hard hand, that's all."

"Please let me know if you hear from Adam, okay? Call me as soon as he comes in."

Joe nodded as Emma got back into her car and drove back to the stables. Emma recognized Ren's car, as well as the Greendale County Medical Examiner ambulance. She nosed her car up to the yellow tape crisscrossing the pen, and parked.

"I'd like to speak to the chief deputy. He called me earlier this morning," Emma said to the uniformed man leaning on the county vehicle parked next to hers.

"You can go on up. Just don't touch anything," the deputy said.

Emma walked into the stables, moving slowly to make herself unobtrusive. Although Joe had shown her the small storage shed behind the stables once, she had never entered the main area where the horses were kept. She was amazed by its grandeur. She knew the Gannons had traveled extensively in Europe and guessed they had modeled their stables from that part of the world. Heavy oak beams lined a vaulted ceiling that was two stories high, topped with an eight-sided cupola. At its apex were two antique brass chandeliers that must have been eight feet tall. The main floor was covered with highly polished wide plank oak floors. The horses' stalls were beautifully finished with sound-deadening rubber floors and coated hardware, designed to minimize injuries. The place smelled like oil soap and horse liniment. It was immaculate.

When she walked by the stalls she could tell that the horses had been disturbed by the shooting. Most were skittish. Some were terrified and were kicking the stall doors.

Emma saw Ren with a group of deputies as well as the medical examiner and his team. She motioned to him, and he walked over.

"You really shouldn't be here, you know." Ren tried to hide a spontaneous smile which spread across his face.

"Well, the deputy let me in. Who am I to disagree with his judgment?" Grinning up at him, she kicked at loose wooden shavings scattered on the floor. "Seriously, Ren, I won't be long. Can you tell if Gannon's death was murder or suicide? Adam would want to know."

"This is off the record, but the ME says it looks like murder. He was shot at close range in the chest. There's blood everywhere. You can't go over there." Ren glanced over his shoulder at the prone body of Robert Gannon, whose feet were protruding beyond one of the ME's squatting assistants.

Emma struggled to see around the ample-bodied investigator. Blood had pooled around the body on the shiny wooden floor. "I've always suspected Gannon had a hand in the murder of Jennifer Patrick," she said. Her eyes were glued to the gory mess. She felt light-headed, her throat constricted. She swallowed several times before continuing. "Looks like I was wrong about that. When you consider the fact that I was shot at on Gannon property yesterday, and today Robert is found dead in his own stables, you've got to conclude that his murder must be connected to yesterday's shooting." Emma glanced up at Ren. "Don't you agree? I think all of the incidents, including the ones directed at me, are connected in some way." Emma slammed her notebook shut. Her face was flushed and her hands were shaking, but she didn't want Ren to notice. She looked down, pretending to brush dirt from her pants leg.

"I always thought you were way off on the theory about Robert. And it's too early to draw any definite conclusions. But yeah, it looks like the shootings have to be connected somehow. They can't all be random acts." Ren stepped closer to Emma and lowered his voice. "But, in case you've forgotten, I'm going to do everything in my power to prevent anything bad from happening to you or the boys again. And as soon as this case is over, you're going to have a very hard time getting rid of me." He touched her shoulder and, feeling no resistance, gave her a comforting squeeze. He stepped back and resumed his normal pose.

Emma pretended to take notes. "I guess I judged Mr. Gannon too harshly. He showed up for Adam, at least half of the time, anyway. You said he was shot close up with a rifle?"

"Yep."

"Why would someone shoot a person at close range with a weapon as powerful as that?"

"Perhaps they hadn't planned on shooting him at all."

Emma sat in the chair in Silas's office watching as he signed a stack of pleadings for filing. She was concerned that Adam seemed more and more impulsive and irrational. She and Joe had stressed how important it was for him to stay in touch, yet she had no idea where he was.

"You don't think Adam could have anything to do with his father's murder, do you?" Silas said.

"I hope not. We don't know where he is now, and since he didn't show up at Joe's place last night, we don't know where he was when his father was killed. But he could always show up and have a perfectly good explanation."

Silas peered over his glasses at Emma and pursed his lips. "Let's hope so. Do you know whether the sheriff has any suspects for Gannon's murder?"

"If they do, they're not telling. But I expect Adam will end up on the list." Emma sank lower in the chair. "Here, take a look at what I found at his parents' place."

Emma tossed Silas the notepad.

"What's this?"

"A conversation between Adam and his parents."

"Why do you have it?"

"Adam left it on the coffee table, and I picked it up."

"I see." Silas thumbed through the pages, stopping to read Adam's comments. "This isn't good."

"Pretty bad timing, especially since his dad ended up dead the following night."

"This sort of thing, coming from a teenager, is usually an empty threat. I'm sure half of the kids in the country say they hate their parents at least once in their lives."

"Most parents don't end up dead afterwards though. Adam also wrote he wanted to kill someone, but he didn't say who."

"Was he speaking with both of his parents?"

"That's what Darcy said. She was pretty upset."

"Also, as you know, we have at least one shoe print from under Jennifer's window from the night she was killed which seems similar to one of Robert Gannon's. I guess we need more information on that."

Beverly, Silas's secretary, appeared at the door with the morning mail. Silas quickly flipped through the envelopes pausing at one from the Superior Court, and tore it open.

"Well, we'd better find Adam pretty soon. We're scheduled for trial in six days."

Belinda Carmichael wasn't fond of her job as the front desk clerk at the sheriff's office, but it was a far sight better than waiting tables at Sue's Burgers. Her clothes and apartment no longer reeked of stale grease. Plus she had a dental plan now, and could even afford to have her nails done once a month. She looked down at her new color, *Vampira Violet*. She liked it. But her matching toenails were hidden underneath her regulation shoes.

The front desk was rarely active and Belinda had little to do but admire the luster of her nails in varying light as she sat at her station. Noticing a tiny chip in the color of her right index finger, Belinda opened her desk drawer to pull out her emergency nail repair kit when she noticed a large envelope tucked in the back of the drawer. She reached in and pulled out the thick bundle. Written on the outside of the envelope was the following: *To: Sheriff Colson, From: Professor Anthony Beasley*, Re: *Letters,* and the professor's telephone number. *Patrick Case* was boldly printed across the top. She had no memory of logging in the bundle only a couple of weeks earlier.

Belinda wasn't ashamed of being inquisitive or tenacious. Her father's nickname for her was Bird Dog, often saying she could track down a cheating boyfriend quicker than he could load his shotgun. Her natural curiosity was piqued by the large envelope. The fact that the contents were intended for the sheriff, that it was private property, or that it could be evidence in a case never crossed her mind. But if she had considered any of those details, she wouldn't have been deterred.

So, Belinda opened and read each of the brittle pages, surprised that the letters inside the packet were nearly fifty years old. All of the correspondence was between Ethel Patrick and Will Gannon. And one letter stood out—the letter where Ethel told Will that Jim Patrick agreed to raise Lyle as his own. In that same letter, Ethel cursed the Gannons and their land for all that Will had done. Shuddering, Belinda carefully placed the fragile letters back in the large gray envelope. She brought it down to the sheriff's office and laid it on top of his desk. Belinda wondered what Ethel would think about her granddaughter's murder and whether Robert's killing was an answer to her curse.

Professor Beasley finally got the call from the sheriff's office asking him to come to the station to speak to Sheriff Colson. He was surprised it had taken them nearly two weeks to get back to him. He grabbed his jacket and keys. It should only take him a few minutes. He lived a couple of miles from town.

Sheriff Colson stood to shake the professor's hand when he entered his office, gesturing for him to take a seat. Professor Beasley glanced around the cluttered space, noting the family portraits, the American flag in the corner, and all of the sheriff's framed commendations hanging on the wall.

"Professor, when was it that you dropped off those letters?" The sheriff rested his elbows on his desk and clasped his hands.

"I wrote it in my calendar. August twenty-ninth. I'm sure of it."

"So what can you tell me about them? How'd you get the letters, what do you know of their history, and what you think they mean?" Sheriff Colson pulled out a small notebook from his desk drawer.

"Jennifer Patrick brought them to me. She had some of the same questions you do. She knew I collected old letters and wanted to know if I thought they were authentic, and if they were, what they meant."

"When did she bring them to you?" The sheriff jotted down notes as the professor spoke.

"About a week before she was killed. She said she'd found them in an old dresser in her room, hidden in a secret compartment."

"Do you think they're authentic?"

"I don't have any other signatures to compare these to, but we should be able to find them easily enough. The letters are authentic in that the postmarks are genuine, and the paper and ink seem appropriately aged. They appear authentic to me, but I'd be more comfortable if I could also see signatures to compare these to."

"What do you think they mean?"

"Well, let me see." The professor reached over to the sheriff's desk and picked up the envelope. "This one is dated October 2, 1945, and says pretty clearly that Will Gannon is Lyle Patrick's father. And there's more. It says:

Will Gannon, you have wrecked my life, the life of your son, Lyle, and the life of my husband who is a far better man than you'll ever be. There is no satisfaction in telling you this, because I know you don't care, but you need to know that I feel great shame that you tricked me into selling our land to you. The Patrick land. The land that Jim loved so much and was so proud of. I will go to my grave ashamed of myself and hating you for what you have done.

Jim will raise your son Lyle as if he is his own. He has forgiven me, although I don't know why. I hope you live long enough to see horrible things happen to the land and those on it. I will curse you and yours forever. I only hope that God does as well.

Ethel Patrick

"And then there's another letter which is even more important."

October 4, 1945

Ethel,

I bought the property from you. Any court in Greendale County would verify the sale. But I'm glad Jim's stepping in with the boy, especially since I can't. My wife would never understand. But I will set up a small fund for him at First Bank.

Will

"That's what you call an acknowledgement. So, Lyle Patrick has a claim to at least part of the Gannon property, if it can be proved that this is really Will's signature. And then, if I were Lyle, I'd be sure to check out that fund at First Bank."

"We all knew that Will Gannon swindled Ethel Patrick out of the Patrick land. But most of this is new information." Sheriff Colson stood up and paced back and forth across the room.

"I don't know anything about that, but it does seem that Lyle has a strong claim here. In any event, I thought you might need the letters. I'll let you connect the dots, or whatever it is you guys do. But, it's pretty clear that Lyle Patrick and Robert Gannon are probably half-brothers. "

The sheriff nodded. "And I guess that made the kids, Jennifer and Adam, cousins."

"You are correct, but no one knew until Jennifer found the letters." Professor Beasley shook his head.

"I wonder why no one in the Patrick family ever challenged the sale of the property to Will. Ethel accused him of tricking her, which implies fraud. Everyone has always said Will didn't pay enough for it. It seems like something they could have pursued."

"You're forgetting the times. This all happened during and right after the war. Neither of the Patricks wanted anyone to know that Will took advantage of Ethel in the way he did. Challenging the sale would have brought their affair to light. And it seems clear that Ethel and Jim never wanted Lyle to know who his actual father was, so he never knew he had a claim to the property."

"I guess you're right. If Jennifer hadn't discovered the letters, we wouldn't know about any of this either. I wonder if she let anyone other than you know about them?"

Professor Beasley stood to leave. "She didn't say. But I'm only a phone call away if you have any other questions."

Sheriff Colson watched the professor leave, then walked down the hallway with the letters in his hand to the open office area where Ren had his desk. Colson walked up as Ren was typing a report and threw the letters down.

"Take a look at these. They were found in Jennifer Patrick's room. We've also got to find out why the hell they sat around our office for two weeks until I saw them today. Find out which clerk was on duty the afternoon of August twenty-ninth."

Ren opened the brittle pages and read the fading lines. His eyes widened in surprise. "Well, this is interesting. Lyle Patrick could be a wealthy man."

"Yeah, today they could do a DNA test to prove he's Will Gannon's son, but they'd have to get some Gannon blood to compare it to. Gannons are getting a little thinned out these days. Who's left? Adam?"

Belinda Carmichael didn't attend the state police academy as the deputies in the office had, but the sheriff insisted she receive some departmental training after she accepted her job. She knew not to discuss sheriff department business outside the walls of the county office. But sometimes Belinda talked to her mother, Connie, about the more exciting cases. She didn't feel too badly about it since there weren't that many crimes in their small town. She knew her mother would be thrilled to hear about the Ethel Patrick and Will Gannon letters. Her mother had gone to school with Lyle and Robert, so this would be fascinating for her. Belinda couldn't wait to tell her what she'd found.

Belinda's mother, Connie, lived in a small trailer park toward the end of town. She had diabetes and since she didn't drive, she rarely left her trailer. Connie spent most of her day with her feet propped up on a well-worn leatherette ottoman watching her favorite soap operas. She looked forward to the visits from Belinda, especially when Belinda gave her reports from the jail. Belinda didn't like to stay long when she visited her mother since the trailer was tiny, only ten feet wide and twenty feet long, and Connie was large, which made Belinda feel claustrophobic. To make matters worse, Connie's cat, which was nearly as old as Belinda and half blind, was not interested in making it to his litter box any longer. Connie was equally disinterested in cleaning up after him. So once Belinda dropped off a few burgers from Sue's and gave Connie the latest stories from the jail, she escaped as quickly as she could.

What Belinda didn't know was that her mother also had a group of old friends from high school she'd speak to on the telephone occasionally. Connie would brag to them about her deputy daughter and her stories from the sheriff's office.

Connie loved Belinda's story about the letters and was on the phone with her friends as soon as Belinda left. The account of Ethel Patrick and Will Gannon was the sort of tale that grabbed their fancy and quickly took flight. By the next day, nearly everyone at Lucky's had heard about the letters Jennifer Patrick had found in her dresser, and that, with Robert Gannon's death, Lyle Patrick might now be the next heir to the Gannon fortune, or at least part of it.

39

September 15, 1990

Ren poured over the ballistics reports for the third time, confirming his suspicions. The bullets found in Emma's trunk were a perfect match with those from the .22 caliber rifle that killed Robert Gannon. The same person must have pulled the trigger in each shooting.

Checking his watch, Ren strode out of the front door of the office, nearly late for his interview with Ben Bailey. He hiked toward the jail, head down, lost in thought about what he'd say. Ben's attorney wouldn't approve of conversations between Ben and the sheriff's office, and any evidence Ren obtained through an illegal discussion couldn't be used anyway. But he wasn't planning to ask Ben about the kidnapping. He only wanted to encourage Ben to talk to him about Jennifer Patrick's murder. Of course, that could lead to a discussion about Lola Mae's case, and that would be just fine. Ren had heard that Ben's withdrawal from whatever drugs he'd been on had been rough. He'd had a seizure a couple of nights ago, fell to the floor, and had to have a few stitches on his head. Ren was hoping he would find a more fragile Ben who was also a little more inclined to talk.

Ren waited in the antechamber and watched through the two-way mirror as the deputy brought Ben to the small interrogation room. Ben had never bothered with his appearance, but he had noticeably deteriorated since Ren had last seen him. He had dropped several pounds since his arrest of a week ago, on a frame that could have already been described as gaunt. His skin tone was gray and clay-like with deep hollows under his eyes, which still bore the jagged claw marks from the night of Emma's kidnapping. Several places on his exposed skin were raw from scratching. His teeth were dingier than Ren recalled and were receding from his gums, giving him a distinct rodent-like appearance. Ren thought he detected a tremor and noticed that Ben was sweating profusely. As Ben sat down on one of the chairs behind the table, he began clawing his arms and neck.

Ren stepped into the interrogation room and closed the door.

"You're not looking so good these days, Ben. What was it you were on? Crack? Meth? I guess you can't get your hands on any in here, huh?"

Ben swallowed, and rolled his eyes to the side. The gashes from where Emma's fingernails had gouged his eyes were scabbed, glaringly red, and inflamed. Ren wasn't sure what Ben was able to see. Cocking his head slightly, Ben looked up at Ren and sneered, "Ain't so bad in here." His speech was noticeably slurred.

"Really? Food's real tasty, too, huh? Looks like you're gaining tons of weight with all that good cooking. Want me to order you some dinner up right now? Let's see. I think I saw what it was on the way up. Fish stew. Think it was cod. That's right. Canned cod soup. Might have a few bones in it. Maybe a few worms as well. I read about those worms in cod. Can't be helped. But you'd probably like that. A little extra protein. Want me to get some in here for you right now?"

Ben swallowed several times. His face blanched.

"Guard, would you get some of that fish stew up here? It's lunch time for Mr. Bailey."

Ben put his arms on the table and held his hands in an attempt to keep them from trembling. Ren could tell from the vibrations underneath the table that his knees were shaking as well. Ben fidgeted in his seat as he glared at Ren.

"You sure it ain't been so bad in here?" Ren said.

"What's it you're wanting?" Ben lifted a shaky hand to wipe the mucus dripping from his nose then rubbed his hand on his county issue jump suit.

"I'm wanting to talk to you."

"What about?"

"About all these murders."

"I don't know nothing about no murders." Ben propped his head up on his hand.

"I don't believe that. Did you know your uncle Robert Gannon was killed the other night?"

"I did not. How could I? I was in here."

"Do you know anyone who would want to kill Robert?"

"Maybe my aunt, Mable Grayson. She's hated him her whole life."

"How are you related to Mrs. Grayson?"

"My daddy's sister."

"Did you ever hear her speak of wanting to harm Robert Gannon?"

"Nah. She just holds a grudge against him. Always has. My cousin talked about it, too."

"Cousin?"

"Her son, Vinny. He's closer to Adam's age."

"Does Vinny live in Jonesburg?"

"Lives with his parents, good as I know."

Ren scribbled the Grayson name in his notebook and made a note to go to visit the family. "Ben, I know you know something about these other murders, or at least about Jennifer Patrick's and Lola Mae's. It makes no sense that you went after Emma unless it was connected in some way to the Patrick girl's murder. And I know someone paid you to go after her, too. You can't afford that fancy attorney of yours. So someone is still paying your bills. Give me something we can use and maybe the DA can work out some kind of plea bargain for your sentence. You're never getting out of here once you're convicted for kidnapping and aggravated assault. If they sentence you consecutively, you could get forty years. You'd be an old man by that time. Let me know what you're willing to do."

"My money ain't no business of yours. I'm doing okay so far, and my attorney's real good."

Adam had hidden out in the camps along the lake once before and Emma had a feeling he might be there again. She pulled onto I-85, pushing the accelerator of her car to the floor.

Ahead of her, to her left, was a black pickup truck, identical to the one driven by Ben Bailey, and those used by the Gannon family. Emma urged her car toward the vehicle. As she neared the rear of the truck, she pulled a pencil from her purse and wrote down the license plate number on a scrap of paper she found along the bottom of her bag. Then, she pulled up next to the vehicle, and drove down the side of the truck, craning her neck to see inside. The driver sped off before she was able to get a good look, but she saw it was a man. She was also able to distinguish some of his features. Something about him seemed familiar, but she couldn't be sure.

Emma turned off the highway, taking the narrow road which lead toward the camps. She rolled down her front window to feel the cooler air from the lake and breathed in the scent of long-needle pines, scrub oaks and the grassy vegetation that clustered about the roadside and the water's edge. She was taken back to the night of her kidnapping, reliving the details. Her fingers clenched the steering wheel as she recalled Ben's two stops that night.

Riding in the back of a truck, her head covered, Emma was disoriented and had no real sense of where she was on the night of her kidnapping. But yesterday Joe had given her directions. She pulled up to the first camp. The Gannon family cabin. She knew she had the right place. The Gannon's place appeared empty. She backed out of the driveway and continued her search.

Shadows seemed to grow longer and more ominous the deeper she traveled into the woods. She felt queasy. Passing two more camps, Emma turned a corner and saw a small wooden cabin. This, according to Joe's directions, belonged to the Gannon's friends, and was Ben's final stop that night. It was also the cabin where deputies had found Adam's fingerprints.

She pulled into the driveway, took a deep breath, and stepped out of her car.

Adam's truck wasn't in the driveway, and she didn't see it anywhere along the perimeter of the property. She walked up to the cabin, and peered inside to see if there was any sign of life. Seeing none, she walked back toward her car, when she noticed a flash of silver and a blue glow in the woods ahead. She trotted down the driveway and across the road. Adam was up to his old tricks again, she thought, smiling to herself. He had broken off several branches from the surrounding bushes and had woven them around the pick-up for camouflage. It had almost worked. His truck was nearly invisible from the road.

Emma walked back up to the cabin. She felt certain Adam would be there.

Ren ripped the GBI's ten most wanted list from the fax machine. It was a motley, sad-looking troupe. They were all men, and although most were sexual predators, there were a few kidnappers and murderers in the group. Ren balled up the list and threw it in the trash. He sat down and rubbed his sore knee. The Gannon family provided the only connection the three deceased victims had to each other. Robert was a Gannon. Lola Mae worked for him, and Jennifer dated his son. The killer wasn't going to be found on the current GBI most wanted list. It was time to pay Darcy Gannon a visit.

Even though Robert Gannon had died only the day before, Mayfair seemed unchanged. There were no funeral sprays on its massive doors. The stables were bustling and Gannon employees were busy attending to chores. When he arrived, Ren noticed an unoccupied black truck, much like the pick-up driven by Ben Bailey, parked on the side of the house. He jotted down the license plate number.

Ren knocked on the door and was invited in. A blast of cool air struck him as he stepped into the fourteen -foot hallway, reminding him that he had entered another stratosphere, another rung on the economic ladder. He'd never be able to attain the financial security enjoyed by the Gannons.

He couldn't even fathom it.

Ren peered through the library windows toward the back of the house. He could see Darcy in the rose garden, somberly dressed in sleek navy slacks and a matching top. She was a striking figure, even in grief. She was speaking to a man Ren recognized as a guard from the county jail. Darcy's housekeeper walked out to the garden, spoke to Darcy, and nodded toward Ren. Darcy waved, then continued speaking to the guard, touching each finger on one hand with the index finger of the other, as if she was ticking off items from a list. As the guard turned to leave, Darcy re-entered the house through the library.

"I'm sorry to see you in such sad circumstances, Mrs. Gannon."

"How nice of you to travel all the way out here to offer your condolences." Darcy extended her hand toward Ren.

Ren grasped her tiny hand in his, surprised at the strength of her grip.

"I know you must be very upset, Mrs. Gannon. But would you mind if I asked you a few questions?"

"That's fine, but you're right. I'm shaken by everything that's happened, Deputy." She brushed away a tear from the corner of her eye. "Who would want to murder Robert? He had no enemies. He had a few vices, but he was a good man." She walked into the library and gestured toward the sofa.

"We haven't announced that Mr. Gannon's death was a homicide. What makes you think he was murdered?"

"I assumed it was murder since Robert had no reason to commit suicide. He was a very happy man." Darcy clasped her hands together.

"Even though you said he didn't have any enemies, hate isn't necessarily a prerequisite for murder. Do you know of anyone who might have had any sort of a motive to kill him?" Ren folded himself into the overly stuffed sofa, and watched as Darcy sat down next to him. He couldn't help but notice a photograph of Darcy as a younger woman on the table behind the couch. She had the sort of beauty epics were written about.

"On the Sunday night before he was killed, we had a disagreement. We all participated in it. I did, Robert did, and so did Adam. It's a very common thing in families, and it doesn't mean Adam wanted to kill his father."

"How did you leave it? Did you part on good terms?"

"Not really. Adam stormed out of the house. He spent the night with Joe, a man who had once been our foreman, and has been staying there ever since. It's been quite upsetting." Darcy clasped her hands, and squeezed them until her knuckles were white.

"How did Adam make his feelings known?"

"Well, there was some verbal communication, but Adam carries a small notebook with him, and writes down words if he wants to make certain he's understood. He wrote down some things that night, and so did Robert."

"Do you have that notebook?"

"No, I don't."

"Do you know where it is?"

"I would imagine Adam has it."

"Do you remember what was written down?"

"I think Adam wrote that he hated his dad. He was very angry."

"Are you willing to make a formal statement that on September thirteenth, which was the night before Robert was killed, Adam and his dad were in a fight and Adam stated he hated his dad?"

"I would prefer that we find Adam's notebook first. If I have that, I can show you exactly what he said."

"It's not important that we have the notepad. I'm sure we'll find it when we speak to Adam. Your statement will be good for now."

"I suppose so." Darcy walked to the library and sat down at her desk. She wrote:

On September 12, 1989 my son Adam Gannon and his father Robert argued. At that time Adam told his father he hated him. He also said he wanted to kill him.

Darcy Gannon

"You didn't say Adam wanted to kill his father earlier."

"He was angry with both of us. It was a very upsetting night. And I probably shouldn't have said anything to you. I need to see our attorney about this." She crumpled the statement and balled it up in her hand.

"Look, you already said he wanted to kill his father. Why tear up your statement now?" Ren said.

Darcy folded her arms across her chest. "Adam was angry, and was trying to write down what he wanted to say. But it was hard to keep up with, and hard to read while it was all going on. So, in retrospect, it would be unfair for me represent what he said."

Ren sighed. "Fine. Before I leave, can you tell me if anything unusual happened the day before Robert was shot?"

"No, except that we had a visit from Miss Thornton that morning, asking us about Adam. And then we went to the stables to see the horses. I had to tend to a foal. I was upset about the argument with Adam. Other than that, it was an ordinary day."

Ren climbed into his car, relieved to be leaving Mayfair. Whether she meant to or not, Darcy had implicated Adam in the death of his father. And Adam's notebook was now an important piece of evidence.

It was obvious no one had lived in the cabin for years. The owners seemed unconcerned about its upkeep. Emma was convinced that Adam might seek refuge there again, especially since the owners didn't press charges for his earlier break-in. She crept up to the back door and peered through the mud splattered window.

Hinges on the screen door were coming loose, causing the door to swing open, and one of the windows was broken. Although none of the lights were on, and the place seemed empty, there were signs of recent occupancy. A coffee maker and a cereal box were on the counter. Emma pushed the door. It creaked open. She tip-toed into the small, grimy kitchen.

It smelled musty, as if it hadn't been cleaned in a while. She checked the coffee pot. It was cold, but there was coffee inside. Surprised there was electricity, Emma opened the door of the refrigerator, and found a fairly new bottle of ketchup. Closing it softly, Emma passed the living room and crept down the hall. She passed the bathroom and two unoccupied rooms, then noticed a small door at the end of the corridor. She opened it and peered inside.

The door led to a basement. She fumbled for a light switch and, finding none, felt her way down the stairs, finally locating a string dangling from the ceiling a few feet from the bottom step. She pulled the string and the basement was cast in a golden glow. The clay walls of the unfinished space were buttressed by several rows of supporting brick columns. Cobwebs were scattered over stored furniture, bicycles and fishing gear. A sump pump whirred away in the corner. Across the room, Emma noticed another door, which was slightly ajar, opening to a small room. The glow from the room's light triangulated across the basement.

Emma entered the tiny space. Her breath caught in her throat for a moment. The tile-covered floor was filled with canvases of different sizes, brushes, and paint. Stacked against the walls were paintings in various stages of completion. A crudely constructed drafting table fashioned from old boards stood in one corner. Emma walked to the side of the room and flipped through some of the paintings. Among them were several finished portraits of Jennifer Patrick. Emma had seen the rough sketches and preliminary paintings, but these were Adam's final works, and they were stunning. He appeared to have moved most of his work from the storage room at the stables to the basement of the cabin. Emma noticed one piece that was propped up against the wall. She picked it up to examine the moonlit scene. The details of the painting could not be mistaken.

Emma sat staring at the painting for several minutes, taking in all of the details. Her hands shook as she propped it back up against the wall. As she did, she noticed an empty magazine from a semi-automatic rifle leaning against a brick pillar a few feet away. She left both items in the room exactly where she'd found them, rushed to her car and drove back to Jonesburg.

40

Emma headed for Lucky's. She was hungry and her head was swimming from what she'd discovered. It was one of those fall days that can seem hotter than any of the days of summer. The sun beat down on her head without mercy as she crossed the sidewalk.

She decided to eat inside even though she hated the noisy din of chatting diners that echoed off of Lucky's terrazzo floors. She found the ring of the cash register especially disturbing and nearly turned around to leave. But she spied Ren, who she was hoping to see, and walked over to his table.

"Mind a little company?"

"Do you have to ask?" Ren smiled and waved his hand toward a chair.

"It's crowded today," Emma said.

"Yep, they're packed. Couldn't get my usual seat at the bar, but then, this may be better for us." Ren scooted his chair closer to Emma and leaned toward her. "It's always good to see you. I've missed you."

Emma smiled and unfolded her napkin after she sat down. "Missed you too." She squeezed his knee under the table, then frowned. "Ren, I've recently heard rumors that Lyle Patrick stands to inherit at least part of the Gannon property. Apparently, it's all over town. I heard it from Silas's secretary. Do you know anything about that?"

"Yeah. There are some letters that came in as evidence in the Patrick murder case. You can come down and look at them. I've been meaning to tell you about them. But I don't think they amount to much."

"What sort of letters?"

"Letters between Ethel Patrick and Will Gannon from around the time of the war. Will Gannon supposedly admits that he's the father of Lyle Patrick. We got them from a law professor at the University. Jennifer asked him to look at them for her. She'd found them in a hidden compartment in her desk. They were brought in to our office a while back."

"A while back?"

"Our former front desk clerk misplaced them and just gave them to us. She's now back working at Sue's Burgers."

"Oh. The letters sound interesting."

"Really?"

"Yes, Ren. Quite. Could I walk down and take a look at them after lunch?"

"Sure. I also spoke to your client's mother this morning. She said she'd like to speak to Silas about a few things, but she mentioned a notebook that Adam had. She said that the night before Robert Gannon was killed, Adam may have written in a notebook that he hated his dad. He also may have threatened to kill his dad that night as well."

"She actually said that to you?"

"Yep."

"Why would a mom incriminate her son like that? You'd think she'd be a little more careful."

"Not really. If Adam threatened his dad, she had good reason to tell me about it. You haven't seen him lately, have you?" Ren motioned to the waiter and requested more water.

"Adam? No, I haven't."

"Do you know anything about the notebook?"

"Now Ren, if I did, I couldn't tell you about it, could I? But if there's a notebook that is considered evidence in the case, it will be produced. That much I can say."

"Okay." Ren smiled. "And, one other thing. I had the bullets found in your car compared to those that were used in the Robert Gannon shooting. They're from the same gun."

"Wow, that's something."

"Now we're wondering if there is more than one shoeprint and if there could have been more than one person at the scene of the Patrick girl's shooting. Not sure if that makes sense."

"Well, that makes sense to me, now."

"What do you mean?"

Emma brushed the crumbs from her napkin, ignoring Ren's question. "I left a couple of things at one of the camps out by the lake, the one where Adam was staying the night I was kidnapped. They're in a small room in the basement. You'll know what they are when you see them. I'd like you to run by and take a look. Sorry to be so secretive, but I just want you to see them and see what your reaction is. I'm going to run out to the Patrick place for a bit."

Emma and Ren finished up lunch and left Lucky's. They walked over to the sheriff's office so Emma could review the letters between Ethel Patrick and Will Gannon. Once Emma read them, she got in her car and headed down the highway toward Lyle Patrick's place.

Emma hadn't been on the road to the Patrick farm since Jennifer's murder. She'd been so focused on the case back then that she hadn't noticed anything about the drive. The landscape changed considerably along this tract of land. Lyle lived in the southern half of the county. The trees along the northern section, where the Gannons resided, were tall oaks and long leaf pines. But the trees along the lower region, where the Patricks lived, were scrub oaks and brush. The northerly hillside was covered with a lush green carpet, yet the fields from the southerly side were covered by a brittle brown blanket that looked as if it might be blown away by the first good wind. Her grandfather would have told her there was a problem with the land from the lower section of the county. He always said that wealth was tied to the richness of the soil. She believed it when she looked at the farms and the land from Lyle Patrick's part of the world. The Patrick land not only made the Gannons the state's biggest landowners, they were also the state's wealthiest and most productive farmers, with holdings in timber as well. Their stables alone, which started as a hobby, made millions breeding their stallions.

Emma pulled up to Lyle's small white farmhouse. She could see that repairs had recently been made to Jennifer's bedroom window. The house itself was simple, and clean, but the flowers in the front bed had been ignored. Weeds had collected and most of the foliage was dead or dying. A truck was in the carport.

She knocked on the door. It was just after one. Emma hoped that Lyle was still home for his lunch break. She heard the lumbering sound and squeaking noise a heavy person makes walking on wooden floors. The door opened.

"Mr. Patrick. My name is Emma Thornton. I represent Adam Gannon. I realize this is highly unusual, but in preparing for his defense, I've run across something that has given me reason to believe your life could be in danger."

Lyle hesitated as he held the door open.

"You mean you represent the person who murdered my daughter?"

"I don't believe he murdered Jennifer, but, yes, I represent Adam."

"And now you're saying my life is in danger?"

"That's correct."

"Is this a threat?"

"No, Mr. Patrick. I—"

At that moment, a shot rang out. Lyle was knocked back into the house and onto the floor. Blood began pouring out from a hole in his shirt. Emma quickly crouched down on her hands and knees, crawled into the house and slammed the door behind them. She checked on Lyle to see if he was conscious, pulled a scarf from her purse and applied it to the wound in an effort to stop the bleeding. He was pale and shaking. His cheeks were flushed and blotchy, and he was perspiring profusely. Fearing he might be in shock, she took off her jacket and spread it across his chest to keep him warm.

"Lyle? Can you speak?" Emma asked.

Before he could answer another gunshot crashed through the living room window. Emma realized that two or three gunshots in the middle of the day in rural Georgia wouldn't arouse suspicion, if they were heard at all. Lyle's nearest neighbors were miles away. She and Lyle would have to fend for themselves.

Emma saw Lyle's eyes flutter. "Do you have a gun somewhere, Lyle?"

Lyle nodded and swallowed. He was breathing hard. He lifted his head and nodded toward a room beyond the kitchen. Emma could see a cabinet filled with shotguns and rifles. "Key's in the desk across the room. Shells are there, too." He dropped his head back to the floor. His breath was coming in short, shallow bursts.

Emma ducked down and began creeping across the floor toward the desk. She felt a sudden explosive pain at the back of her head. Then nothing.

41

Ren watched as Ben Bailey was escorted into the room. Lamar Johnson, Ben's attorney, had been waiting with Ren for several minutes. They hadn't spoken during that time, and barely made eye contact. Johnson was a retired Marine and had kept the haircut and demeanor. He'd been a prosecutor in the JAG Corps but preferred criminal defense work. Johnson represented most of the criminals in Greendale and the surrounding counties. He was tough. Ren had seen him at the gym. He was one of those guys that worked out every day and had the biceps to prove it. Ren guessed he didn't take any crap from his clients. But since Ben didn't have a legitimate job, Lamar must not be too particular about where his fees were coming from. Where was the Marine honor in that?

Ben shuffled into the room and sat down. His appearance hadn't improved since the last time Ren saw him; in fact, it had deteriorated. His skin was ashen and his hands were trembling. The purple-red scars across his eyes stood out against the pallor of his complexion, giving him a ghoulish appearance. The officer who escorted Ben into the room stood guard next to the door in the hallway. Ben sat down next to his attorney.

"You called this meeting, Ben. What's this all about?" Ren scooted his chair closer to the table.

"You gave me the idea, Deputy," Ben said, wiping his nose with a dirty hand. "Remember when you said the DA might work something out with me if I gave you somethin' to use as a plea bargain? Well, I have something for you to give him." Ben peered at Ren with his good eye.

"I can't make promises about what the DA will do, but I'm happy to listen to your proposal, Ben."

"I thought you said the DA would reduce my sentence if I gave him something he could work with. Something he could use to solve some of those murders. Ain't that right?" Ben eyed his attorney.

"What Ben means is that we're prepared to talk to you about the Jennifer Patrick and Lola Mae Robinson murders in exchange for leniency regarding the kidnapping and aggravated assault charges in Ben's case. Before we speak we also want protection from prosecution on those two murders. So we want to enter into a non-prosecution agreement, before we talk."

"If what you're saying is true, it's obvious you were involved in those two cases. So I need substantially more information before I can go to the DA. You've got to give me something to see if it's worth his time to deal with you. Then maybe an agreement can be worked out that everyone can live with."

Ben looked at Lamar Johnson, who nodded.

"Can you give us a few minutes?" Lamar Johnson said.

"Sure, I'll be back in about five." Ren stepped out of the room and walked down the hallway. He stopped at the end and looked back down the corridor and through the windows in the room he'd just left. He could see Johnson and Ben Bailey with their heads together. Johnson was talking and looked persuasive. After several minutes Lamar Johnson stood up, walked out of the room and gestured for Ren to come back in. Ren rejoined them, and sat down in the empty metal chair.

"Ben's going to talk now. But he's going to keep it brief. This will have to do, Deputy."

Ren nodded.

"Yeah, well, Robert Gannon had been paying the attorney's fees in my case," Ben began. "He'd been doing that to keep me quiet since he discovered that Adam had hired me to kill Lyle Patrick. 'Course, Adam killed Jennifer."

"Why would Adam want Lyle dead?"

"That I don't know."

261

"What gun did Adam use?"

"The AR-15."

"How many rifles were at the scene?"

"Two."

"Why did he hire you if he was there too?"

"I can't answer that. I guess it made the double shooting easier."

"What happened to the plan to kill Lyle?"

"My rifle misfired. That was that."

"Anything else?"

"Adam also hired me to kill Lola Mae Robinson."

"That makes no sense. Why would Adam want her dead?"

"How would I know? Maybe she knew something about the Patrick girl's murder."

"Why'd you decide to talk now?"

"To reduce my sentence, like you said. No other reason."

"So you're saying you killed Lola Mae Robinson, too?"

"Depends on our agreement. I'm not ready to say any more without a full agreement."

"How'd Lola Mae die? Do you know that much?"

"Blow to the head."

"Do you know where she was buried?"

"That's enough for now, Deputy," Johnson said.

"We're going to need more details, Lamar."

"You have enough to go to the DA. We can discuss the details after we have the agreement in place." Lamar gripped the back of his chair, as if he were about to pick it up and knock it over someone's head.

"Lamar, this doesn't add up. Ben can make up stories all day long to plea bargain, but if I find a hole in his story I can promise you that he's never getting out of prison. I'll do my best to guarantee that. Lie to me now, and cause me to take a lie over to the DA and he'll live to regret it for the rest of his life. Go tell your client that. This is not the time for games."

"Give us another few minutes, if that's okay with you."

Ren nodded his approval and walked down the hallway again to allow the duo to discuss Ben's statement. A few minutes later Lamar motioned to Ren, who re-entered the room and sat back down at the table across from Ben.

"Looks like you were correct, Deputy. Ben would like to change his story." Lamar remained standing.

"I'm not surprised, but I have to say that this makes anything you say at this point less believable, Ben. But, by all means, go ahead."

"My legal fees had been paid by Robert, but he paid them for me to keep my mouth shut about my work for him with the horses. I think he may have suspected his wife had something to do with the murder of the Patrick girl, too. And he was right. She's the one that shot her. Like I said earlier, I was there to shoot Lyle, but the gun misfired."

"Is there anything you can tell me that would help me prove that anything you're saying is true? Some of this is very hard to believe, Ben."

"That night, as we were turning to leave the Patrick place, Darcy gave me the rifle to put in Adam's truck, but she accidentally pulled off the magazine. I was already halfway to my truck then, so she picked it up off of the ground as she was leaving, and later hid it behind a trap door on the floor of a storage shed at the stables. She also had me wear a pair of Robert's old shoes. I gave them back to her later. They may be there too. And, like I said, I killed Lola Mae. Darcy hired me to do it. Paid me for it."

Ren strode down the steps of the county jail, crossed the street to the parking lot to his car and climbed in the front seat. It was hot inside and still smelled like that morning's donut and coffee. The DA wasn't in, but he'd left a message. He didn't know if Ben was feeding him a line of bull or not, but he'd check it all out. He also picked up a warrant for the Gannons' shed.

He decided to drive out to Joe Casey's place. If he happened to see Adam while he was there, it would even be better. But he wanted to run a couple of questions by Joe, and hoped he could shed some light on what Ben had told him. Bailey was a piece of work, the single most unreliable man in the county. He'd say anything to reduce his sentence.

Fifteen minutes later, Ren pulled off the highway onto Gannon property drove up Joe's gravel driveway. He didn't see Adam's truck. He bounded up the porch steps and knocked on the front door. Joe opened the door, and invited Ren in.

"Coffee?" Joe asked.

"Thanks, Joe. Would you mind telling me if you pay rent to the Gannons, or do they just allow you to stay here?"

"I had an agreement with Mr. Will Gannon and Mr. Robert. So did my parents. The house was part of our salary. So far, Miss Darcy hasn't said anything to me about changing anything."

Ren scribbled down Joe's answers. "How would you describe your relationship with Ben Bailey? Have you ever worked with him? Do you even have any sort of relationship with him?"

"I know who Mr. Bailey is, but I don't really know him that well. What I know I don't like." Joe sipped his coffee.

"What if I told you that Ben Bailey told me Adam Gannon paid him to kill Lyle Patrick, and that Adam killed Jennifer?"

"I'd say that's crazy. Adam don't have that kind of head or heart. He'd never hire someone to kill anyone. And why would he want to kill Mr. Patrick? It don't make sense. I know Adam didn't have nothing to do with no murders. I can say that." Joe looked at Ren without blinking.

"What if I also told you that Ben Bailey said that Robert Gannon was paying his attorney's fees for his silence about his involvement?"

"He might be paying his attorneys fees, but if he is, then something else is going on. It ain't Adam that's done the wrong. That much I can say. Ben Bailey ain't someone you can trust. It all seems fishy to me, especially if it's coming from him."

"Ben Bailey also changed his story later and said that Mrs. Gannon killed Jennifer. What would you have to say about that?"

"I would just say that you can't trust someone who changes they story so often."

"Were Robert and Adam ever close as father and son?"

"Nah. Not really. Adam being deaf and all was difficult for Mr. Robert, I think. Same thing with Miss Darcy."

"Are Adam and his mother close?"

"Well, I don't think I could say that. Darcy's mother died when she was real young and she was raised by her dad. So she don't know much about how to be a mother, except that she's real good with horses, foals especially. If a horse gets sick, or if a mare goes into foal, she's right there. She'll stay with them all night if she has to. Her dad was a trainer for the Gannon stables, you know. That's why she loves horses so much. Only thing she knows or understands is horses 'cause that's what her dad taught her. That and guns. Her dad taught her how to shoot and how to ride. She's good at both. I don't mean she don't love Adam. She just don't know how to be with him like a mom should be."

"Ben also told me that Adam was involved in the murder of Lola Mae Robinson, the Gannon's housekeeper, and that Adam paid him to kill her and bury her body."

"I don't know nothing about how Lola Mae died, but I know Adam wouldn't have no cause to hurt her or to want her dead. I also know that right before she died Lola Mae was worried about talking to Miss Emma when she was out visiting at Mayfair. That's all I know."

"Are you saying that you think the Gannons had something to do with Lola Mae's death?"

"No. I'm just saying that she was real nervous about saying something to Miss Emma, that's all."

"Joe, I noticed Adam's truck isn't here. Do you know where he is?"

"I haven't seen Adam in a couple of days now. My nephew's truck is also missing. He left it here for a few days while he was out of town. The keys are missing too. I'm wondering if Adam might'a borrowed it."

"Any idea where Adam might be?"

"Not really, unless he's down by the camps again. That's where he went the last time he decided to hide out. That's the time Miss Emma was kidnapped, remember?"

Ren nodded.

"But after his last arrest, Miss Emma asked me to make sure he knew to stay in touch with us, that it was important. Plus, he has to check in with the court every week. So, I don't know why he's run off again." Joe rested his hands on his walker.

"I'd like to take a look at that storage shed next door." Ren showed him his warrant.

Joe sat up straight in his chair. "Sure. It'd be easier if you just walk on down there by yourself and take a look around. Everything's unlocked."

Ren walked down to the shed and opened its creaking wooden door. He waited while his eyes adjusted to the light he'd turned on. The shed was the catch-all storage spot for the farm, the equivalent of a kitchen's junk drawer. The stable's left over saddles, worn out harnesses, odd horse tack and even some used boots were stacked along the wall. He breathed in the familiar and comforting odor of old leather.

Ben said the trap door was on the floor in the storage shed, but where? Ren searched each corner of the room, then fanned out toward the middle, finally spotting a small hole in the floor. Stepping closer, he could also see the outline of a trap door and shiny hinges on the floor. He grabbed a screwdriver from the workbench, opened the door, and peered into the recessed storage area underneath, disappointed to see that the door concealed nothing but an old pair of muddy boots, worn slightly more on the left heel than the right.

Within thirty minutes, Ren was following the winding back roads along the county lake toward the fishing camps. It didn't take him long to find Adam's truck which was still hidden in tree limbs and brambles. Ren was surprised that Adam had returned to the same cabin he'd visited before, and that he'd hidden his truck in exactly the same place. It was as if he wanted to be found. Ren crossed the road and approached the camp house. Within five minutes he found the small basement studio. When he discovered the painting and magazine propped up along the wall, he knew he had to make a drive out to the Patrick place. If what Ben said was true, and Lyle had been a target that night, he could still be in danger and should be warned. Ren picked up the painting and the empty magazine, placed each in plastic bags for protection, and set them in his back seat before he headed out. He'd send a squad car out to search for Adam the next day.

42

Emma opened her eyes. She was surrounded by inky darkness, and the dank odor of mildew and damp clay. She knew she was underground. Perhaps in a basement or a cellar. A headache reminded her of the gunshots that had been fired at Lyle's house. One must have grazed the back of her head. Her shoulders stabbed when she tried to move. A rope was tied around her wrists and then looped around an overhead crossbeam, immobilizing her upper body. Light shone from a crack in the door at the top of the stairs. Tools, boxes, and storage items were stacked in the corners. She didn't know what had happened to Lyle.

Emma heard two sets of footsteps overhead, then heard two people speaking. One was definitely a woman. She couldn't catch everything but was able to pick up the word *letters*. Did they have Lyle upstairs? Were they threatening him about letters? Was that what the shooting had been about? Were they looking for the letters Jennifer had found?

The woman said, "Tell me what you know, Lyle." Then something that sounded like "kill you."

Emma realized that getting out of the house with Lyle in tow was unlikely. She had no plan of action, and no skill set for saving herself or anyone else. She had no weapons either, unless she could find something in the basement. She had two choices. She could try to escape by herself, or she could help Lyle. She couldn't do both. And her escape would mean certain death for

Lyle.

Emma repositioned her thumb so that it was in the middle of her palm to narrow the width of her hand. She moved her fist back and forth to expand the ropes. Then she twisted her wrists against the ropes until they were chaffed and nearly bled. After several minutes, she was able to work her hands free, then untied herself. She stood, scanned the basement, searching for a weapon, and found an old baseball bat, and a crowbar under a stack of detergent boxes. The crowbar was heavy, awkward, and difficult to maneuver. Giving the bat a swing in the air for practice, she made her way up the stairs.

The door to the main floor was unlocked. Emma opened it slowly, peeking through a small crack to make sure all was clear, and walked in. The kitchen was cluttered with strewn drawers and furniture, but otherwise empty. The small office next to the kitchen was in no better shape, with its overturned cabinet drawers, and desk contents spilled out on the wooden floor. Emma heard voices down the hall, sneaked across the entrance to the hallway and peeked down the corridor. She moved close enough to recognize Darcy's voice.

"Wasn't this Jennifer's room, Lyle? Was this her dresser?"

Emma could hear Darcy's footsteps moving across the room.

"When Jennifer came to see me, she told me something about finding some letters. Said she found them in some old furniture in her bedroom. Maybe in this dresser?" Darcy said.

Emma heard the dresser drawer open.

"They're not here. Have you seen those letters, Lyle?"

"Never heard of them."

"Are you sure? Jennifer didn't talk to you about letters from your mama and Robert's daddy written around the time of the war?"

"I don't know what you're talking about." He wheezed with each breath.

"You're useless to me, Lyle. I don't see that we have much more need of you or your little attorney friend. Oliver, go get Miss Emma. They're both done."

Emma picked up her bat, and started to step out, but someone grabbed her arm. Startled she turned around, shocked to see Adam. He put his finger to his lips, silencing her.

Adam and Emma crouched behind an over-stuffed chair next to the hallway entrance and watched as Oliver headed for the basement. Emma recognized Oliver from the day of Dr. Whittley's psychiatric testing at the county jail. He had seemed extraordinarily interested in the procedures.

Oliver scrambled back up the steps out of breath. "She's gone, Darcy."

"Gone? Didn't you tie her up?" Darcy stormed down the hallway and stood a few feet from Emma and Adam. "How could she have escaped? There's only one exit. We'll take care of Lyle first. She can't have gone far." Darcy held up the rifle, aimed it at Lyle, and motioned with its tip for Lyle to move down the hallway toward the basement.

Adam stood up from behind the chair where he had been hiding and said, "No, Mother" clearly enough for everyone to understand.

Darcy twisted her head around to look at Adam, at first keeping her gun aimed at Lyle. "Well hello, Adam. This is a surprise. What do you mean no?"

Adam didn't move and Emma couldn't tell whether he had understood what his mother said. His face remained stone-like as she spoke, without a flicker of emotion registering in his eyes—not hatred or fear or pain. Darcy slowly moved her rifle's aim from Lyle to Adam.

Emma couldn't help but compare the two. Adam, at more than six-foot-two towered over the diminutive Darcy. But there was no doubt Darcy, with her .22 pointed at Adam, was the more lethal of the two. She was not only capable of brutality, but her chatter made her seem unbalanced. She had a strange glint to her eyes, as if her pupils were dilated. She was breathing rapidly.

"The last time I saw you, you told me you hated me. That's not a nice thing to tell your mother, you know. Oliver, bring Lyle up here closer to the rest of us."

Oliver dragged Lyle by his good arm into the den. Lyle had been bleeding from his wound and was pale and weakened. Blood drenched his shirt and had seeped down his pant leg. A bloody trail trickled behind him in the hallway. Oliver deposited Lyle in a crumpled heap at the end of the corridor.

When Darcy turned to Lyle, Adam lunged at his mother and tackled her. She fell to the floor, causing the rifle to discharge as she dropped it. Emma sprang from behind the chair and took aim, striking Oliver in the back of his head with the bat. He was out immediately. Emma grabbed Oliver's pistol from his holster and aimed it at Darcy, but Adam was too close to his mother for her to fire.

Darcy, struggling under Adam's considerable size and weight, managed to free an elbow and jammed it in his throat. Adam gasped for air as Darcy freed herself, scrambled to her feet, and grabbed the rifle. She pointed the weapon at Adam again. Emma clinched Oliver's pistol, and kept it aimed at Darcy.

Just then, they heard the front door creak. Heavy shoes stepped along the wooden floors of the front room.

"Emma? You here?" Ren pulled out his pistol.

As he rounded the corner and saw Darcy holding her rifle on Adam, he stopped but kept his pistol raised.

"There's no need for any more violence, is there Darcy? Why don't you put down your weapon?" Ren said.

Adam took a step toward his mother. Darcy set her sight at Adam, pointing the barrel directly at his heart.

Emma held her breath, watching in horror as Adam reached out for his mother again. Emma moved toward Darcy to get a better shot at her, but it was too late.

Darcy pulled the trigger.

43

The ambulance dashed down the single lane road toward the county hospital. Emma could still see the paramedics working on Adam through the illuminated back window. She didn't want to know if her shot or Ren's had been the one that had killed Darcy, but she was glad Oliver would be okay. She'd knocked him out, but the EMTs said he was coming around and that they were taking him in for observation. Ren thought he'd be booked in the county jail by the next day.

Given the chance, Darcy would have killed them all. Emma's only regret was that she and Ren didn't get to Darcy before Adam was shot. Emma knew only one person Adam would want to see if and when he woke up. Joe Casey's place was fifteen minutes away.

Emma and Joe walked into the third floor surgical waiting room at Greendale County Hospital. Ren was already there, the mint colored walls and fluorescent lighting giving his face a pale, pasty look. Emma was so happy to see him she burst into tears, and forgetting their agreement, ran over to hug him.

Ren grabbed her and hugged her so hard she couldn't breathe for a few seconds. "I'm so glad you're okay." He kissed her right on the lips, and hugged her again.

For once, Emma didn't check for onlookers but instead held on to Ren's arm. "Have you heard anything from the doctors?"

"No, not yet. They said they expected to be in surgery for several hours though. If the caliber of the bullet had been anything other than a .22, he'd be dead, that's for sure. Good thing Darcy chose to use such a small rifle."

"Yeah, bless her heart."

"Care to bet whether the casings from Darcy's rifle match those found at Robert's murder scene and the ones we got from your trunk?"

"Only if I get to bet they were all from Darcy's rifle."

Joe sighed and sat down. "Miss Darcy was always missing something. She proved that today, for sure." He glanced up at Emma. "I want you to know Adam and I are both very thankful for everything you've done. You fought for Adam. And you believed in him and tended to him, sort of like you might tend to one of your own."

Emma sat next to Joe and held his shaking hands. "Adam saved my life. I wouldn't be here if it weren't for him."

"He came to trust you and he never trusted anyone before, 'cept me." Joe's eyes brimmed with tears.

They heard footsteps and turned to see a surgeon dressed in scrubs approaching them.

"Is there anyone here from Adam Gannon's family?"

"I'm Emma Thornton, a law clerk for Adam's attorney, Silas Steele, and this is Chief Deputy Ren Taylor. Joe Casey here is the closest thing Adam has to family."

"Mr. Casey, it looks like he came through the worst part, but you can't go in just yet. You should be able to see him within the hour. The nurse will come and get you."

"If I could dance that's what I'd be doin' right now!" Joe raised his arms in the air for Emma's hug, and fist pumped Ren. "Halleluiah!"

"Doctor, can you tell us anything about Lyle Patrick's condition?" Ren said.

"Is that the other man that was brought in with a gunshot wound around the same time?"

"Yes."

"He's not my patient. Do you know if he has any family here?"

"I guess you could consider Adam Gannon family. I don't know of anyone else we could even call," Emma said.

"Well, they're still working on him, but last I heard they stopped the bleeding, and that's a good sign. His heart was still beating when they brought him in, and that gave him a ninety-five percent chance of survival, even with that gut shot he sustained. So, you should feel encouraged about Mr. Patrick."

Emma thanked the doctor and motioned to Ren, signaling a need for a quick chat. They met by the water cooler at the end of the hospital corridor.

"What a day, huh?" Emma smiled, brushing away tears of relief as she filled a paper cup with water.

"You could say that." Ren looked at his shoes, and then back up at Emma. "I couldn't believe what I walked in on at the Patrick place. Darcy was insane. I hate to say it, but I'm glad she's gone."

Emma nodded. "I'm glad it's over. Now maybe life can return to normal."

"Normal? Adam's lost his parents. His mom was not only a murderer, she probably killed his dad, and tried to kill him. Poor kid. And Lyle not only lost his daughter, he's about to learn that he's actually a Gannon. That's going to be a shocker."

"Maybe 'normal' isn't the right word, I just hope that Adam and Lyle can get on with their lives. Adam should continue with his education. That would be good for him. And even though Lyle will need to prove he's a Gannon, once he begins, I don't think it will be too difficult to do."

"Not with those letters."

Emma shook her head. "The estate will have to go through probate, but eventually, Lyle and Adam could end up with a joint ownership of Mayfair. That could work out for both of them. Lyle knows how to run a place like that, and Adam knows a little more about the horses. They are family, after all."

"Yeah. And they could both use a break." He leaned against the wall and crossed his arms. "Since you're predicting outcomes today, what does your crystal ball say about our future?"

"Future? Well, Deputy Taylor, I think I can predict a nice relaxing dinner somewhere, sometime soon." She smiled.

"Anything else?"

"It's a little early to talk about all that, don't you think? I'm not sure what I'm going to do after school, or where I'll go. One of my professors has been offered a position as dean at a law school in New Orleans. He said if he accepts it, he'd like me to consider a position as a legal research and writing professor there. But I'm not sure I'd take it. And I haven't had time to think about it. Too much has been going on."

"Well, dinner sometime this week sounds great to me."

"Me too."

Emma reached out for his hand and squeezed it. She knew he would stay at the hospital with her as long as she wanted him to and that Joe would be there for Adam. She'd call her neighbor to see if her kids could sleep over. It might be a long night. But the worst was over.

"Did you bring Adam's painting with you? The one that was in the basement of the camp house?"

"It's in the back of my car. Want to take a walk and take another look at it?"

Emma nodded. "I'd like to see it again."

Together they walked out to the hospital parking lot and Ren unlocked his car. The painting was there, along with the magazine to the AR-15, just where Ren had placed them earlier.

Emma removed the plastic covering from the painting, held it at arm's length, and took in Adam's precise brushstrokes. The canvas told the story of the night of Jennifer Patrick's murder. That Darcy killed Jennifer and that Ben Bailey was poised to kill Lyle. Adam was there that night, too, arriving at the site too late to stop anyone, and watching in terror as the shooters fled the scene.

Emma held the painting up to the setting sun. She admired Adam's careful technique and color choices. Turneresque in its illumination against the dark sky, the painting had an inner glow, except for the little bare spot in the corner where some of the paint had been rubbed off. It was magnificent. Each feature of his mother's face was reflected in the moonlight, revealing a harsh, calculating beauty.

"It's evidence now." Ren reached out toward the painting, barely touching it.

"It's remarkable that he did this. How far would Darcy have gone if Adam hadn't finally led us to it?"

Emma glanced at Ren. They both knew the painting was much more than an account of the night of the murder. It was about strength of will, and learning to trust. The sort of trust that would allow Adam to step out from the silence he'd always known, and tell his story, his truth, the only way he knew.

Acknowledgements

The book started with a short story, which I timidly entered into a contest, never expecting to win. These ideas were slowly developed, over years of encouragement, into the novel it is today. I owe much to my daughter, Laura Desporte Akin, and to my son Charles L. Desporte, Jr., for their support and encouragement. They've inspired ideas which helped shape the story, not only the love Emma Thornton has for her kids, but certain qualities, especially Emma's sheer grit and keen intelligence which I also see in both of my children. They have been my steadfast champions and I am theirs.

And thanks also to Jamie Hubans Desporte, Bailey Toksoz, Yong Takahashi, Catherine Shmerling, Carolyn Jarboe, Monica Hardy, Aleta Magana, Elizabeth Whitaker and Mari Ann Stefanalli, for all of their help, practical and emotional, through the years leading up to this publication. Bailey Toksoz's beautiful photography graces the cover of the book.

I'm grateful to Harriette Sackler and the team at Level Best Books, including Shawn Reilly Simmons and Verena Rose, for guiding me through the publishing process. Harriette, in particular, has shown more patience and kindness than I'd previously thought possible in this business.

I'd also like to acknowledge my gratitude to Corry Wilcox and Jennifer Rideneor for lending their expertise in the field of audiology and deaf education which helped immeasurably in the development of this story. Corry read the entire book. Her commentary gave an authenticity to Adam's character I could not have found otherwise.

Also, even though I'm an attorney I've never practiced criminal law in Georgia. Jennifer DeBaun gave her time most generously to a review of this book. I am very grateful for her considerable expertise.

Several other people have also read the book and critiqued it. Specifically, I'd like to thank authors Roger Johns and Ellen Byron for their willingness to read and comment on a first-time writer's work. Their kind and encouraging words are so appreciated, and their talent and dedication to their craft will always be an inspiration.

I'd also like to thank my beta readers, who took valuable time to read and comment on the story: O.W. Tolbert, Jr., Marjorie Miller, Carolyn Jarboe, Marilyn Schulman, Leigh Reveley Kellogg, Janet Attanasio, Susan Reger, Mark Reger, Rick Homan, Norma Nixon Shofield, and Meg McCallum.

Thanks also to the readers of the very first draft of the manuscript, writing group members, Ron Aiken, Ralph Elliot, and Leanna Adams. Their insights helped shape the story.

I'd like to thank the entire writing community, especially the members of Sisters in Crime, Guppies, and Mystery Writers of America, as well as the Atlanta Writing Club, and Broadleaf Writers Association for all of their support, and the education they provide for new writers.

Finally, I'd like to thank my family, especially my husband, whose suggestion that I retire came just at the right time. His support is much appreciated.

About the Author

C.L. Tolbert grew up on the Gulf Coast of Mississippi, a culturally rich, beachy stretch of land with moss covered oaks and unforgettable sunsets. Early in her career she earned a Masters of Special Education and taught children with learning disabilities before entering law school at the University of Mississippi. She spent most of her legal career working as defense counsel, traveling throughout the country in litigation for corporations and insurance companies. She also had the unique opportunity of teaching third-year law students in a clinical program at Loyola Law School in New Orleans where she ran the Homelessness Law Clinic and learned, first hand, about poverty in that city. The experience and impressions she has collected from the past forty years contribute to the stories she writes today.

After winning the Georgia State Bar Association's fiction writing contest in 2010, C.L. developed the winning short story into the full scale novel, *Out From Silence.* Her second manuscript, entitled *The Redemption,* will be published in 2020. Retiring after thirty years of law practice, she lives in Atlanta with her husband and schnauzer Yoda. When she's not writing, she volunteers for Atlanta Legal Aid Services and visits her children and grandchildren as often as possible.

Visit C.L. Tolbert on cltolbert.com.

Made in the USA
Columbia, SC
25 May 2020